MW01712567

LEGERDEMAIN

The Shattered Mage Saga

P.S. RAMSEY

For Kylie,
Hope you like it!
Peggy

Sword & Science
An Imprint of COM Publishing

Sword & Science

www.swordandscience.com

LEGERDEMAIN
Sword and Science
Sword and Science is an imprint of COM Publishing, LLC
43422 West Oaks Drive, #292, Novi, MI 48377-3300
www.com-publishing.com
www.swordandscience.com

PRINTED IN THE UNITED STATES OF AMERICA

Copyright © 2007 Peggy S. Ramsey

Trade Paper back Publication April 2007
Electronic book Publication May 2007

ISBN 9780979029905
Library of Congress Control Number: 2007922973

Cover Art and Interior Illustrations provided by
Dark Elf Designs, LLC.
Cover Art Copyright © 2007 by Brian Germain
Interior Illustrations Copyright © 2007 by William Messner-Loebs, Brian Germain

Senior Managing Editor – Kris Kelly   Senior Editor – Nadine Messner-Loebs
Design Layout – Chris Jefferies

This book is a work of fiction. Names, characters, places, and incidents are the product of the author's imagination or are used fictitiously. Any resemblance to actual persons, living or dead, business establishments, events, or locales is entirely coincidental.

The scanning, uploading, and distribution of this book via the Internet or any other means without the permission of the publisher is an illegal act punishable by law. Please purchase only authorized electronic editions, and do not participate or encourage electronic piracy of copyrighted materials. We appreciate your support of the author's rights.

Without limiting the rights under copyright reserved above and with the exception of quotes used in reviews, no part of this publication may be reproduced, stored in or introduced into a retrieval system, or transmitted, in any form, or by any means (electronic, mechanical, photocopying, recording, or otherwise), without the prior written permission of both the copyright owner and the above publisher of this book.

---

1 2 3 4 5 6 7 8 9 10

Dedicated to the memory of my writing teacher,

Annabelle McIlnay,

who taught us all about nouns and verbs, the evils of passive voice, and how you need to know the rules of grammar before you can break them. I know it's a cliché, but if not for her, this book would not exist.

Thank you, thank you, a million times, thank you.

I'd also like to thank —

— Everyone who ever spent an evening in Annabelle's writing class and listened to me whine, dither, 'splain, and complain about my writing, with special appreciation going to Joan Johnson, Bob Maier, Chris Nadeau, Marion Patrick, Nora Smith, and Allison Sterling.

— Tom McCormack, for keeping the butterfly lights on for us.

— Brian Germain and William Messner-Loebs, for the beautiful artwork (and the lessons on description).

— Nadine Messner-Loebs and Kris Kelly, for finding the errors that Christine and I did not.

— Chris Jefferies, for saving us from having to turn layout into a "learn by doing" experience.

— My "virtual" writers' group, the AWC, especially Carolyn "Relentless" Rogers.

— My friends and family — Dad, here's your book!

— Christine Owens, most of all, for keeping the band together, and letting me go first.

LEGERDEMAIN

The Shattered Mage Saga

P.S. RAMSEY

Legerdemain

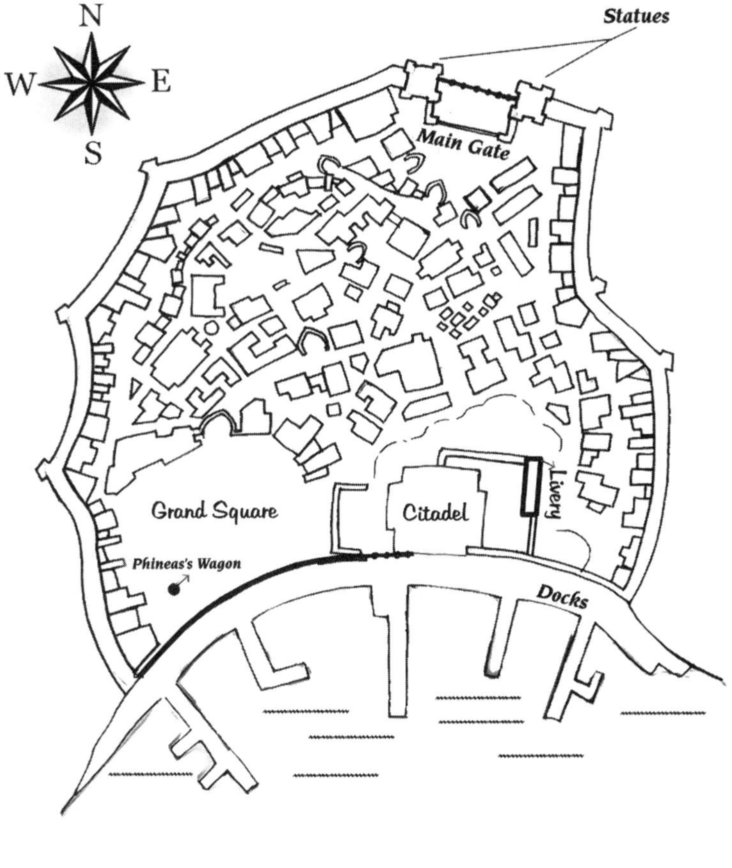

PHINEAS DELAYNE, MAGE

Chapter 1

"You've come to see magic, have you?"

The old man with the silver hair and golden tongue surveyed the crowd as if he owned the lot of them. "You wish to be amazed? Astounded? Astonished?"

A few of the sun-reddened faces nodded in agreement; the rest stared like the cattle they were. These simple citizens had stopped by the gaudy caravan-style wagon on their way from market to farm, or farm to tavern. Now they had to decide whether this diversion was worth a pause in their journeys, or a longer wait for refreshment. Since most who stopped remained rooted in the dusty town square, the answer was undoubtedly yes.

"You think you've seen magic before? Bah! Any shifter worth his cups and balls can run a trick past your eyes and call it magic." The showman paused and cocked his head, his bright eyes gleaming in the fading light. "But I, Phineas DeLayne, will show you wonders you've never seen. Things you never dreamed you'd see."

No one noticed the wiry boy of sixteen, with eyes as gray as the over-sized workman's cap covering most of his head, working his way through the crowd. At least, not until he spoke. "Aw, old man, come on with you!" he shouted. "Only a fool believes in magic."

"Call me a fool, will you?" Before the last word left his lips, the old man seized a bejeweled staff from a rack at the rear of the stage and directed it at the boy. "No such thing as magic, eh?" The tip glowed bright red and the boy rose into the air as if snatched up by invisible hands. "Perhaps you are right."

Applause and murmurs of astonishment surrounded the boy, almost drowning out his cries for help. "Let me down," he yelped. "I ain't done nothing to you."

"Ah, but that is where you are wrong." The showman pointed and torches flared to life at both corners of the stage. "You interrupted my performance. You questioned my integrity. The first is inexcusable; the second, unforgivable."

The boy squirmed, arms and legs flailing. "I didn't mean it," he howled. "Let me down, ah, please, let me down."

"As you request." The staff ceased glowing and the boy dropped to the hard-packed earth amidst a circle of knees and ankles, falling so hard it nearly dislodged the three stolen purses tucked into his tunic. Amidst the cheers and applause, he scrambled to his feet and raced off in a hasty retreat.

"One doubter gone," Phineas DeLayne smiled and addressed his now-rapt audience. "Spare me some of your time and I will show you some real magic."

Once out of sight, Eric cursed softly and glanced over his shoulder to make sure he wasn't being followed. "You didn't have to drop me that hard this time, you old drunk," he muttered as he sought a quiet shadow to count his take.

An alley stair provided shelter as he tipped one, two, three pouches into his flattened palm. Twelve coppers, six bronze, and one silver, barely enough to feed them and their beasts through to the next town. The last pouch also contained a small quartz talisman meant to ward off thieves. Eric grimaced and dropped it into his own pouch with the rest of his collection. People should know better than to believe in such magic.

He was old enough now to feel some guilt about taking from those who could ill-afford it, but when it was steal or starve, his conscience usually lost. He learned long ago that if they had to rely on the old man for sustenance, they'd be nothing but a pile of dried bones by now.

Before returning to the street, he removed the workman's cap and shook his mouse brown hair loose to his shoulders, then reversed his tunic so the blue showed instead of the brown. He didn't know why he bothered. No one would notice him — no one ever noticed him. The only thing he didn't change was the lightweight scarf wrapped loosely around his neck. He tossed the empty purses into a pile of trash in the corner and resumed his course down the street.

The market street was barely worthy of the name. It and the lop-sided square comprised more of the town — Dunnap; he'd heard someone call it. It was the first time Eric had been here, been anywhere near this far west, but Master Phineas claimed to know it from the old days. A half-dozen open-front stalls lined either side of the narrow street, their faded eaves and awnings slanting this way and that. There wasn't much to choose from; most of the venders were making ready to end the day.

A stumpy man wearing a bloody apron roasted chunks of meat over a barrel fire. When he caught Eric staring, he gestured extravagantly. "Step forward, young sir. Nothing but the finest, hand-raised venison for my customers."

More like the finest dog, Eric thought. Or maybe a goat, if he was lucky; though he was certain his rumbling stomach wouldn't care. It had been weeks since they'd run out of the leathery meat he'd bought for their journey, and even the horses were starting to look tasty.

Ruefully, he shook his head, and moved on to the baker, where he bought four loaves of coarse bread off the back of the wagon for half the price the man quoted. He made a similar bargain for a small wheel of cheese, but had to pay full price for a sack of beans and another of dried corn. On the next street, he found a stable, where he bought grain for the horses and replaced a broken leather strap on the harness.

While he waited for the leather monger to return, he watched a trio of stable boys make a game of their sweeping. None wore slave collars. Were they the tradesman's sons or young men set out by their fathers to learn a trade? Either way, Eric envied their freedom and their lighthearted manner.

His errands complete, he circled the perimeter of the square and made his way through the shadows to the rear of the wagon he and Master Phineas called home. On the stage in front, the man himself was just finishing his performance.

"Did I disappoint? I think not! Did I give you something to tell your neighbors? I think so!"

Eric mouthed the words along with his master as he stowed the supplies and fed their mismatched team of horses. "Now," he muttered under his breath as Master Phineas shouted the words. "If you will be so kind as to show your gratitude with a coin or two. I shall be gone by morning, so now, good people, now is the time to show your appreciation."

"Now" was also the time for Eric to complete

his final task of the performance, the part he always dreaded. He gave the horse a slap on the rump and, feet dragging, mounted the step at the rear of the wagon, took a deep breath and gripped the door latch with a damp hand.

It was nearly dark inside; the only light creeping in through the woven lattice that faced the stage and a glowing ring with gems embedded in the floor. A figure shifted within the circle of pale, jewel-colored light, and Eric heard a hiss of frustration. He waited, frozen there, until Master Phineas ended the performance.

"Good night!" Master Phineas called. "Good night and thank you for your time, and your generosity!"

That was his cue. "Sleep," Eric commanded, and all the torches fell dark.

Once the crowd had dispersed, Eric struck the stage by the light of a pair of oil-burning lamps while Master Phineas counted the money. "Bah!" he grumbled. "This is not enough to buy a round for a hermit at the bottom of a dry well." He tipped the coins into his leather pouch and tossed the basket aside for Eric to fetch later. "How did you do?"

Eric shook his head. "These are poor people." His voice strained as he hoisted the rope that folded the stage back against the side of the wagon. "I barely got enough to restock our larder and feed the beasts."

"Supplies? Bah!" The old man stood and brushed dust from his faded crimson breeches. "Who gave you leave to spend my money?"

His bluster fell off Eric's shoulders like so much rain. "Our empty stomachs, that's who. Mine and the horses'. And yours." He hesitated. "Have you eaten anything today?"

Master Phineas snatched up his tattered wool cloak and threw it around his shoulders in a dramatic gesture. "You know very well I was at the roadhouse promoting my performance all afternoon. They've plenty of food there."

"But did you eat any of it?" Eric turned his face away and tied off the last rope. The old performer was a good man, but a bit overfond of the drink, with a tendency to get distracted if there was too much of it around.

"That's none of your concern." Master Phineas extended a gnarled hand. "Is there any of it left, or did you spend it all on whores and trinkets?"

Eric sighed and gave the stage a rap to make certain it was secure, then surrendered all the copper bits left in his pouch. He did not surrender the bronze coins he had stashed in his worn, leather-bound casket in the wagon; that bit of resourcefulness had kept them from starving on more than one occasion.

"Gone before morning," Eric called as the old man tottered off in the direction of the nearest tavern. "Remember."

"Silence, boy, of course I remember. It's my line, is it not?" Master Phineas dismissed him with a wave. "Folks will think you're my bride, not my servant." He started away again, but stopped when he reached the edge of the lantern light.

He turned, and his ruddy features softened. "The next town will be better, you know. Legerdemain. It means magic." His eyes brightened and his shoulders squared. "There, we shall live like kings, and be worshipped as gods."

Chapter 2

Legerdemain.

Master Phineas had talked of it for months, some days speaking of little else. To hear the old man tell it, the walls were built of gold and the streets paved with silver. Eric was used to such speeches, and adjusted his expectations accordingly.

The road to the fabled city was not an obvious one. All Eric had to guide him was the tattered remains of a map Master Phineas claimed to have created on his last visit to the city, eighteen years earlier. The parchment was thin and fragile, and the ink was so crooked and faded that Eric had to copy it onto the back of another map, just so he could use it. At every opportunity, he asked wayfarers and innkeepers for better directions, but most either hadn't heard of the city, or looked at him as if he were crazy for trying to get there.

"Legerdemain!" the barkeep at Dunnap had exclaimed. "Why do ya want to go there for?"

"Never been," he replied cryptically, because the streets are paved with silver seemed a stupid answer as did the fact that the name meant magic. "Thought it sounded promising for some shows, maybe make some silver."

The fat man snorted a laugh. "Your master's a magician, ain't he? Why don't he just wave his hand and send you there?" He snorted again as the early-morning drinkers chortled their approval.

Sensing a total lack of help, Eric thanked the man for his time, rolled up his map, and returned to the wagon. While the old man snored, he topped off their water barrels, took one last look at their paltry larder, and pointed the horses west.

The next three weeks saw them traveling an unending succession of switchbacks and mountain paths, leading them through the heart of the Eskell Divide, the heavily forested spine of land separating Legerdemain from the rest of the world. Eric stopped frequently, both to rest their weary horses and to restock their supply of fresh water. These pauses caused Master Phineas no end of frustration — especially since his supply of redsmoke wine grew weaker by the day. Eric was used to adding water to the barrel to make it last longer, but now the color was growing so pale, it wouldn't fool the old man for much longer.

The rutted track seemed infrequently used, and their heavy wagon was ill-suited for such a trek. They saw no other travelers once they entered the mountains, and after nearly three weeks of solitude, Eric began to wonder if they were traveling in the right direction. The old man insisted on both the veracity of his map and his memory, and since their supplies were running dangerously low, Eric had no choice but to press onward. They did not have enough food for the journey back.

It wasn't until the end of the third week that they finally met some other travelers. Three ox-drawn wagons, all laden with household goods, approached from the opposite direction. Eric halted his team, set the brake, and hailed the lead drover.

"Well met, sir," he called. "Is this the road to Legerdemain?"

The man, a sturdy laborer with a potato-shaped face and sandy hair, narrowed his eyes at Eric, and then shifted his gaze to the woman seated in the cart. Her sun-reddened face was surrounded by wisps of straw-colored hair, and she clutched a tightly wrapped bundle to her chest, which Eric presumed to be an infant. Two other children of indistinct age and gender peered at him from over the side of the cart.

Eric nodded at the little family, but got no response other than a hard stare. He looked back at the man, wondering if they spoke a different language. "Do you understand me, sir?" he tried again. "Is this the road ...?"

"I understand your words, lad," the man interupted, his accent harsh. "Just not why you'd be traveling to such a lost place as Legerdemain."

"Lost?" This brought Eric up short. "What do you mean?"

The man looked at his wife once more, then back to Eric. "I don't know what you're after there, but I'm afraid you're wasting your time. If I were you, I'd turn that fancy wagon of yours around and head back the way you came."

Eric felt a rush of apprehension. "Why is that?" he asked, not at all certain he wanted to hear the answer.

The man grimaced as if thinking of it pained him. "It's been my home all my days, and my father's days as well, but the city's not the place it was. It's twisted hard now, though I can't rightly say why. That's why me and mine are headed east." He jabbed a thick hand at the collection of carts, all containing people similar enough to be kin. "You're welcome to travel with us, if you choose."

Eric shook his head, disheartened by the notion that they had wasted all this time and travel. "We must press on, I'm afraid. Our supplies are low, and the horses are beat. How far is it?"

"Suit yourself." The man shrugged and spit. "You're two, maybe three days out. Just stay to this road, and once you clear the mountains, you'll see it." He paused. "Just be wary, lad, and mind you don't cross them at the citadel. Legerdemain is a fearful place, even for those that know it."

Eric wanted to ask him what he meant, but the man chirruped to his team, and the beasts heaved the cart up the trail. He waited until the wagons and their empty-eyed occupants had passed, then released the brake and urged the horses onward. He was glad Master Phineas hadn't wakened from his stupor for that conversation, and the quiet of the afternoon gave him time to ponder what the traveler had told him. This wouldn't be the first time the old man had led them on a fool's errand.

As promised, once the mountains opened up, the city appeared on the horizon. The road wound down from the mountains, cutting a path through the purple-gray fields and ending at high marble-faced walls. Bright spires pierced the mist and shot back the red morning sun. Beyond was a gray dimness that seemed the End of the World.

Overcome by wonder, Eric hooked the reins on the handrail and stood to get a better view. Shivering in the cool sea air, swaying with the wagon's movement, he stared open-mouthed at the vast expanse until the horses halted of their own accord. Water to the horizon, until it touched the sky. For a boy born in the desert, it was no less than a miracle.

"Boy!" The old man's voice barked from behind

the narrow door leading to the wagon's interior. "Why have we stopped?"

Eric shot a glance over his shoulder. "Come see for yourself."

"Insolent creature! I shall have you flogged."

Eric smiled at the bangs and clattering behind him that said Master Phineas would soon appear. He had been threatened with punishment every day for the last ten years, but the old man had yet to raise a hand to him. Like most everything Master Phineas did, his threats were all for show.

His master's silvery head appeared, followed by its hastily-dressed owner. His scowl evaporated behind a grin of delight. "That's it, my boy!" he said, clapping Eric on the shoulder. "Legerdemain means magic. Did you know that?"

"Yes, Master Phineas." He smiled. "You've told me. Several times."

"Don't be clever." The old entertainer's voice was jolly. "Within the space of a moon's turning, we shall own this town. I promise." He wavered unsteadily, then dropped onto the wagon's splintery seat. "Drive on, boy, drive on!" he proclaimed. "Tonight, we shall dine as kings!"

Infected by Master Phineas' enthusiasm, Eric resumed his seat, unhooked the reins, and urged the horses onward. Tall grass shifted and whispered around them, while the rising breeze brought an unfamiliar damp smell of salt and water. The road grew more crowded now, and Eric saw more outbound wagons that appeared to be full of their owner's worldly possessions. The traveler's words echoed in his ears, and he tried in vain to temper his eagerness to reach the city. But from this vantage, it didn't look dangerous. It looked beautiful.

Dusk fell before they reached the flatlands, and,

despite the old man's protests, Eric insisted on stopping for the night. Master Phineas celebrated their imminent arrival by downing the last of his wine. Though it was barely pink, such was the power of suggestion and the general state of his well-being that he was snoring before the sun had fully set.

Eric climbed on top of the wagon and watched the sun disappear into the ocean. By now, they were close enough to see the white-tipped waves crashing in from distant lands. He had always known such a thing existed, but never expected to see it for himself. Despite the drover's words, Eric couldn't help but feel excitement at the prospect of their arrival in Legerdemain. Maybe it meant magic to Master Phineas, but to him it meant freedom.

Though their destination loomed on the horizon, it still took the best part of the morning for Eric to guide the wagon out of the foothills and onto the worn stone road leading to the great city. The air grew thick with salt and moisture, and the weight of it filled his chest. "Just another city," he murmured, in a failed attempt to ease the knot that had settled in his stomach during the damp night.

While the city lay to the south, small farms surrounded by stone fences boxed off the land to the east and west as far as he could see. He couldn't identify the crops, but the fields were lush and green, and rolled as if in response to the ocean on the horizon. Rough-skinned laborers dotted the fields, wearing broad-rimmed hats and working up the soil. Eric hailed the first dozen he saw, but stopped when he received no response more friendly than a guarded stare.

Even more curious was the fact that the fields

grew less prosperous as they neared the city. Tidy white-washed farms gradually gave way to weathered sheds, leaning crazily away as if shouldering the wind. These fields were still cultivated, but the plants were as wan and thin as those who tended them. Most wore slave collars.

Eric hunched his shoulders and forced himself to look away. The sudden chill he felt was swallowed by the soaring walls of Legerdemain. He had seen larger cities, but none older. He was close enough now to make out the green striations on the gray-black stone. Great stonework statues of men and beasts guarded the walls on either side of the gates, but their faces and features were eroded. It was as if those who lived here inhabited the skeleton of a long-dead civilization.

As afternoon waned, the road grew crowded with out-bound farmers heading home and in-bound way-farers seeking shelter within the town walls. A massive spiked gate hung over the road at the exact point where the pike-wielding guards halted the inbound travelers. Three officials wearing black and silver cloaks inspected the wagons and queried their occupants.

Eric guided the team to the end of the line, dried his palms on his breeches, then reached around and rapped on the wagon door. "We're here."

The wait was excruciating, and Eric had time enough to grow nervous, relax, and get nervous all over again before they reached the spike-toothed gate. After the third rap, Master Phineas finally emerged, primped and polished as if ready for the stage. "Leave this to me," he whispered as he gathered the folds of his crimson cloak.

Eric nodded, then dropped his gaze. They had no money for a bribe; if they were to enter the city, it would be on the old man's considerable wits.

The first official, a portly man wearing a crested

baldric and an imperious manner, examined the wagon. He looked at Master Phineas, then gestured to the faded paint. "I'd admit you as a trader, but I can't for the life in me figure out what you're selling."

"A trader!" The old man feigned indignation. "You insult me, sir! I have performed my arts before kings and commoners from here to the Western Sea, and all before your father was but a glint in his father's eye. A trader! Bah!"

The official stepped back and stared at Master Phineas. He was clearly unaccustomed to being challenged, especially in such an overdramatic manner. "Well, then," he said, deciding to play along. "Since I can't admit you on balls alone, tell me, what is it that you do?"

Master Phineas fixed his audience of soldiers and travelers alike with a steely glare. "I had hoped my reputation preceded me, but perhaps you are not accustomed to the finer arts." He produced a slender amber wand as if from nowhere, and worked it through his still-agile fingertips.

"A juggler?" One of the men suggested. "We had one of them a few weeks ago. Saw him drunk at the tavern just t'other night. Dropped his balls all over."

"Bah!" Master Phineas roared and pointed the wand at the group of men. Of course, nothing happened, but only Eric expected it, and the circle around them widened. "I am no mere juggler; I am Phineas DeLayne, master magician and purveyor of the dark arts. Now I suggest you hold your tongue, else you find it flapping on the cobblestones like a hooked fish."

"Magician, you say?" The first official spoke. "I can admit you as that, aye." He nodded. "Our good King has a taste for that sort of entertainment." His lips curled in a smile, but it was by no means warm or friendly.

"Then he is a man of exquisite intellect and breeding." Master Phineas beamed and the wand vanished into his sleeve. This was just as well, as it had no more magic than a twig plucked from a rotten tree. "Now, do be a good knave and stand aside. I've a performance to prepare."

There was a long pause, in which Eric fully expected the guard to order them both arrested and hung for impudence. Instead, he waved them through the gate. "Pull your wagon into the yard. The steward will see to your papers."

Eric guided the wagon through the iron gate and into the enclosed yard. While he waited, he adjusted the workman's scarf around his neck and pushed his thick mouse brown hair off his forehead. The ocean breeze carried with it the scent of cooking meat, and his stomach rumbled in response. They had run out of everything but flat bread four days ago.

The steward, an older man with a stern countenance, emerged from an arched doorway in the stone guard tower. He held up a hand for silence even before Master Phineas started to speak. "I'll give you a pass for two weeks, no more. You'll need to register." With ink-smudged fingers, he flipped back the cover on his wax pad and plucked a stylus from his baldric. "Just you and the boy?"

Master Phineas stiffened, and for a moment, Eric thought he might lie. "I have another servant in the wagon."

"Servants?" The steward's brows arched. "Free or bound?"

The old man looked at Eric and sighed. "Bound."

The steward stopped writing and looked up. Eric felt his cheeks flush. With his free hand, he reached up and loosened the workman's scarf that hid his slave collar. It was a simple iron ring, but to Eric, it represented the weight of a thousand worlds.

"Mind he keeps that in sight." The man frowned and scribbled on a small piece of parchment. "Else you'll lose him to the galleys."

"I'll see that he does." The old man accepted the rolled parchment. "Are we free to enter?"

The steward looked them up and down, gnawed the inside of his cheek, and nodded. Not wanting to give Master Phineas another chance to speak, Eric slapped the reins on the horses' backs and the wagon lurched into the city.

Eric guided the horses through Legerdemain's narrow cobbled streets. His head swiveled at the sights. Food vendors, cloth merchants, jewelers and armorers clamored for attention with an unfamiliar high-pitched lilt. His stomach rumbled again. They would feast tonight, even if he had to creep back here and steal something.

Master Phineas sat beside him on the wagon bench, uncharacteristically silent. Eric assumed the old man was doing the same thing he was — gawking — but when he looked over, his master's face was knotted with worry.

Eric felt a pang of alarm.He leaned closer to make himself heard over the din, then asked. "What is it? What's wrong?"

"Not like I remember." Master Phineas said, more to himself than to Eric. "It is not right." He was quiet for another moment, then caught himself and clapped Eric on the shoulder. "'Twill be fine, though," he said as he stood. "You'll see. It may not be the Legerdemain I remember, but they'll still treat us like kings." His forced smile fell away again as he shook his head, then disappeared back into the wagon. To Eric, he seemed as if his memories had betrayed him.

After that curious exchange, Eric looked at the city with new eyes. Though he had nothing to compare it to, he realized that the old man was correct. Something was not right. The merchants seemed prosperous, and while the buildings were old, they appeared well kept and fully stocked. These were citizens — free citizens — who should have no cares, yet they went about their business in a joyless manner. Their movements were quick and wary, and they seldom, if ever, smiled. Even the children seemed oddly dour, and few responded to Eric's greetings. The brightly-painted wagon attracted more suspicion than curiosity, and Eric found himself wondering if they'd manage to attract an audience here at all.

Chapter 3

The street twisted and turned, until finally opening into a wide square that extended to the ocean. The sound of the hooves changed as they moved from cobblestones to onyx colored tiles; the hollow clop echoing in the damp air. The guards on duty in the square looked at him hard, studied his pass, then waved him through without comment.

After careful consideration, he halted the wagon at the far end of the square opposite the arched entrance. It was a perfect position — those roaming the town in search of diversion could not help but notice them. Eric pressed his boots against the worn floorboards and stretched. His head swiveled as he scanned the sun-washed stone and ornate marble buildings. The first home he remembered would fit in the entrance to one of those buildings, and there was more than enough room in the square for his entire village.

Eric took one final look at the ocean and set to work. Muscles strained, wood groaned and flecks of paint drifted to the ground as he lowered the stage from the wagon's side. He swung out the legs, braced the rear right corner with an empty oil cask, then stomped around on the worn boards to make sure it was stable. A boy from the livery stable trotted over, and they haggled over coins for the horses' keep. Eric noted with jealousy that the boy wore no collar; he was a freeman's son, learning a trade. Someday.

With a sigh, he covered the painted circle on the boards with a faded Sephasian carpet. Next, he inspected the torches at the front and placed incense-filled braziers at the rear. Salt air snapped the purple and silver pennants he hoisted at the four corners of the stage. Finally, he placed a wrought iron stand at the rear against the lattice, and filled the empty slots with amber wands identical to the one Master Phineas had produced from his sleeve.

Townspeople stopped, watched, then continued on their way. By the time dusk fell, those so inclined had made their way home, and those who remained clustered in groups at a cautious distance from the stage. Eric smiled. It seemed they would have an audience after all. He lit the braziers and torches, then ducked into the rear compartment of the wagon to change into his working clothes and get ready for the performance.

Eric removed an iron key from his coin pouch and unlocked a small interior compartment in the front of the wagon. Their reason for coming to Legerdemain sat pressed into the corner, scarecrow arms wrapped around bony knees, his pale face obscured by greasy hair that hung past his shoulders. Eric caught the boy by the slave collar and hauled him to his feet. "Let's go, feeb," he said. "Time to work."

The boy, Simon, followed obediently as Eric led him into the main compartment. He wore Eric's cast-off clothes, which hung from his shoulders and hips in tatters. His pale blue eyes blinked against the light, but registered nothing.

Eric halted him in front of the lattice window that looked out over the stage. Below the window, a golden circle inside another — symbols layered between — was painted on the floor. Blood red gems imbedded near the symbols pulsed as Simon entered the circle.

Eric stepped back to within arm's reach. He whispered a protection charm he knew to be nonsense, took a deep breath, then reached over and clasped Simon's wrist. "Wake up," he whispered, then sprang back a hair's breadth from the monster's clawed fingertips. Eric's heel caught a loose board and he stumbled, striking his right shoulder on the rough worktable.

"Getting slower," Simon cackled. "Almost had you."

Eric swore and rubbed his shoulder. This happened every time. The mad creature thought it was a game.

The awakened Simon paced the inner confines of the circle, a step in each direction. "Where is this?" His words ran together and his eyes, now the color of a moonlit sky at midnight, darted in their sockets as he took in his surroundings. The glow of the gems followed his movement. Though he wore the same clothes and skin as the feeble boy, this was not the same person.

Suddenly, he stopped and confronted Eric. "Where is this? This is different."

"You'll know soon enough." Eric stood and brushed the dust from his clothing.

"Tell me you tell me you." Simon stopped abruptly, his head cocked as if listening to something Eric couldn't hear. "What?" His head tilted in the other direction. "What is it what is ..." his voice trailed off into gibberish and his body grew still.

Eric gaped at him. What indeed? This was not the night for Simon to finish his journey into complete madness. But before he could decide what to do about it, Master Phineas came banging through the rear door. "What's keeping you, you lazy whelp?" he barked. "I just had to chase a half-dozen thieves and brigands from my stage. Why isn't the boy ...?"

This time, it was the old man's voice that trailed off. Eric looked from Simon to Master Phineas, and saw that most of the blood had drained from his face. "What is it?" Eric asked.

Master Phineas gave himself a little shake and some of his bluster returned. "Malingering, that's what. Both of you." He jabbed a gnarled finger at Simon. "Tell me what happened to him?"

"I don't know." Eric gave a shrug. "He was awake and threatening me like usual, and then he just — stopped."

"Stopped, eh?" The old man seemed to grow more agitated with every breath. He motioned Eric out of the way with a dramatic flip of the wrist and approached the ring. "Boy!" he barked. Eric had never heard Master Phineas address Simon by his name. "You heed me! Boy!"

Simon remained as he was, eyes and ears trained on something no one else could sense. It may have been a trick of the fading light, but Eric could have sworn Simon's eyes were now the color of morning sky.

"Boy!" The master's voice rose. "Heed me!" He extended a gnarled hand over the edge of the circle, and the gems gave a weak pulse. Master Phineas narrowed his eyes in concentration and growled a string of nonsense syllables. At first, nothing happened, and the old man repeated the phrase in a guttural chant. His voice swelled, as did the beads of sweat on his ashy skin. Finally, the ring responded, sending jagged flickers of pale blue light arcing between the gems. The light crisscrossed the center of the ring, and Simon cried out, startled, when it touched him. He circled wildly, trying to escape, but there was nowhere for him to go. After a few, frantic moments, he sank to his knees, sobbing and rocking.

Master Phineas withdrew his hand and the light stopped pulsing. He regarded the huddled boy on the floor with a hard stare. "He'll mind now," he barked at Eric, without looking away. "Wake him up."

Eric crept to the edge of the circle and crouched beside Simon. The strong smell of urine filled the wagon; Simon had wet himself. Eric's heart hammered and his mouth was dry. As pitiable as Simon looked now, Eric knew from experience that he'd be doubly dangerous when he awoke. He took Simon's wrist. The boy's skin was damp and cold.

"Get on with it," Master Phineas growled. "I'll lose my crowd."

Master Phineas shoved him backward. Eric stumbled against the rear door and watched as the old man once more brought the ring to life, punishing the mad creature. This time, Simon stood against the pain, baring his teeth and growling like a caged animal. Blood streamed from his nose and mouth, vivid against his pale flesh.

"You will obey!" Master Phineas demanded. "This night, you will obey, or I will send you to Otherworld with my own hands."

Simon screamed with laughter and tried to throw the magic back at him, but, as powerful as he was, he could not breach the outer ring. The two stood locked in a futile battle, Simon withstanding, even seeming to welcome, the pain from the light, and it was Master Phineas who finally had to withdraw.

"You will obey," the old man repeated, stepping as close to the circle as he dared. "You will not ruin this night."

Simon chuckled and smeared the blood from his face with the back of his hand. He sent a shower of sparks flashing at Master Phineas, who jumped back even though he knew better.

The old man covered his flash of fear by turning to Eric. “Once the show is over, put him down and clean him up. One way or the other, we will be rid of him.”

Eric nodded once. He had seen them battle before; charging the ring seemed to make Simon more powerful and better able to perform. But he had not seen it go on for so long. He looked to Simon, whose eyes remained fixed on Master Phineas until the old man left the wagon.

As soon as the door closed, Simon chanted, “Let me out let me out let me out. We will be rid of him. Rid.”

Eric had seen this before too. Just as Master Phineas never spoke Simon’s name, Simon never spoke at all in Master Phineas’ presence. All of his insane chatter, he reserved for Eric. “You aren’t going anywhere,” Eric told him. “At least not yet.”

“Yet? Yet?” Simon fixated on the word.

“That’s right,” Eric retorted. “Guard the wagon.”

Simon flashed a malevolent grin and faced the stage. Legerdemain was a city of magicians, and Simon was the reason they had come all the way to this far-flung city. Surely, someone here would pay handsomely for a slave of Simon’s particular abilities. If Master Phineas’ plans and prognostications held true, he would be the key to their future — one without hardship and hunger, without uncertainty and unending travel. A key to freedom.

Eric touched the iron collar on his own neck. Though he’d worn it all of his life, the weight of it still burned him. “You will obey,” he told Simon. “The Master will be out soon.”

Chapter 4

Princess Daria paced the confines of the seaside salon, her anger outstripping her fear. Two of her attendants hovered in the hall, as did the pair of ever-present guards assigned to insure her safety. She glared at them and tossed her long black curls over her shoulder.

Those guards were the cause of her current agitation. Newly assigned by the Court Magician, Lord Vassant, they shadowed her every movement and prevented her from leaving the citadel compound. For your protection, Princess, the captain had assured her smoothly, though she could not imagine what she was being protected from.

Daria exhaled through her teeth and stared through the lattice doors to the night-dark ocean. How long had it been since she had been out on the water, or even outside the citadel walls?

Nervous about the coming confrontation, she smoothed her skirts and brushed imaginary dust from her bodice. Each time she spoke to Lord Vassant, his words made perfect sense as they fell from his lips. Each time she found herself nodding in agreement. It wasn't until later — much later — that she questioned everything he told her, astounded that she had agreed with him at all.

A single set of boot steps sounded in the hall. Daria whirled to confront Vassant. Instead, her father, King Lysander, stood in the doorway. "Hello, my treasure," he said, his dark face crinkling in a smile. "Steward told me I'd find you here." He dropped his cloak on a low bench beside the door and held his arms out to her. "Have you missed me?"

Her anger dissipated as she hurried toward him. "Papa!" she exclaimed as they embraced. In his arms, she felt much younger than her fifteen years. "Where have you been? I haven't seen you in …."

"Hush." He placed a gloved finger on her lips. "I have been busy, but it's nothing to concern you." His brown eyes were tired, but he seemed genuinely happy to see her. "But these are dangerous times, and as much as I would prefer to spend my time in your company, I have a duty to protect our kingdom. And you." He touched her nose with his fingertip. "Which is why I have had guards assigned to you."

"You?" Daria tilted her head. "But I thought Lord Vassant …."

"He only did so at my request." His demeanor grew serious. "I have enemies, Daria, enemies who would seek to strike out at me through you. As much as it pains me to limit your activity, I only do so out of fear for your safety."

"But who?" Her brow furrowed.

"That is not your concern." His voice, though gentle, took on an urgent tone. He cupped her face in his hands and placed his thumbs on her lips. His warm touch made her feel disoriented. It was the confusion she felt when ....

"You know I love you." He spoke softly, drew her closer. "You know I would never do anything to harm you." Daria's throat tightened and her eyes filled with tears. "My dear friend Lord Vassant does what he has to do to protect you. As he always has and as he always will."

The magician! Fear tugged at her mind. She tried to back away, but his grip tightened. "Vassant ...." she whispered.

"Loves you as I do. And you must obey him as you do me." His voice grew solemn, and he removed his hands from her face. "I am a busy man. Perhaps you haven't noticed, but I have a kingdom to attend to." His voice, while not harsh, let her know that he was not humoring her.

"Of course." Daria stepped back, momentarily lost in the conversation. Her eyes dropped briefly to the floor, but she forced herself to look back at him. "Is there any way I can help you? Learn from you?" His short outburst of laughter pained her. "Why is that so funny?"

Her father collected himself and smiled at her in a patronizing manner. "My dear, you are only a child. Why would you want to trouble yourself with such things?"

"I'm not a child," she stammered, sounding more childish than she intended. "I am your heiress. I should be learning ...."

"We will not speak of this further. You asked to see me, and I am here. If there is anything else you desire, speak it now. But I will not have you annoying me like ..." his voice trailed off.

Daria, somewhat wilted by his words, looked up at him. He seemed to be listening to something in the outer halls. Daria strained her ears, but heard only the normal passage of servants. "What is it?" she asked.

He ignored her, a smile growing on the lower half of his face. That smile, more than anything that he did or said, worried her. He turned to one of the attendants waiting in the hall. "Fetch Rialle." When the girl didn't move quickly enough, he barked the order again.

Daria's heart plummeted. This elevation of a former servant to trusted advisor was yet another symptom of his growing strangeness. Though they tried to keep it from her, she knew what the servants whispered, that the cold, calculating Rialle was much more than an advisor to her father. The thought sickened her, and she refused to believe it.

Rialle appeared in the doorway, as if she had been waiting just outside to be summoned. She dressed above her station, wearing fine brocade robes of ice blue silk and spun silver. Her pale eyes flickered over Daria and dismissed her as if she were the one who was a servant, instead of the other way around. Daria seethed as the elegant blonde woman positioned herself at her father's elbow. "How may I serve you, Highness?"

The King motioned for Rialle to come close, then spoke so only she could hear him. Her reaction was not one of romance, but of surprise. "Are you certain?" she asked.

"Ah, yes," her father smiled again, a smile Daria did not recognize. "Quite certain." He turned to go. "Have a carriage made ready." It wasn't until he reached the door that he seemed to remember that Daria was still there. "You must forgive me, my dear," he said, sounding not at all sorry. "I have business to attend."

Chapter 5

Outside the wagon, the audience grew silent as Master Phineas mounted the stage. Taking his cue, Eric wrapped the long scarf around his neck to cover his collar and stepped up to the window to scan the crowd for prospective targets as the old man began his performance.

"You've come to see magic, have you?" he queried, his voice as bold as that of a god.

"Obey the master," Eric whispered to Simon.

Master Phineas stepped into the circle carved into the stage and produced an obsidian orb from the folds of his sleeve. Simon gave a low growl as the globe in the old man's hand began to spin. As it moved, its glow bathed his noble face. "You want to be amazed? Astounded? Astonished?"

Eric took one last look at Simon, whose unblinking blue-black eyes were fixed not on their master, but a point somewhere distant. His bloodied face showed no strain, only rage. "Enjoy the show," Eric muttered, then moved out into the mass of spectators.

He slipped through the crowd, anonymous as an apple in a barrel of many. He lifted two coin purses as he listened to the patter and idly sought an inattentive third. He had just selected his target when he heard the crash of glass. Eric darted left and scrambled for a clear view of the stage. Master Phineas stood over the shattered globe as the crowd began to jeer at him. The combination of rage and humiliation on the old man's face sent Eric scrambling for the rear of the wagon. By Bartoch, now what?

He jerked open the door and found Simon standing before him. Eric staggered back in astonishment. "What?" Only his grip on the handle kept him from falling. "Sleep," he shouted, not caring who heard. "Sleep!"

Simon only stared at him. He seemed to have lost focus and gone dormant without being told. He babbled a string of nonsensical syllables, and, when Eric didn't respond, Simon lunged at him and caught him by the arm.

Eric jerked back in reflex, but there was no malice in the boy's mien. Stunned, he allowed Simon to pull him over to the window, heedless of the flashing circle beneath their feet. Still speaking nonsense, Simon jabbed a finger out the window.

Eric looked through the lattice and out onto the stage, expecting to see their angry master ready to skewer the pair of them. Instead, Master Phineas stood with his robed back to them, watching a procession of soldiers advance across the square.

Simon pressed his face against the lattice and increased his babbling. Eric jerked hard on the fool's collar. "Be quiet!" His heart thumped in his chest. Should he stay hidden, or go to Master Phineas?

It happened quickly, though Eric's mind drew out the memory like fine-spun thread. A handsome nobleman emerged from the cluster of uniforms, wearing a greatcoat of crimson and burnished gold. The din of the crowd fell to a hushed whisper as he approached the wagon, and the empty space around them grew larger. In the fading light, his eyes burned black against his fair skin, and the smile that split his face held no warmth. Eric wanted desperately to believe he meant them no ill will, but there was nothing benevolent about this cruel young man.

With great ceremony, the haughty noble raised his left arm and extended his long fingers. A cluster of blood-red flame bloomed and grew in the palm of his hand. "Legerdemain has a magician," he proclaimed, and hurled the fire at the stage.

Eric screamed as the flames consumed Master Phineas' robes, then his flesh. "No!" he bellowed, but the sound vanished in the roar of the spectators. Beside him, Simon laughed gleefully. Eric whirled and struck him, open-handed, against the jaw. The blow knocked Simon backward and he stumbled out of the circle, crashing against the wall.

Simon's laughter ceased; his head swiveled, and Eric realized the folly of his actions. Simon raised his hand, and Eric saw the beginnings of a crimson flame. His heart stopped in his chest as he drew a breath and shouted, "Sleep!"

This time it worked. Simon dropped like a puppet with cut strings. He scurried back to his corner and covered his head with his hands.

"You always were a clever boy, Eric." Master Phineas' shade manifested between him and the door. His eyes, dark in life, blazed brightly with the glow of Otherworld.

Eric's knees buckled. "Master."

"I haven't much time. Neither have you." Master

Phineas stepped toward him, but his boots made no sound on the boards. He pointed at Simon. “Wake him. Turn him loose on the crowd. It’s the only way.”

Horrified, Eric stared up at the shade. “What?” His jaw trembled. “No!”

“Yes” he barked, his ghost-voice as sharp as it had been when he was alive. He drifted closer and jabbed an elongated finger at Simon. “You want your freedom? Here is the key. Use him now, before they realize.”

Eric looked from the spirit to the crouching Simon. Phineas brushed his chin with an icy hand. Repulsed, Eric looked away. “I can’t control him. He’ll kill me. He’ll kill everyone.”

“A worthwhile risk,” the ghost insisted. “Do it.”

His muscles frozen in fear, Eric forced himself to shift position to his hands and knees. Careful not to crawl through the impatient shade, Eric crept to where his meager cache was hidden. His hands shook as he pried up the floorboard and removed the leather-bound box that contained all of his money and possessions, including the letter that would set him free. Free. The thought struck him then. He looked up at the billowing shade. “You’re dead,” he whispered. “I am free.”

“Not yet, you aren’t!” Phineas crossed the room like a windswept cloud to where the feeble boy sat rocking. Simon lifted his face, and amidst the swirl of death magic, their eyes met. Simon showed no fear, no rage, and no comprehension of what was happening around them.

“Turn him loose,” the spirit urged. “Avenge me.”

Eric shoved the box into a satchel. “I won’t! It’s too dangerous.”

“What does that matter to you?” The ghost’s eyes blazed red. “Don’t be a fool, Eric. You’re not free yet. They’ll take him, and they’ll take you.”

Eric shook his head and cradled the satchel against his chest. “Coward!” Phineas’ voice raised the hairs on the base of his neck. “I will see you in Otherworld!” The shade’s final shriek nearly split his skull as the wagon door splintered inward.

Chapter 6

Eric, prodded by a pike-wielding soldier, stumbled into the Grand Square. Rows of armed men in blue tabards had replaced the spectators, and in their midst stood the magician, still gloating and bloated with power.

Eric's fear became rage. "Murderer!" he cried and broke from his captor, his hands outstretched and grasping.

Before he covered half the distance, the force of a dozen winds caught him up and slammed him against the wagon. Breathless and dazed, he regained his feet and lurched forward for another assault. This time, his fingertips brushed the crimson coat before the laughing magician hurled him back across the stage.

Desperate, he braced for another run. Heat seared his left hand; Eric jerked away, then crab-scrambled on his heels and elbows away from Master Phineas' charred remains. The old man's spine was arched, his arms outstretched in final supplication. Tendrils of smoke wafted up from the raw hole of his mouth and his once bright eyes were black.

"Care to try again?" the magician taunted. "Three times lucky?"

Eric swallowed his bile, drew a hard breath, then another. The world dissolved with his wits; he wanted to hide his face and scream until his throat burst.

Shapes moved through his blurred vision. Two soldiers dragged Simon from the wagon. He dug his heels into the ground and his black hair streamed out as he shook his head from side to side. One of the soldiers raised his cudgel and barked, "Be still, damn you!"

"Don't hit him!" Eric shouted. "He doesn't understand!"

The blow fell. Simon yowled and jerked away, still fighting. "Please!" Eric pleaded, then called, "Simon!" The mad creature turned. Terror became recognition, and he lurched toward the stage. "No!" Eric commanded. "Be still!"

Simon immediately stopped struggling and went limp. The soldier with the cudgel shoved his cowering captive face down on the tiles. His partner eyed Eric, then advanced, only to be halted by a pale slip of a woman with eyes as blue as ice chips. "Well now," she said softly, gliding toward Eric. "What have we here?"

"You didn't have to kill him." Eric's breath spiked in his chest. "We did nothing!"

"Were you not paying attention?" The malice in her smile made Eric flinch. "Legerdemain has a magician." She gave a languid gesture with her right hand. "Lord Vassant."

As if to punctuate the remark, the magician lifted his hand. Crimson flame burst from his fingertips, splashing the square with red light. A gesture dashed the magefire against the stage, which shuddered and burst into flames. The force of the blast knocked Eric to the ground. The soldiers surrounded him before he could rise; he felt a boot on his spine, and a spear point pricked the back of his neck.

The woman spoke. "Take them to Sniley. I'm told he's short of stock."

Eric shifted his head and stared at the smoldering remnants of his life. His skull felt hollow; his guts became stone. It could not be real, but the burning in his eyes told him otherwise.

Someone yanked the satchel from his grasp. He staggered back as the scarf was ripped from his neck, exposing his collar. "No!" he shouted as the woman's words took on their true meaning. "I was to be freed!"

"Is that so?" The soldier hauled him to his feet and hooked him to the other end of the chain attached to Simon's collar. "And what about the fool, here? He a free man too?"

"No!" Desperate to explain his situation, Eric twisted away and searched for the lady. Surely, she would understand. He scanned the crowd. On the far side of the square, a liveried footman was helping her into an ornate carriage.

"Wait!" Eric shouted, but she did not turn. He started toward her, only to be brought up short by the chain. His captor jerked him in the opposite direction, and he stumbled, numbed by fear. With one last look at the smoking wagon, he realized that perhaps Master Phineas was the fortunate one.

Chapter 7

Rialle allowed the footman to hand her into the carriage without so much as a backward glance at the mess Vassant had left in the square. The satisfaction she felt was a tangible thing; not at the charlatan's demise — for that was nothing — but at the attention she commanded from the townspeople. The touch of their gaze upon her gown, her hair, her skin, was better than that of a lover.

She settled back against the plush velvet upholstery and watched Vassant's restless movements — finger drumming, shifting, stomping and puffed exhales. When she could bear it no longer, she spoke. "Is something troubling you?"

"The old man didn't even fight." The magician groused like a thwarted child. "Why did he not fight?"

"I don't know." Rialle studied her reflection in the carriage glass. "You killed him before I could ask."

With the speed of an adder, Vassant snapped out a hand and caught her wrist. Rialle drew back her lips and gasped. "Do not be insolent," he snarled, giving her hand a twist. "I know what I felt." He released her with a jerk. "He should have fought back."

Rialle massaged her bruised flesh. "Perhaps when he felt your prowess, he knew he had no chance." She made no attempt to keep the sarcasm from her voice.

"Perhaps." Vassant steepled his fingers, oblivious to her indignance. "But this, this was not at all satisfying."

Rialle scowled at his petulance. His affected airs grew tiresome, as did the charade of playing his chamberlain. Only a few years separated them but, while she was the wiser of the two by far, he was the one with the power. Literally. She lifted her gaze and looked across the carriage at the magician. His eyes were closed, and his head moved loosely against the cushion. He played the nobleman with everyone but her — only when alone together did she see the pale young man beneath the glowing facade. She stroked his cheek with her fingertips, and his lips curved in a faint smile.

"Don't try to distract me," he murmured, without opening his eyes. "I wish to sulk."

Rialle smiled, closed her eyes and lost herself in the gentle sway of the carriage. Each season brought charlatans and posers from the mountains, all seeking favor with the King, and all claiming powers beyond imagining. Vassant handled most of them without leaving the palace — a mental shrug and they were no more.

In their years of power, only four true magicians had come to Legerdemain and all had fallen as this one had. Five dead now — six, counting Vassant's former teacher, the old witch he vanquished to take the Court position. Her smile broadened. Three years past, and the witch's death still pleased her most of all.

But this one was different. It had taken all her considerable wit to persuade him not to rush the square unattended. She knew she had nothing to fear from him; but in that moment, she had flinched before the madness in his eyes. Now this. He had expected a tumble and got a peck on the cheek. No doubt, she would be expected to compensate.

Vassant's head jerked up. "Servants!" he exclaimed, rapping his hand on the side of the carriage.

Rialle came to attention. "Is there something you require?"

"No, no, no." He thumped with each word. "The old man had servants. What became of them?"

Rialle considered this. There were two — the plain boy, who had put up a fuss, and a pretty, feeble creature. "I sent them to Sniley. Why?" Her brows arched. "Do you want them?"

"No, no," he interjected. "I want you to talk to them." His eyes flashed in the semi-darkness of the carriage interior. "Something is amiss here, and I will know what it is."

Their arrival at the citadel saved Rialle the trouble of fabricating a suitable response. She waited as Vassant exited the carriage, then allowed the footman to hand her down into the courtyard. From the corner of her eye, she caught a glimpse of his face in the torchlight. The servant was an older man, and though his face remained impassive, she thought she saw a glint of contempt in his eyes. She gave a private smile — just because you are content to remain at your station, does not mean I am.

Chapter 8

The walk from the square to the seaside citadel was a blur. Chilled bone-deep by the damp air and sickened by what he had witnessed, Eric followed blindly. Master Phineas was dead. His mind could not go beyond that point. When he closed his eyes, Eric saw the charred body as if the image were seared on the inside of his eyelids.

Memory of the ghost struck a cold bolt through his gut. Kill them, the Master's shade had told him. Kill them all. Eric looked to his left, where Simon plodded mindlessly along beside him at the end of his chain. He could still do it. They were close enough that their shoulders were almost touching; the guards would never notice if he reached over and took Simon's wrist. One touch, one word, and none of this would be happening. It would all be over.

But his hands were as paralyzed as his heart and his mind, and Eric plodded on. Too late, he realized he should be watching his steps, watching their path, so he could retrace it later if needed. Stupid, so stupid. It was as if his wits had been stolen along with his freedom.

The screech of metal on metal interrupted his self-recriminations. Before them, a massive iron gate crept upward into the blackness of an imposing tower. Spitting torches fought the night, and pennants flapped in the salt-air gloom. When they passed through the arched gateway, Eric felt as if he had entered Otherworld.

At the north end rose a shining keep, ringed around with flaming torches the size of a grown man. The soldiers' boots echoed off the stone, the sound almost lost amidst the laments of strange fowl and the ever-present ocean roar.

The mass of soldiers thinned. Their captor and two of his fellows led them toward a series of low buildings at the far end of the compound. The captain hammered on a heavy wooden door with his pike. "Come now, Sniley!" he shouted. "I've got something for you!"

Eric shivered in the night air as the door stared blankly back at them. Some sort of prison, he imagined, and protests rose and fell in his throat. A mistake. The weight of his collar, something he'd worn his whole life, made it difficult to breath. "A mistake," he said, finally.

The door swung inward. Eric's jaw clicked shut. A one-eyed hulk of a man wearing naught but a nightshirt peered at them from the gloom. He lifted his lantern. "What you want? I've just found my bed!"

"Lord Vassant cooked another magician in the square. These two are leftovers." He tugged the chain. "His trinket said give 'em to you."

"Did she now?" The man stepped closer and eyed the pair. "By Sancte, if you balled 'em together they wouldn't make a decent rower." He raised the lantern. "Not worth the bread to keep 'em alive."

A slave trader. Eric's blood froze. "No. No. No! I don't belong here. A mistake. There's a letter ...."

"Quiet!" The soldier cuffed him with a gloved fist, then addressed the trader. "I can take 'em back, tell her you didn't want 'em?"

"Nay. Bring 'em in." The man stepped back and opened the door. "A poor trader's got to take what he can. They give you any trouble?"

"This one squawked a bit when his master fried." The soldier prodded Eric with his pike, forcing him to stumble over the doorsill. "But he's been a good little slave ever since."

Eric caught himself before he fell. Awash in fear, he spun to face the soldier. "I am not a slave. I am a free man."

The soldier laughed and produced two coin purses. Eric recognized them as the ones he had stolen from the spectators. "If you ain't a slave, then you're a thief. And thieves get their necks stretched." He jiggled the coins in his hand. "Tell me, boy, what are you?"

Eric wanted to shout — better to die a free man, but his mouth would not form the words. His hands fell hopelessly to his sides as Sniley led them through the gloom into a low raftered hall. Pale faces watched their passage from outside the glow of the lantern. "Here you are, boys." Sniley hung the lantern on a hook. "Hope you like the accommodations."

The empty stall was three paces across and filled with moldy straw. Eric dug in his heels and shook his head. "This isn't necessary."

"Oh, aye." The soldier released Simon and shoved him against the wall. Simon whimpered, but did not fight as he was tethered to an iron ring in the wall. "I leave you loose; you lie here like a pair o' lambs 'til morning?" He snorted. You must think I'm daft as your friend there."

Sniley caught the soldier's arm and pointed at Eric. "Put that one across the aisle, away from his mate.

Keeps the mischief down."

The soldier snorted again but did as the keeper asked. Eric resisted enough to earn an ear-ringing clout and a sharp jab to the stomach. His hands went to his collar. The iron felt tight, and the weight of the chain enormous. Panic snatched at him with cold gray claws as the lock snapped shut. "I don't belong here."

"Yet here you be." Sniley reclaimed his lantern and tottered off down the aisle, leaving them in darkness.

Exhaustion dragged Eric into a leaden unconsciousness; his weary mind spun nightmare, memory, and dream together.

His life played out before him like a wheel. He ran in packs with other children, learning to steal. He traded what he had stolen for food; too young to know he could take the coins and buy more than the meager rations his master doled out.

He had no waking memory of being sold — but in his dream, a strange man with white hair and wild eyes walked through the old master's yard, touching each child on the forehead. At each child, he shook his head and scowled.

Eric expected nothing and wanted to get about his day's work. There was a new vendor at the far end of the market who was blissfully lax about minding his wares. Eric was eager to see if yesterday's losses had taught him anything. But the strange man placed his bony palm on Eric's grimy forehead and a jolt shot through his body. One moment he was standing there waiting, the next he was on the ground, bawling. Amidst the sounds of his own tears, he heard the old man say, "This one."

His new master, called Phineas, took him on a

long wagon ride. Eric's fear melted as he realized that Master Phineas meant him no harm. There was to be no more stealing, and he ate more in one day than he used to see in a week. Best of all, Master Phineas talked to him and taught him things. He had a charmed voice, better even than the market fabulist. Eric became lost in his words, so that he did not notice the hours pass or the scenery change. It was the happiest time he ever knew.

Their journey ended at an isolated cottage deep in an ancient forest. Master Phineas approached the little building at an odd angle, and did dozens of incomprehensible things while Eric sat shivering on the wagon seat. Finally, the gray door swung inward and the old man motioned him to follow.

"Come," the Master beckoned. "There's someone I want you to meet."

Eric forced himself down from the wagon and through the narrow door. The cottage was bare of furniture, and a brightly painted circle of silver and gold covered much of the floor. A boy, not much bigger than Eric, sat motionless in the circle's center. He was cat-thin and had black hair that hung well past his shoulders.

"Interesting. Yes. Very." A woman spoke from behind him. "He hides well, that one."

Eric jerked around. The woman was no taller than he was, with a narrow face and long white hair that fell to her waist in twisted strands and braids. Though her skin was unlined, Eric knew somehow she was old, very old. Her dark eyes glittered as she watched Master Phineas go about his magic, unlocking the circle.

"What is he?" She pointed to Simon then prodded Eric with a gnarled finger. "Magician? Demon? Madman?" Her voice quivered in amusement. "Angel?"

"I don't know," Eric stammered. "I've never seen him before now. I've never seen you either."

"Ah, but you shall." She placed a finger to her lips. "But it would be best if you did not remember." She seized his shoulders, spun him around and forced him to watch as Master Phineas brought the boy in the circle from his slumber. "Ask your master what he is."

"You wish to know?" Phineas said as he undid the final ward. "You wish to know what I've created?"

The boy jerked to life. His deep blue eyes scanned the room, then fixed on Eric. Terror struck deep, in a place Eric hadn't known existed, and he stumbled back against the closed door. He turned to the woman, thinking she would protect him, but she was gone, replaced by the mad creature spitting pinwheels of flame from his fingertips. The old man's robes caught fire, and as he burned, he said, "You should have used him when you had the chance."

Chapter 9

Blasted him right away, he did." The boy laughed. "Never seen anything like it."

Daria leaned forward on the window seat and arched her neck to see the speaker, though she had a pretty good idea who it was. One of the older pages had been pursuing her chambermaid, Talya, with particular vigor. From the permanent flush on the woman's cheeks, it appeared his attention was not unwelcome.

"You were there?" Talya exclaimed.

"Aye." The page gestured expansively. "The old man had just begun his pitch when Lord V stepped out of his carriage and Wham!" He slapped his hands together. "Old man weren't nothing but a pile of ash."

"Weren't you frightened?"

"Naw." The page hooked his thumbs in his belt and affected a swagger. "I see to Lord V's wants and wishes sometimes — he knows me, knows I'm the one who knows what he likes."

"Daria!"

Daria's head snapped back. She looked at her

nurse, then back at the needlework in her hand. It was supposed to be a flower. "I'm sorry Bethel," she said, holding the cloth against her chest. "But this is just so pointless."

"Every lady should know how to stitch," Bethel sat down beside her. "I learned as a girl, I taught your mother — may the spirits hold her — and I am determined that I will teach you too." She held out her hand. "Now let me see."

Daria looked out the window and wondered just how far the scrap of linen would fly if she gave it a good hard toss. Instead, she handed it to Bethel. "Has there been any word on the hiring of a new tutor for me?"

An upward flick of the nurse's eyes told Daria this was a foolish question. Of course there was no word; this was just one of her many grievances, and one of the many ways in which she was becoming lost in her own home. Her education had ceased three years ago when her tutor abruptly resigned and departed for his home on the other side of the mountains. Since then, her father had assured her he was seeking a replacement, but had difficulty finding someone who was both suitable and willing to travel to Legerdemain.

"I know it is hard to imagine," Daria said. "But I miss having lessons."

Bethel finished clucking over the misshapen needlework and handed it back to Daria. "Well, clearly my lessons aren't satisfactory."

Daria laughed. "I love you, Bethel, but no, they are not. And I am not going to waste the afternoon sitting here." She tossed her handiwork to the other end of the bench. "What is my father doing this afternoon? Perhaps I shall join him."

"I don't know, miss, I've not seen him." Bethel hid her eyes as she retrieved the cloth and began picking away the errant stitches.

"What about Lord Vassant? Have you seen him?"

"You wish to join him?" Bethel asked, a hint of humor tugging at her lips.

"I do not." Daria snorted and sat back. In truth, she had always been more than a little uncomfortable around Lord Vassant, even back when he was simply Vassant the Apprentice, studying under Maraguase, the former Court Magician. He was always watching her, always a little too familiar, as if his proximity to the court gave him leave to presume friendship.

Thinking of Mara made Daria sad; she missed the old woman in ways she couldn't miss her own mother, whom she had never known. Lord Vassant wasn't even a pale replacement for his predecessor; he was an insult to her memory. Mara wouldn't have blasted a poor old itinerate magician; she would have invited him for a meal and spent the evening discussing their craft.

Daria seethed anew. The more she considered it, the more it offended her. She gestured toward the open door with her chin. "Did you hear what Talya's page said? Lord Vassant roused himself from his tower and killed a street performer last night. Why do you suppose he did that?"

"That's not my concern, miss." Bethel lifted her eyes from the sampler. "And not yours either."

"Oh yes." Daria rolled her eyes. "My concern should be whether or not the green thread and the blue thread are aligned correctly." She stood. "I am going to speak with Lord Vassant. I wish him to know who is the master here."

Chapter 10

Eric woke with the taste of dust in his mouth. The air was cold and damp, and shivering made his body ache. Must have forgotten to latch the wagon door, he thought as he rubbed his eyes and shoved himself into a sitting position.

The weight of the chain on his collar brought him up short. His eyes snapped open. Instead of waking from a nightmare, he had awakened into one.

Fighting panic, Eric blinked and looked around, trying to gather the remnants of his scattered memories. Mote-filled light streaming through glassless windows did little to dispel the gloom in the long, low-ceilinged building. Cobwebs hung from blackened rafters — ghost cloaks, the other children had called them. Eric shivered again. Where had that memory come from?

A narrow aisle separated two rows of cramped stalls, divided by partitions. In each, rag-clad, hollow-eyed slaves sat chained to the wall. Every stray breeze stirred the air and filled his nostrils with the smell of unwashed bodies and human waste.

Across the dirt aisle, Simon sat pressed into a shadowy corner. In this state, he seemed piteous, but Eric remembered his laughter as Master Phineas died. The chain slithered between his shoulder blades as he moved to the edge of the stall and glared at the fool. "This is your fault," he whispered, his words as hard as a curse. "You could have saved him."

At the opposite end of the row, a broad-shouldered boy distributed hunks of bread. Eric felt his stomach roll. Most of the others were standing, arms outstretched for their paltry rations.

When his turn came, Eric ignored the offered bread. "I need to speak to your master," he said, making his voice deliberately calm. "There has been a terrible mistake."

The boy shook greasy blond hair from his eyes. "Take it," he grunted, pushing the bread toward him.

Eric accepted the loaf. The boy moved on, bypassing Simon. "Hey!" Eric shouted and gestured across the aisle. "What about him?"

"Rupe only feeds them that stand."

Eric turned. In the next stall stood a thickset man with red hair and a scraggly beard. His tattered tunic revealed a deep brand on the center of his chest. He gnawed his chunk of bread and stood patiently while Eric stared.

Finally, he swallowed and asked, "You as innocent as you look, boyo?"

Eric had to stop himself from nodding. "What is this place?"

"Galley livery." He took another bite of bread. "Let me see your hands."

Eric held out a hand. The man grabbed his arm and yanked him hard against the partition. "Ladies' hands," he jeered, jamming a grimy hand into Eric's face. "Look there." The palm was as hard as the flesh on a farmer's heel, and the base bore a callus nearly an inch thick. "Working the oar." The man laughed and made a rowing motion with his free hand. "You'll find out, soon enough."

Eric jerked back, unable to break the iron grip. "Let me go!" He raised his free hand to strike, but the other slave hooted and snatched the loaf away. His weathered face crinkled in a grin as he twisted Eric's arm and sent him sprawling into the dank straw.

"You'll not last here." He laughed and stuffed the stolen bread in his mouth.

Eric rubbed his shoulder and glared at the slave. "I don't intend to."

The water cart came next. Rupe filled the pails that sat in the corner of each stall. Eric watched as a slave on the opposite side of the aisle stood and urinated without a shred of shame. Like animals, he thought.

After he had slaked his thirst with the tepid, murky water, Eric tore a strip from the hem of his tunic and dipped it in the pail. Hands trembling, he washed as much of the dust and grime from his face as he could manage. The branded slave continued to taunt him about the great galley vessels. Eric tried to envision rows of men, chained to the benches, pulling the oars, hour after hour, day after day. If this were his fate, at a month's end he'd be as mad as Simon.

Sniley appeared at mid-morning, dressed in merchant's robes and wearing a patch over the missing eye. He halted before Eric's stall, Rupe at his elbow. He held a leather-wrapped goad with a hook at the end. "Even in the light, you ain't much," Sniley grunted. "Lift yer tunic."

Eric hesitated and was rewarded with a poke from

the goad's metal tip. Startled, he raised the garment to the middle of his chest, only to get poked again. "Are you daft as well?" the man growled. "All the way."

Cheeks burning in humiliation, Eric lifted his tunic hem up over his head, as far as the chain would allow. Sniley bid him turn, then turn again. His head and arms enclosed, he didn't realize there was another observer until she spoke. "Not so bad as you imagined, tradesman?"

Eric recognized the voice — it was the lady from the previous night. He felt her fingers touch his flesh.

"See," she said. "He's thin, but well-muscled. And look, not a mark on him. That should raise the price a few bits, eh?"

"Aye." The master agreed, but there was grumbling in his voice. "A poor trader takes what he can get."

"That you do, tradesman. That you do." Her fingernails lightly scraped Eric's stomach, then withdrew. "You may lower your garment."

Eric did as she ordered. Their eyes met. She seemed surprised, but not angry that he dared look directly at her. Her attire was that of nobility, but there was something street-born about the set of her jaw and the hardness of her mouth.

Her thin lips curved in a smile. "You're a bold one." She folded her arms, resting her manicured hands in the crooks of her elbows. "Didn't your late master teach you any manners?"

"Don't mind him, Madam Rialle." Sniley hefted the goad. "He's been fussin' all morning about how he don't belong here." The keeper laughed. "Like every rower in the barn at one time or t'other."

The sound of her name caught Eric's ear — Rialle. His mouth formed the word, and when she saw it, she smiled. "What did the old man call you?"

“Eric, mistress.” He steeled himself and waited. From the corner of his eye, he looked at Simon — still crouched in his corner. A plan formed in Eric’s mind. Legerdemain only has one magician, she had told him. Would knowledge of a second be worth his freedom?

Rialle studied the boy. There was nothing remarkable about him, save the dignity in his gray eyes. While she watched, he brushed the loose straw from his hair and tunic. Her contempt for the dead man grew. It was poor practice to allow slaves to think this highly of themselves.

She looked at the second slave, a finely constructed boy with unkempt black hair and empty blue eyes. “And what did your master call him?”

“Simon. He’s ...” the boy hesitated.

Rialle fixed her gaze on him. When he flinched ever so slightly, her lips curved. “What was that? I don’t believe I heard you.”

His eyes dropped. “He is feeble, mistress.”

“Feeble!” Sniley erupted. “With all I must bear, now I’m feeding a fool! By Sancte and all her daughters, I have no use for a fool!”

“Be silent!” Rialle ordered, then crossed the aisle and knelt beside the second slave. With delicate fingers, she brushed the fine hair from his forehead. The boy watched Eric like a devoted cur. Intrigued, she cupped his chin and forcibly turned his head so he had to look at her. Pretty as they were, his pale eyes were devoid of intelligence.

Sniley continued his noisy protest. "Surely, Madam Rialle, you cannot expect me to bear the expense of keeping a fool. If he cannot pull an oar."

She silenced him with an upraised hand. "The old man kept him," she answered. "He must serve some purpose." Again, she turned Simon's head toward her. He squirmed under her touch, and when he would not be still, she struck him.

Eric reached out. "You don't have to hit him."

His outburst ended in a gasp as Rupe drove the butt of his goad into Eric's stomach. Rialle looked up at the panting boy. "Tell me, Eric, to what use did your late master put this creature?"

Eric's eyes filled with rage. His lips moved, but he did not speak. She gestured to the trader's boy, then pointed at Eric. "Restrain him."

Sniley's boy hooked his pike into the ring at the rear of the stall. Using it as a lever, he forced Eric back against the wall.

Rialle stood and returned to Eric's side. "He was good to you, your master, wasn't he?"

The knob of his throat moved as he swallowed. "Yes," he whispered.

"Of course," she continued. "You were meant for finer things, weren't you?"

He nodded. She had him. "Answer two questions for me, and perhaps I can find you more suitable employment."

Though he said nothing, his eyes grew hungry. Rialle studied him. "I am told it was you who drove the wagon and set the stage — what purpose did young Simon serve? Surely your late master was not wealthy enough for charity."

Eric looked long and hard at Simon, as if making up his mind, then he shook his head. "Master Phineas kept Simon as a pet." The flush of his cheeks betrayed his emotions. "If you must know."

Rialle laughed. It made perfect sense. The plain but loyal servant labored while the beautiful fool warmed the old man's bed. "Good boy," she whispered, moving closer. "Now, second question. What was the extent of your master's power?"

His chest heaved. "I don't understand."

"What could he do?" Rialle narrowed her eyes, sensing blood. "You saw Lord Vassant, could your Master Phineas do as he did?"

Eric met her gaze. "No, mistress, he could not."

His deceit amused her. "You are lying, Eric."

"No, mistress." He hesitated, seeming to gather the loose strings of his tale. "The glowing orb and the stage ward. A few simple tricks, nothing more."

Rialle knew she ought to order him beaten until he loosened his tongue. His was a pointless lie. She chuckled. His loyalty to a dead man amused her.

"You disappoint me, Eric." She turned to Sniley. "Put him on the first outbound galley."

"No!" Eric shouted. "You promised!"

"And you lied." Rialle shrugged. "Perhaps some rowing will stir your integrity. And in a few months, if you return alive, I'll ask again." She turned and called over her shoulder. "If Lord Vassant is still curious, and I haven't completely forgotten about you."

"What about the fool?" Sniley whined. "You don't expect …."

She whirled and faced him. "What I don't do, is care. If he can't row, kill him. Better yet, send him to a brothel. Surely you know the type to take a pretty mindless creature like that?"

Sniley grew silent, already counting his coins. Rialle took one last look at Eric, who stared at her in horror. By Sancte, he'd actually believed her! Perhaps he wasn't as clever as she thought.

As soon as the lady was gone, Rupe released the pressure on the pike. Eric stepped away from the wall and into the butt of the trader's goad. The blow caught him mid chest and dropped him to the moldy straw.

Sniley's depressive visage hovered over him. "Best you look sharp," he growled. "I've a customer coming, and I don't aim to feed the two of you another day." He thumped Eric in the chest with his fist. "And not a word about the fool, hear?"

Eric gritted his teeth and watched him go. Yesterday, he was the next thing to free. Now, he was chained to the wall and destined for the galleys. Why didn't he tell her about Simon? Why?

The red-haired slave's head popped over the partition. "An offer like that? From a woman like her?" His voice was more incredulous than cruel. "Are you daft, boyo?"

Eric closed his eyes. He had to decide who was more dangerous — Simon, or Rialle?

Chapter 11

Rialle was shocked at the intensity of her anger. How dare the boy lie to her! She turned and climbed the stair to the Ocean Walk. Startled guards cleared her path as if she were a fearsome beast. The stiff salt breeze tossed her blonde hair and drove the slave stench from her robes. She leaned on the stone rail and looked across the misty waters of the ocean. The rhythm of the waves calmed her.

The failure in the livery nagged at her. The boy, Eric, seemed in every way a slave, and yet he lied to her. Why? He had everything to gain by cooperating, or so she had told him. She turned and looked at the livery. She was sorely tempted to go back and order him beaten, but returning would make her appear foolish, and Rialle was not one to appear the fool.

Perhaps she should bring the boy before Vassant. He would wrest the truth from him with a touch, but there was always the risk he would do with Eric what he had done with the old man.

Rialle shrugged. What did it matter? She would

let Vassant deal with the boy; if there was anything left, the galleys could have him. Her mind made up, Rialle turned to order him delivered to the castle and found a slack-jawed servant standing before her. "Lord Vassant requires your presence."

Though it was nearly midday, Vassant lay sprawled over his draped bed in his dressing gown. Light streamed through the domed glass ceiling, staining the crimson rug with the soul of a rainbow. "Where have you been?" he demanded.

"Inspecting the new stock. As you requested." Rialle lifted a palm full of starkroot incense from a blue crystal bowl and dropped it into a serpentine brazier. The air in the magician's chamber was thick with age and dust. Servants were not permitted into his sanctuary and the time when she attended those needs was long past. "Did you rest well?"

"I did not." He flipped a pale hand toward the carved teak door. "She is demanding to speak to me. Again."

Rialle frowned. "Did you learn what she wants?"

"That is why I have you." His arm fell back to the coverlet. "Go, now, before I lose my patience."

"Of course." Rialle swallowed the urge to add 'my lord' to the end of her reply. The reflex reminded her of the street magician's arrogant slave. Her frown became a grimace as she crossed the room and passed Vassant's peculiar cloak rack. It was fine and well that he exert his power, but to make a trophy of it was pure arrogance.

She shuddered, slipped the gold key from her bodice and moved through the outer chamber toward the heavy wooden door. Daria waited on the other side, a fisted hand upraised in readiness to knock. "I will speak to him!" she commanded.

Taking firm control of her tongue, Rialle spoke, "Lord Vassant is resting. You may not have heard, but he was forced to exert himself last night in the interest of your safety, and the safety of the city."

"Nonsense!" Daria placed a hand on each hip. "I am told he murdered a street performer in the town square last night."

Rialle glanced at Daria's guards and reminded herself to instruct them on the proper containment of their charge. She looked back to the Princess, and cocked her head. "This concerns you?"

Daria hesitated long enough for Rialle to swallow a smile. As she suspected, the Princess was speaking for the sake of making noise. Still, she did not give up. "Lord Vassant oversteps his authority. Mara did no such things when she was Court Magician."

This time, Rialle did smirk. The haughty little Princess had exposed her throat. "Perhaps that is why Lord Vassant is now Court Magician, and old Mara is naught but moldering bones." She reached for the girl as if offering a comforting hand. "It is for the best, really."

Daria jerked away. "I will see him," she said, and pushed her way into the chamber.

Rialle's eyes widened in shock as the Princess darted past. "Stop her!"

Daria's indignation turned to outrage as one of the guards seized her arms before she was halfway across the salon. "How dare you!" she cried. "My father will hear about this!"

"Hear about what?"

Daria lifted her head and saw her father emerge from Lord Vassant's private chamber. "Hear about what?" he repeated.

The guard looked at Rialle. She nodded, and he released the girl who rushed into her father's arms. "He grabbed me!" she exclaimed, and jabbed a finger at the guard. "Did you see?"

He held her by her shoulders, leaned down, and looked into her face. "What I saw was a loyal soldier following orders." His grip caused her to wince. "What I also saw was a willful, disobedient child attempting to go somewhere she does not belong."

Rialle watched the girl's face as her mind warred with what she thought were her father's words. What a willful creature she was! Each time, the pacification seemed to take, but it never lasted, and she appeared as she had moments earlier, twisted in indignation.

But not now. Daria's resistance disappeared. She looked up into the face of her father — a face which, a moment ago, had borne the visage of the weary, petulant Vassant. His masquerade as King Lysander was impeccable, but the price was steep. Vassant emerged from each encounter more spent than the girl.

"How can I get through to you, Daria?" he said softly, shifting his right hand to the side of her face. "I only have your best interest at heart, you must realize that."

"But." The word emerged as a whimper. "Why don't I ever see you anymore?"

"I have a kingdom to govern — duties ...."

Vassant stopped mid-sentence. He swayed back, then forward, and the illusion of King Lysander shimmered over his face. Rialle stepped toward him, then forced herself to stop. She could not be seen approaching the King in such a familiar manner. Her blood ran to ice as she watched him falter, watched his grip tighten on the Princess, and the image shift again.

"What is it, Sire," she asked, coughing out the word. "Are you unwell?"

"He lives." Vassant's voice rose to a roar as his own visage returned. He shoved the Princess away from him. "The magician lives!"

Chapter 12

"Galley master coming!" Rupe's bellow reached every corner of the livery. "Oarsman to yer feet!"

Eric's head jerked up. Out of options, he looked across the aisle at Simon, who hadn't moved since morning. "You could have saved him." Eric spoke aloud. "You could have saved us all."

Eric looked down at his hands. Beneath his rage lay the deeper, uglier fear — he could have saved himself.

"On yer feet, be lively!" Rupe thumped down the aisle. "Earn a beating, die on a war galley."

Eric swore under his breath, stood, and moved to the edge of the aisle. Sniley and a stranger moved up the row of stalls. The trader fawned over his guest — a great lump of a man with a greasy, overfed bearing.

"Perhaps these two will suit your needs, my good Hakan." Sniley's voice was subservient, even more so than when he spoke to the magician's consort. "New hands, in off the streets just last night."

"Perhaps." Hakan's high-pitched voice emanated

from the folds of his face. "At least they seem young enough to live until I clear the harbor."

Eric started to speak, but Sniley cut him off with a glare so fierce it nearly stoned him. "Lift yer shirt," the trader barked. "Show the good sir all those muscles and that pretty unmarked flesh."

When he didn't move fast enough, Rupe prodded him. "Yer'd him," the servant barked, mimicking his master. "Show yerself."

Eric's face burned red with anger. He gripped the hem of his tunic, lifted the rough dusty cloth and displayed himself. He sickened as he heard the trader describe his fine points as if he were a prospective carthorse.

"How much?" he heard the phlegmy voice ask.

Sniley named a price. Hakan named another. Unbidden, Eric lowered his tunic and looked at the doughy man. "I won't work for you." He spoke as bravely as he could with a dry mouth. "You'll have to kill me. Your coin will be spent on a dead man."

The two men gaped at Eric. Then they laughed, Hakan far more heartily than Sniley, who seemed amused only to appease his customer. "Do you think you can choose not to row?" the fat man asked.

Eric's threat weakened Sniley's bargaining position and the sale was quickly sealed. They moved on to Simon. The order to "raise yer shirt" was met with a blank stare. When Rupe advanced, Eric called, "He doesn't understand."

"Doesn't understand?" Hakan looked from Eric to Sniley. "What do you mean he doesn't understand? How could he not understand?"

Eric began. "He's …."

"A mute!" Sniley interjected quickly. "Deaf and dumb as a pier stump, but no less a rower for it." He barked a laugh. "I should charge more for him, as you can work him all day and not hear a word of complaint."

"I think not." The galley master shook his head. "More trouble than he's worth, and I've a few more traders to see."

"Fa!" Sniley spat a gob onto the cobbles. "You'll not find better stock in all o' Legerdemain." He thumped his chest. "I get first pick."

"Be that as it may." The galley master looked down on him. "I believe our business is concluded."

"No, sir." Eric spoke. "Him and me." He pointed at Simon. "We're a team. Where I go, he goes."

Hakan looked at him absently then turned back to Sniley. Eric pressed on. "I can get him to work, no problem. But we have to stay together." The lies came to his lips with ease. "I promised our mother."

This caught the attention of both men, and for a moment, Eric thought he had won. Then Hakan laughed, and after a moment, Sniley joined in. Even Rupe smirked.

"I hope you row better than you lie," the galley master laughed. "Any fool can tell you aren't brothers — there's not a common feature between you. Lovers, perhaps." He arched a brow and inclined his head. "Is that it, boy?"

Desperate, Eric nodded. "Yes sir." He even managed a little blush. "I didn't mean what I said earlier. You take us both, I'll work for you, both of us will."

"I think not." Hakan pointed at the oblivious Simon. "He seems not at all upset at the parting." He smirked. "Methinks you overestimate the bond."

Out of both lies and options, Eric felt panic. His hands fell to his sides as he watched Rupe unhook the chain that bound him to the wall. Sniley and Hakan moved off down the aisle. Eric looked at Simon. If there was a chance, it was now. What did he fear most?

Rupe shoved him. Eric stumbled and felt his skin grow cold. He twisted back, saw Simon try to follow. When the chain caught him up short, he whined and reached after them.

"Back, you!" Rupe brandished the goad. The metal tip flashed in the sunlight.

Simon caught the goad in his outstretched hands. Rupe howled in outrage, but his anger was lost in the cheers of the other slaves. He pivoted and jerked the weapon free. "I'll learn you!" he barked, and drove the weapon into the captive's midsection.

The chain went slack. Eric jerked away, expecting the tether to pull him up short. Over the ragged sound of his own breath, he heard the links rattle across the stone floor. He gasped. He was loose! Eric lowered his head and charged for the door.

"Get him!" Sniley bellowed. "Get him!"

Eric's hand closed on the latch. He twisted back and saw Simon struggling with Rupe. The servant yelped as the terrified Simon bore him to the ground.

Sniley's voice grew shrill. "Be damned, all of you!" He hefted his goad and slammed it down across Simon's shoulder. The boy flinched, but did not release his grip on the hapless Rupe. Already the servant's face was red, and his struggles seemed to lessen.

"No!" Eric screamed, but soon he had troubles of own. The door swung inward and a beefy guard slammed the butt of his staff into his stomach. Gasping, Eric scrambled back down the aisle. In the space between heartbeats, his eyes met Simon's. "All right," he breathed. "All right."

He lunged forward, caught the boy by the wrist and shouted, "Wake up."

Simon reared back, a cry of pure joy on his lips. Sniley stayed his pike and stared gape-mouthed as blood red flames danced from Simon's fingertips. The image of

Lord Vassant flashed before Eric's eyes — Simon's gestures, his stance — they were all the same!

Without taking his dark blue eyes off the trader, Simon stepped back and gestured at the whimpering Rupe, who burst into flame before he had the chance to scream. The trader's pike clattered to the floor. "Hit me again," Simon snarled as the flames swelled. "Hit me again."

Sniley scrambled back and screamed, "Stop him!" When Simon reached the end of his chain, the trader's face twisted with short-lived glee.

"Demon!" he shrieked. "By Sancte, I'll kill you!"

Simon threw another ball of fire at the trader. Sniley's mouth opened in a fiery shriek; his arms flew up and he toppled backward into the nearest stall. The smoke thickened, and the cheers of the slaves became screams as the fire spread. Simon yanked the chain, and when it did not break, the magician blasted the ring from the wooden wall.

Eric staggered, realizing his captors had fled. He opened his mouth, to shout Simon down, but his lungs filled with smoke. He could barely breathe, much less speak. Their eyes met. Dark recognition flashed on Simon's face, and the last thing Eric heard was the sound of the magician's laugh. He is loose, he thought, and the world went dark.

Chapter 13

Daria's mind reeled as her father's hand grew hot against her cheeks and a sharp jolt swallowed his words. A scream rose, then died, trapped in her chest. Her mouth fell open, her knees weakened. Her father's howls blocked out all. His hands fell away; she staggered back and dropped to the thick carpet.

"He lives!" Her father cried, only it wasn't her father, it was Lord Vassant. "The magician lives!"

"Get her out of here!" Daria recognized Rialle's shrill voice. "Take her to her chambers and see that she remains there."

At once, Daria was surrounded. Hands grasped her roughly and stood her up as if she were a child. Bethel hovered over her, mouthing queries and endearments. Daria waved her away. She needed time to clear her racing mind. This was not right, not right at all. Where her father had been was now Lord Vassant railing against the old street magician.

Realization struck as her mind cleared. Vassant had tricked her. Stunned, Daria broke from the cluster of servants and raced into the hall. She had to get away, gather her thoughts. She heard Rialle shouting orders from within the Salon. She knew she should countermand the bitch, but she had more faith in her feet than in her authority.

Daria dashed the length of the hall, past Vassant's chambers and down the Grand Stair. Her palms were slick on the marble rail, and her leather heels skidded on the polished tiles. She leapt the bottom two stairs, turned a sharp right and followed the shadows to a heavy oak door.

After a quick glance to make sure her pursuers were still out of sight, Daria grabbed a heavy bronze ring, tugged it up, down, and to the left. She heard a dull click, shouldered the door open and slipped into the forbidding silence of her father's library.

Chest heaving, she closed and relocked the heavy door. Only she and her father's chamberlain knew how to open it, and he would need to be found. Meanwhile, Daria had a chance to breathe and decide her next move.

Light streamed in through the high windows, and dust motes danced in the muted rays. A fine layer of dust covered books and scrolls scattered across the desk. An intricate spider web ran from the back of the chair to the bookcase. There was a goblet sitting on the corner, its contents long dried away to a moldy powder.

Reality slapped her again. Her father hadn't been here for a very long time. Daria sank down into his chair. The cold leather provided no comfort. This was his favorite place, and he hadn't been here in so long the servants had stopped cleaning.

She fought back panic. What had Mara taught her? Daria heard the words as if the old woman were whispering in her ear — "There are those who will seek to beguile you, child, use your mind and your abilities to prevent it."

She ran an unsteady hand over the arm of the leather chair. If she closed her eyes it was easy to imagine him — her real father, not that abomination from the Salon. He was here in the scent of the books, the muffled quiet of the thick shelves. With a trembling finger, she set the orrery in motion "What should I do, Papa?" she whispered as she watched the globes spin against the harsh face of the cold hearth.

The hearth! Daria crossed the thick woven carpet to the stone fireplace. With trembling fingers, she traced the carved crest of waves on the wide teak mantle. Could she remember the pattern? Six, seven — her hand stopped at the eighth whorl. It was her eighth birthday when her father showed it to her — that's how you will remember, he had said.

Daria held her breath, pressed down and a waist-high panel swung outward. Silently thanking her father for the lesson, she crouched down and entered the stale passage. It was dark, but she needed no torch — these passages had been her favorite playground as a child.

Daria closed the panel with her foot and crawled three paces to an intersection with room to stand. Searching her memory, she chose the right branch; this led to a descending spiral stair. Her gown caught and tore on the rough stone, but she paid no heed. At the bottom, she turned left and traveled a long, narrow corridor keeping one hand on the wall to guide her. The air was close and damp, and she shuddered as cobwebs brushed, then clung to her skin. The squeaking, scrabbling sounds of fleeing rats bid her to retreat, but the two-legged vermin in the citadel proper scared her far more.

In her haste, she passed the napery door, and she was forced to backtrack. Daria crouched and pressed her ear to the rough wood. She heard running footsteps and the excited chatter of voices, then nothing. She waited — mouth dry and heart racing. It wouldn't do to be seen; she didn't know who were Vassant's creatures and who were not.

When the silence rang in her ears, Daria clicked open the tall, narrow panel and peered into a cluttered storage room. It was empty, save for castle linens, stacks and stacks of cotton and muslin — sheets, spreads, napkins, and aprons.

Aprons! Daria entered the storeroom and stripped off her stomacher and silken robe. The smallest apron was still too large, but she pulled it over her head and wound the ties twice around her waist. She yanked on a scullion's cap to hide her dark curls and added a couple of smudges of dirt to her face to complete the costume. She had no mirror to judge her handiwork, but it had to be less conspicuous than her normal garb.

Daria took a deep breath. She needed distance, and time to think. She placed her clothes in the bottom of a basket and covered them with napkins, then placed the basket in the back corner of the room and slipped into the servant's hall. Each time someone passed, she lowered her head. All around, voices tangled in murmured babble; everyone seemed in an agitated state. Had her disappearance already caused such a stir?

But as she moved into the wash yard, the sea breeze carried the scent of burning wood. Daria craned her neck and saw a pillar of smoke rising from the East. A perfect distraction — fortune was with her. With a barely disguised smile, she moved in among the servants and away from Lord Vassant.

Chapter 14

He lives!" Vassant insisted as he paced the confines of the Salon like a caged bear. Vases shattered as he passed; pottery shards littered the rich carpet like seashells. His nostrils flared. "What a creature he must be!" he cried. "To have survived that! I must have him."

"You have had him." Rialle muttered, more concerned about what Daria did or did not remember. She did not know the consequences of stopping in the middle of a spell, but it couldn't be to their benefit. She had chased the gaping servants from the room, with strict orders to corral the wayward Princess and lock her in her chambers.

"I'll find him." Vassant knocked open the outer doors with a gesture, sending leaded glass flying. Rialle followed him onto the balcony overlooking the inner compound. At the eastern end, a column of thick gray smoke streaked the blue sky.

"There," Vassant breathed, stretching out a robed arm. "That is where he is."

Rialle studied the courtyard. At that end of the compound lay the stables, the smithy, and the galley livery. The livery! The old man's two slaves; if they hadn't been shipped out, they would still be there. Could the dead act through the living?

She looked at Vassant. Only the last shreds of sense kept him from bolting over the railing and dropping to the cobbles below. "Is it as strong?" she asked.

"More." His eyes closed and he breathed deep. "Much more." The words ended in a moan of pleasure.

The wind brought the scent of smoke and shouts for help. It was the livery that was burning. She was certain of it. How many slaves had there been —thirty, forty, all chained to the walls and doomed. Which meant that Eric and his feeble friend would die, and with them the last remnants of the rival magician.

"Do you still feel it?"

"Silence!" Without a second glance, Vassant turned and reentered the Salon. "Come," he growled. "This time he will not get away."

The main yard was bedlam — soot and cinders filled the air. The roar of the fire, the shouts of the soldiers fighting the flames couldn't drown the screams of dying slaves. Harried grooms led strings of panicked horses from their stalls. A long row of bare-armed men passed dripping buckets toward the blaze while their captains barked orders.

Rialle covered her mouth with a kerchief and followed Vassant through the maddened throng. He was unaffected by the smoke while she could not draw a breath. "Where are you?" he shouted, spinning around.

"Show yourself!"

Rialle felt fear, not from the chaos but the strain on Vassant. First the rival magician, then Daria, now this — never had he needed to expend such power. She reached out and caught his arm but he thrust her away, sent her stumbling back. "Come to me!" he bellowed. "I command it."

Spectators shrank from the raving magician. Rialle ordered the guards to form a circle around Vassant and kill anyone who tried to broach it, then latched onto the first person that looked competent. "What happened here?" she demanded.

The soot-stained man coughed and shook his head. "Don't know." He wiped his mouth with his hand, smearing grime across his cheeks. "Do know no one got out."

All dead. Rialle cursed. No answers. From the corner of her eye, she saw something move within the wreckage of the livery. Shielding her face against the heat, she blinked and moved closer. Again, she saw it, a fire-limned figure moving toward her. Voices dropped off then rose in horror as more sighted the creature. I am not mad, Rialle thought, then turned to see if Vassant had spotted it as well.

He had. Vassant, still surrounded by the squadron of guards, approached the burning building. His dark eyes narrowed, and the mask of his face moved in recognition.

Rialle twisted back to the livery and gasped. From the fire's edge, the old man's slave, the feeble one, stared at Vassant with fear and wonder. Not possible, she thought, yet there he stood, untouched amidst the conflagration.

"Take him!" she shrieked. "He is the one!"

Vassant remained motionless, his eyes locked on the boy. Then he lifted his right arm. Rialle braced for a burst of fire but instead he crooked his fingers and beckoned to the strange creature. She saw his lips form the words, "Come here, little one."

Simon danced through the flames and threw back his head in wild laughter. His lips moved, but his words were lost in the roar of the flame. Rialle gaped in amazement. How could this be?

Vassant's fingers twitched. "Come." He moved toward the fire, beckoning to the boy as if he were a stray dog. Stray dogs bite, Rialle thought, and as she did, Simon grinned and gestured outward. The fire in the livery rolled toward them in a crushing wave. Screams and heat filled her ears as the workmen fled and the soldiers broke rank around them. She looked to her own magician, who staggered backward against the force of the blast. For a brief instant, she saw fear in his eyes, and this terrified her more than the fire or the slave mage.

Vassant steadied himself and fought back, arms outstretched, throwing up a towering ward that dashed the flames back with an invisible breakwall. His face was drawn in concentration, and his eyes were closed tight against the strain.

"Help him!" Rialle shouted, rallying the soldiers and the workmen. "Douse the fire. He can't hold it back forever."

As Vassant pushed forward, the livery's roof gave way, crashing to the ground in a great shower of sparks. Heat blasted the guards and workmen fighting the fire back across the square and windswept smoke flung embers over the spectators. "No!" Vassant screamed as he forced the flames back to their original source. "You stay here and you fight me."

The ward fell, but the fire was once more contained to the shattered building. Vassant staggered, then started once more toward the fire. Rialle clutched his arm. "It's too dangerous," she shouted. "Don't be a fool!"

The force of his anger knocked her from her feet. Her head rang as it made contact with the cobblestones. Stunned, she stared at him in rage and horror. Vassant glared at her, then spun drunkenly and faced the guards. "That boy is mine! Do you understand?"

He swayed on his feet, and for a moment, she thought he might collapse. The soldiers watched him warily, but none was brave enough to steady him. For a moment, Rialle was tempted to let him fall, but now was not the time to show weakness. She pulled herself to her feet and directed four of her trusted men to escort him to his quarters.

Vassant seemed about to protest, but Rialle did not give him the chance. She seized his arm once more, drawing him away from the crowd. "Do not let them see you falter," she hissed in his ear.

At first, she wasn't sure if he heard her. Then he nodded, and regained some sense of composure. "I'll join you in a moment," she said. "Once I've dealt with this debacle."

She stood her ground until he was safely inside the citadel. Strands of damp hair stuck to her face and her attempts to brush the filth from her silk robes left black smears on the pale blue. Summoning what dignity she had left, Rialle turned and faced the captain of the guard, forcing the man back a step before addressing him. "You find that boy and bring him to me."

Though he stood a full head taller, there was fear in his eyes. "But Lord Vassant ...."

"Told you the boy is his." Rialle advanced on the guard, forcing him to take another step back. "Lord Vassant and I are one — I see no contradiction."

Chapter 15

It was night when he woke, and for the second time in as many days, Eric had no idea where he was. The closeness of the air told him he was indoors, yet his skin felt seared, as if he had slept a day in the desert sun. His mouth and nose were clogged with dust and soot. His first deep breath made him choke. He shoved himself onto his stomach and coughed until his eyes watered.

When the spasm subsided, the memory of the livery fire swept over him. He had turned Simon loose and the world had burned. I should be dead, he thought, yet here I am.

Pale moonlight seeped through a narrow window, casting shadows in blue across the odd contours of the room. He cautiously extended his arm across the rough, round surface beneath him. His sensitive touch told him he lay in a hollow of filled sacks — flour maybe, or grain. He extended his reach and his fingers brushed cloth.

Eric froze. Over the hammering of his heart, he heard the rhythmic breathing of sleep. Simon. He would have rather found a coiled rock viper in his bedroll.

He remembered nothing of their escape from the fire. He must have run, and Simon followed. Was Simon awake or dormant? Eric slowly withdrew his hand and breathed a deep sigh of relief when the slumbering magician did not stir.

Fatigue overcame him and he drifted toward sleep. The soft sound of footsteps snatched him back. Eric's heart thumped. He lifted his head and peered into the murky shadows. He heard the creak of a door and shielded his face with his arm. A soft glow appeared, followed by a candle-bearing servant girl wearing an apron several sizes too large for her. Black curls escaping from beneath her cap framed a delicate, dusky face. She moved tentatively, as if confused. He might have thought she was meeting a lover, but she appeared too miserable. Hiding, then.

Eric's mouth twisted in a half smile. Perhaps he was not the most wretched creature in all of Legerdemain. Though his conscience urged him to provide assistance, he was in no position to provide any. Odds were the best way for her to get out of whatever trouble she was in would be to turn in a couple of runaway slaves.

The candle's light danced over the mottled stone walls. She lifted the candle higher and turned in his direction. Her dark eyes widened. Eric drew a quick breath. Through the thin fabric of her shift, he saw her chest rise and fall, and Eric realized she was more terrified than he was.

From the passage he heard the tromp of boots. "Did you check the storerooms?" a tired voice asked.

"Once and twice," its mate replied.

"Make it thrice and we'll call it a night. I got no call to run into that monster in the dark."

The girl shied away, looking frantically for a place to hide. Eric crept to the edge of the stack and held out his hand. “Come!” he mouthed.

She glanced at the door, then back up at Eric. “I won’t hurt you,” he whispered. “Just hurry.”

With a grimace, she blew out the candle, reached up and clutched his hand. His spent muscles screamed in protest as he hauled her up the mountain of sacks.

They crouched — side-by-side, hearts pounding — as the boot steps drew closer. The door creaked inward, and a stubble-faced guard swung a lantern over the sill. He gave the stack a cursory scan. “Ain’t no one here but us rats,” he chortled. “You still got that flask?”

“Aye.” The second guard ambled in, a dull gray jug in his hand. “Let someone else find that ungodly thing.”

They were searching for Simon. Eric glanced at the girl. Her dark eyes were fixed on the guards and her jaw was clenched. As if aware of his gaze, she turned and looked at him, then caught sight of the sleeping magician. Her eyes widened. Eric placed a finger over his lips and she nodded.

Together, they watched the guards make themselves comfortable on the lower tier of sacks. Watching them drink, Eric became painfully aware of his own thirst. His throat burned and his stomach tightened He needed water, then food. His last meal had been, when? With Master Phineas, while they were still on the road?

Eric knew he should stay awake — had to stay awake — but weariness soaked every muscle and his eyes still burned from the smoke. The guards’ hushed conversation lulled him. The last thing he remembered was the delicate smell of the girl’s hair. “Whatever you do,” he whispered in her ear. “Don’t wake him.”

Daria held herself so still her muscles ached, so still she scarcely dared breathe. Even after the strange boy beside her drifted to sleep and the indifferent guards resumed their rounds, she remained motionless, paralyzed with terror and fatigue.

What had she done, running away like that? What would she do? There was no one for her to turn to. Her every instinct told her to run to her father and bury herself in his arms, but how many times had she thrown herself into Vassant's embrace instead? The thought made her throat tighten, and she swallowed hard to avoid a sob.

What could she do? The question rolled through her mind until an even more terrible truth emerged — if Vassant was impersonating the King, where was her father? Her fears screamed the word "dead."

Her father was a busy man, he was the King, he had duties that kept him away from her. He asked Vassant to take on his guise to handle the more mundane tasks. And one of those mundane duties was talking to his daughter.

No. She shook her head. That could not be. There was danger; her father had enemies. Vassant was impersonating him to keep him safe. Because her father had enemies, he was in hiding. But, if that were true, why wasn't she with him?

Something rustled in the darkness. Daria held her breath and listened. She heard the rhythmic sleep sounds of the two boys. An animal scurried across her ankle. She stifled a shriek, brushing against the boy next to her, then froze against the possibility that he might awaken.

In her brief glance, she had recognized neither of them, but they had to be servants, perhaps stable boys or laborers. She had no idea the servants lived like this. Why had the one helped her, unless he thought she was one of them? What would he expect in return?

Tears streamed down her face, and she didn't dare move even to brush them away. Her shoulders shook and her breath caught in her throat. All this time, she had known things were wrong, but the truth of it was devastating.

There was more movement beside her. Daria jerked away. It was the boy who had spoken to her, his hand traveling the length of her arm. What did he want? She held a scream between her lips as his rough palm brushed against hers, then their fingers linked and he gave her hand a gentle squeeze.

Chapter 16

Rialle sat in the grandest chair in Lord Vassant's salon and watched over him while he slept. Despite his fatigue and near delirium, he had been determined to go after the boy, and she'd done everything short of physical violence to force him to rest. Sleep claimed him as soon as he reached the bed, and now he lay sprawled and snoring like a common laborer.

Dusk had come and gone, leaving hours of blackness in its wake. She hadn't stirred herself to light a lamp or summon a servant to start a fire. The darkness suited her mood; it was better for stewing and brooding.

Vassant was a fool to have shown such weakness in the courtyard, and even more foolish to have tried to go after the boy. She should have reined him in earlier, and there was a time she could have, but the fiction they'd built around themselves had become real for the arrogant magician. He may believe he was almighty and immortal, but he most certainly was not. And if he was lost, then everything was lost.

Her only consolation, her only wish, was that Simon required rest as well, and he too would be sleeping. She'd been in the service of mages long enough to know that that kind of display of power didn't come without a price. There were no further reports of violence or fires, so he'd most likely gone to ground somewhere to gather his strength. Every able-bodied man, soldier and servant alike, searched for him, but all carried strict instructions to let him be and report his whereabouts to her. It seemed a strange wish, but she hoped that her soldiers did not find him until Vassant was fully recovered, however long that might take.

Those few she trusted searched for the Princess as well. Rialle didn't want it well known that the girl was missing, and it seemed odd that this was the least of her worries. Perhaps a night in the world, away from her servants and her comfortable bed, would bring Daria to her senses. This seemed a futile wish; the Princess was determined to be contrary.

Perhaps something good could come of this terrible night after all. Rialle smiled in the darkness. Perhaps it was time the Princess shared her father's fate.

Chapter 17

The next time Daria woke it was daylight. Warm yellow light slanted through high narrow windows along the far wall. She pushed herself upright and rubbed the sleep and grit from her eyes, hoping things would be different when she opened them again. They were not. Dust coated the inside of her mouth and every inch of her body. She pulled off the cap and shook out her hair. Never had she been this dirty.

Or frightened. Now, with time and distance between her and Vassant, Daria realized the depth of her predicament. The panic of the previous evening was replaced with the cold realization her father was in peril. She had to find him. Her shoulders slumped and she buried her face in her hands. She was cold, tired, and hungry. And alone.

Only that wasn't true. Daria lifted her face and looked at the other two fugitives slumbering in the hollows between the swollen grain sacks. The closest one, the one who had taken her hand, had mouse brown hair and reddened skin, and his clothes were worn and singed. In the dark, she thought him nearly grown, but now she saw he was not much older than she was.

The second was a boy as well, though it was hard to guess his true age. His head was thrown back, his arms and legs akimbo. Don't wake him, the first one had said. Curious, she crept along the rear ridge of sacks until she was above and beside the second boy. Soft black hair fanned out around his pale face. His delicate features were peaceful in sleep; he seemed untouched by whatever had befallen his comrade. She extended a hand.

"Don't," a rough voice croaked.

Daria gasped and looked up. The first boy was awake. "Don't," he repeated.

She withdrew her hand. "Who are you?" she stammered. "What are you doing here?"

He hauled himself to a sitting position, his head almost brushing the rafters. "I could ask you the same thing."

"You don't ...?" Her voice trailed off. He didn't recognize her! Daria stared at him in amazement. "You don't know who I am?"

He pressed his arm to his stomach and coughed, wincing with each spasm. "Should I?" he asked, when he was able to speak.

"No." Daria crawled back to where her cap lay, eager to get away before he realized who she was. She twisted her long hair into a knot and pulled the cap over her curls. "You didn't see me, and I promise I didn't see you."

"Wait." He reached out a hand, but stopped short of touching her. "Where are we?"

Daria studied him. Her desperation was mirrored in his eyes. "The granary," she replied. Curiosity got the better of her. She jerked her head at the second boy. "What's wrong with your friend?"

"He's not my friend." The boy swayed a bit and steadied himself with his hands. "And I don't have the time or the breath to tell you what's wrong with him." He swallowed and grimaced. "Is there somewhere nearby I can get water?"

"There is a well for the horses." Daria looked closely at the boy. He wouldn't make it off the stack, much less across the stable yard. For the first time, she noticed the servant's collar around his neck. A length of chain hung down the middle of his chest. Both boys wore them. Her eyes widened. "You're slaves!" she said.

"What of it?" His eyes narrowed and his voice grew defensive. "It didn't matter when you needed help last night."

"No, no, that's not what I meant." Her words tumbled out, but she couldn't hide her disappointment. A servant might be able to help her, but a slave was even more powerless than she was. A slave might even be dangerous. She looked at him again. She knew she should be wary, but nothing about him fostered fear. "What happened to you?" she asked softly.

He looked at her but remained silent. "Whatever it is," she added. "I am certain I'm in far more trouble than you are."

"I doubt that," he whispered.

Daria saw the trace of a smile on his lips. Despite everything, she smiled back. She moved to go, but a small voice within her heart bid her to wait. You can trust him, the voice told her. Daria looked at the boy and knew, just knew, that the voice was right. She could trust him. "You wait here," she said. "I'll get you some water."

His surprise pleased her. "Why are you helping me?"

"Because you helped me," she replied and started to climb down.

"Wait," he called. She turned and he asked, "What is your name?"

"Daria." It was out before she thought.

"Daria," he repeated and smiled. "I am Eric."

Eric listened until the girl was gone. He wasn't sure if she would return, but she seemed as eager to avoid the soldiers as he was. He stretched and swallowed, wincing at the sand-dry scratch of his throat. His skin was tight and every muscle ached; he felt as if he had been beaten with a flaming truncheon.

Simon lay to his right, head thrown back, mouth open. Anyone else would have thought him dead, but Eric had seen him sleep like this countless times after one of Master Phineas' performances. If floating the glowing orbs left him spent, his performance in the livery might put him out for a week. It was still hard to believe the feeb, with whom he had shared his wagon for most of his life, was capable of such destruction.

Eric studied the sleeping boy. Was he active or dormant? Eric remembered nothing of their escape. Had he shouted the command that turned Simon off? By Bartoch's Balls, what if he had wakened while the girl was here. He'd thought she would never shut up, and despite the promise of water, he doubted if he would ever see Miss Daria again.

Eric knew a thief when he saw one — beneath her too-large apron, she wore a thin shift of fine linen and green satin shoes. Most telling of all, the hand he grasped was too soft to belong to a servant.

Eric smiled. A thief was someone he could deal with. But first, he had to deal with Simon. His skin flush with trepidation, Eric reached out and touched the boy's shoulder. "Simon," he hissed, braced to move.

Simon moaned and stirred. Eric prodded him again. "Come," he urged. "Before she gets back."

His eyelids fluttered, then opened. Eric braced, the word "sleep" unspoken on his lips. Without rising, Simon took in his surroundings. Eric saw intelligence, but no malice. His apprehension grew. Was Simon active or dormant? Eric could always tell. Until now.

Eric crept closer. "Do you know what happened?"

Simon tracked him with a half-lidded gaze, cocking his head at the question. But he did not answer. Eric was about to try again when he heard footsteps in the corridor. The air shimmered as if over a fire, and Eric knew the young magician had returned.

"Do you know what happened?" Simon intoned, his lips twisting into a faint grin. "What happened, do you know?"

"Sleep!" Eric shouted, far louder than he intended, then dove down behind the shield of grain sacks.

The footsteps stopped outside the door and the door creaked inward. Daria appeared, carrying a heavy oaken bucket with both hands. She closed the door with her hip and looked up, her dark eyes scanning the stacks. "Eric?" she called, in a loud whisper. "Are you still here?"

Assured she was alone, Eric rose to his hands and knees and let her see him. Relief washed over her face. Eric clambered down with a grateful smile, dipped both hands into the water, and drank deeply. The cool liquid slid down his throat, removing the thick layer of dust. When he had drunk his fill, he splashed water over his face and forearms.

"That's not all," Daria said when he had finished. She patted a lump in her apron pocket. "I've got food."

A very good thief, Eric thought, his estimation of her rising considerably. Together, they returned to their hiding place, bringing with them the bucket. Daria came up short when she saw Simon sitting up. "Hello," she said, her voice apprehensive.

"That's Simon." Eric eyed the bulge in her pocket, his stomach rumbling. "He's feeble, he doesn't understand." He pushed the quarter-filled bucket toward Simon. "Drink."

Simon hesitated, then lifted the bucket with both hands and tried to drink from it as if it were a cup. Water splashed down both sides of his face, soaking his hair and his clothing. Daria laughed, and Eric joined her.

She produced a rough gray sack from her pocket. "I think it's someone's lunch." She tumbled the contents onto the nearest grain sack. The bag held a dry, fist-sized chunk of black bread, a smaller piece of green spotted cheese and a wrinkled apple.

"A feast," Eric exclaimed. He rubbed his fingers together but touched nothing. It was her find, and she had the right to divide the spoils. But when she made no move to do so, he looked up. Daria stared at the food. "What's the matter?"

"Nothing." She shuddered. "I guess I'm not as hungry as I thought." She gestured toward the food. "You take it."

Eric was too hungry to question his good fortune. He broke the bread in two pieces; tossed one to Simon then stuffed the other into his mouth. While he chewed, he studied Daria. A mantle of worry had settled about her shoulders, and she seemed to have grown younger somehow. When he had finished chewing, he said. "You can trust me."

"I know. It's just ...." She shifted, exhaled, opened her mouth to speak then stopped.

Eric spared her the trouble of an explanation. "Look, we're both in trouble or we wouldn't be hiding. I've never seen a servant wear shoes like yours, and your hands are too soft for anything but a lady's maid." He swallowed the last of his bread. "What did you do, steal from your mistress?"

"How dare ...!" Daria's voice dropped off, then her shoulders stiffened. "So what if I did?" She gestured at the length of chain hanging from his collar. "Is that the new fashion in neckwear?"

"A misunderstanding." His cheeks flushed as he gathered the links and dropped them inside his tunic. "You didn't have to come back." Eric paused, then added. "But you did." He softened his tone. "That must mean you want my help."

She looked at him, then nodded. "There was supposed to be an exit here." She gestured at the rear of the room. "But there are all these sacks."

"Exit?" he asked.

Daria nodded. "There are passages throughout the citadel, ways for the soldiers to get in and out."

Eric took a bite of cheese and gestured toward the window. "Do you know of another exit?"

She nodded. "But it's on the far side of the compound, and lets out right on the shoreline. We'd have to climb to get back into the city."

"I can climb." Eric jerked his head at Simon. "So can he, I suppose." He paused. "But why would you want to get back into the city? Do you have friends who might help?"

"I don't know. Possibly." Daria's face tightened,

and in the depths of her eyes, he saw the traces of panic.

Eric covered her hand with his. "We can worry about that later. Right now, we have to get away. Agreed?"

Daria nodded. "Agreed."

"Good." Eric smiled. "You tell me the way out and I'll see to it that we don't get caught."

With a sense of purpose, Daria settled back against the sacks of grain and watched Eric prepare for their escape. She felt as if she had just been roused from sleep, alert for the first time in months. Daria was certain her father would not have left her in Vassant's care, not willingly. She had to find him, which meant she had to get out of the citadel, which meant she had to trust Eric.

Fortunately, that was easy to do. But why should she trust him? They had just met. Her only experience with slaves was from a distance; she had never met one. Now, she was trusting one enough to flee with him. She only knew she felt safer now, in Eric's company, than she had in the months under Vassant's care. But how could she trust her instincts, which had been so wrong up until now?

As she pondered, Eric pulled his sooty tunic over his head and shook the dust from his shaggy hair. He shifted the chain from the front of his collar to the rear, so it dangled down along his spine, then secured the end around his waist with a strip torn from one of the grain sacks.

"So it won't rattle," he explained. He then turned the dirty tunic inside out, which both served to hide the soot marks and change the color from gray to brown. This simple act transformed him from a fugitive to a nameless servant working the castle grounds.

"You've done this before, haven't you?" she asked.

Eric smiled and nodded. "If I had a hat, you wouldn't recognize me."

The other boy, Simon, sat motionless as Eric repeated the process on him, hiding the chain and changing the color of his shirt. Daria longed to ask Eric why he was dragging along an obvious fool, who could not possibly be an asset and almost certainly would be a liability. When she could bear it no longer, she spoke. "Why? I mean, I don't have to guess why you're running, but why him?"

"You mean, why am I bringing Simon?"

"Yes." Daria leaned in and studied Eric's face. "I mean, we could move so much faster ...."

"If I just left him." Eric tilted his head and looked at her, not angry, not exactly, but with weariness far beyond his age. "Do you want my help or not?"

She nodded. Eric exhaled. "Then Simon comes with us." He cleared his throat. "I need you to show me the layout of the castle grounds. Can you do that?"

"Yes." Daria spoke eagerly. "If only I had something to write on, I could show you." She glanced around the grain room, her gaze settling on the dusty window. "There!" she exclaimed, moving toward it, "I can draw it for you on the pane."

"Wait, no!" Eric caught her by the ankle, then jerked his hand away as soon as she stopped. "Someone will see you."

"Oh." Daria's face fell. "I'm sorry."

"That's alright," he said reassuringly. "It was a good idea." He smiled. "And I'm sure we can find you somewhere else to sketch — it's not as if there is a shortage of dust in here."

They scrambled down the grain sacks. Daria drew a map of the castle grounds with a stick on the dirt floor. Eric questioned her in detail, asking again and again if she were sure about this and that. Though she had lived there all her life, twice Daria found herself smoothing over lines and redrawing them in another place. He questioned her about the activities of the guards and the servants, most of which she could not answer. Eric told her it didn't matter, but it did matter. No wonder Vassant had been able to trick her so easily — she knew little of what happened outside her own sheltered life.

When this was over, she would make it her business to become more informed about what went on in Legerdemain. Her Legerdemain.

Eric studied her sketch for a long time, then carefully scrubbed it out with the heel of his hand. "You ready?" he asked. She nodded. "You'll have to do everything just like I say. If you have questions, ask now."

Daria had questions, but knew Eric couldn't answer them any better than she. "You just get us out of here. I'll do whatever I can to help."

He smiled, nodded, and set about arranging their escape. She watched him heft several of the grain sacks as if testing their weight; each appeared too heavy to be lifted by a single person, yet Eric moved most of them.

"Less conspicuous if you're carrying something," he explained. His gaze settled on a ripped bag. He widened the tear enough to let most of the grain spill out, and then stuffed it full with empty sacks from a barrel in the corner. When he hefted it to his shoulder, it looked as though he was toting a full sack of grain.

"How's that?" he asked.

"Amazing," she answered truthfully. "Will you make one for Simon as well?"

Eric shook his head. "I'd never be able to explain it to him." He studied her. "What about you? Is that frock the same color on both sides?"

Daria blushed and nodded. "I'm afraid I don't have as much experience at this as you have." She clamped her mouth shut as soon as she spoke, fearing he would take this as an insult. Instead, he smiled.

"That's all right," he answered. "No one has as much experience at this as I do."

At his instruction, she removed her shoes and stockings and hid them in his false grain sack. After a few more questions, he had her tuck all of her hair up into the cap, as the servant girls did, and draw the rear of her apron up between her legs and tuck it beneath the tie in front, so it appeared as if she were wearing a strange pair of trousers.

"I look ridiculous!" she exclaimed.

"No." Eric surveyed her critically. "You look like you've just come from the laundry." He picked up the bucket and handed it to her. "If we had any water left, I'd soak the hem of your skirt to make it look even more real."

Daria held the bucket with both hands, squared her shoulders and lifted her chin. Eric laughed. "No. No. Now you look like you're proud to be doing laundry. Servants are weary, keep your gaze down like you've walked this path a thousand times and don't need to look where you're going, and walk like the bucket is very heavy. You aren't hurrying, we are just servants, and servants don't hurry if no one is watching them." He paused, as if considering this, or, more specifically, why she didn't know this already.

Daria gritted her teeth. "My mistress was very

kind to me," she snapped back. "I was proud to serve her and always hurried about my tasks."

"Of course you did," Eric answered, not sounding convinced. "But now you are a laundry maid, and you hate your life. Remember that." He gestured toward the door. "Come. I want to get out of here before it gets dark."

Why? Daria started to ask, then realized why. Because servants wouldn't be out after dark.

Eric hefted the false bag of grain onto his shoulder and motioned for Simon to follow him. "You stay a few paces behind us. Keep your face down, but your eyes on me and match my speed. Whatever you do, don't panic and start watching out for whoever it is that's looking for you. And don't run." He paused and smiled. "Unless I do."

"Understand." Daria held her breath as Eric opened the door. The dirt floor felt gritty beneath her bare feet; she was unaccustomed to walking without shoes, even indoors. Eric moved into the corridor, through an open door, and along the perimeter of the main yard with Simon bobbing along unconcerned at his side. He did not look back to see if she followed.

Chapter 18

Rialle paced the length of the parlor outside Lord Vassant's chambers, her arms hugged tightly across her chest. Her slippers scarcely made a sound on the emerald carpet. She saw nothing; her mind was as distant as the horizon.

Why didn't the slave mage protect the old man?

Why was there an old man at all?

Why did the other boy, Eric, lie to protect him?

"Attend me!" Vassant called through the heavy wooden door.

Rialle inhaled deeply, still smelling smoke. The last question was easiest. Eric had no choice. It was a position with which she could sympathize.

"As you wish." Rialle grimaced as her hand went to her throat. She was still uncomfortable wearing anything around her neck. She drew a long chain from the depths of her bodice; at its end dangled the key to Vassant's chambers, still warm from her body. She jammed the key in the lock, heard it groan and click, then shouldered the door inward.

Vassant lay as he had the day before, sprawled across his vast bed, an arm crooked over his face. He was half-dressed, and what clothing he wore was in disarray. His hair was tangled and sweat-soaked, and his skin was pale with exhaustion. If she didn't know better, she'd have sworn he was recovering from a night of debauchery.

"Have you found them yet?" he asked, his voice weary.

"Not yet." She lifted his heavy brocade robe from the floor where he had let it fall. "But I will."

"See that you do." He stared wide-eyed at the stained-glass aperture in the ceiling and made fists of his hands. "I must know how he comes and goes, and why I cannot find him now."

Rialle watched him, her hands clenching the heavy material. Was this how the crone Maraguase had felt when Vassant appeared, his talent burning white-hot? Her hand went to her neck again. To look at him now, spent and jaded, it was hard to imagine a time when they had both served the old woman.

"I require sleep." Vassant's eyes darted in their sockets. "Yet my mind races."

"Allow me." Rialle replaced the heavy robe on its stand. Her fingers brushed the mannequin's stony flesh and she froze. Inadvertently, she looked into the King's terrified eyes, and quickly looked away. It was not enough for Vassant to dispose of Legerdemain's former ruler; he had to make a trophy of him as well. With a shudder, she readjusted the robe so the mannequin's face was covered. If there was a worse fate than spending eternity as a dressing dummy, Rialle could not imagine it.

Banishing the image from her mind, she gathered her skirts and settled herself beside Vassant at the head of the bed. He shifted, so his head lay in her lap, and she massaged his temples. His flesh burned beneath her fingertips, and though his eyes were closed, she saw them darting around in their sockets.

"Sleep," she whispered, blowing the word gently into his ear. "Sleep." Gradually, his features softened and he slumbered. Rialle brushed the hair from his forehead.

At first, Rialle had merely admired Maraguese's handsome young apprentice, until she realized what a powerful ally he could become. As she served the old woman, she courted him: fed his vanity, made him believe the old witch was withholding her art — holding him back. Although he was erratic and even cruel, Rialle made him more powerful, and herself indispensable to him. Nothing was ever enough for him. It was a quality Rialle admired, and, in time, exploited. Maraguese had been a fool not to recognize his potential. Rialle was no fool.

She still felt the old woman's presence in the odd corners of the citadel. Though Vassant assured her otherwise, she often wondered if perhaps the old witch wasn't stashed in a forgotten chamber, serving the same function as King Lysander.

Her hand found her throat again, and she forcibly returned it to its task. This nervousness was foolish — Maragause was dead. Rialle had a princess to find and a magician to pen.

Chapter 19

The castle yard teemed with activity, and no one seemed to notice three more servants in amongst the chaos. From the corner of her eye, Daria saw a crew of workers digging through the wreckage of a burned building, loading chunks of charred wood and other debris onto ox-drawn carts. The noise was deafening; sea birds screamed, the ocean sang and crashed in the distance, workmen shouted to one another as if nothing at all was amiss. Pairs of soldiers walked the top of the walls, occasionally surveying the yard below, but no one looked at them. No one.

Their destination was a small wooden gate on the seaside of the compound. Mindful of Eric's instruction, Daria followed along gamely, while rough stones dug at her tender soles, and the rope chafed her hands. Though he had not spoken the words, in her mind, she heard him remind her that a laundry maid would be used to this, and would not limp or pick her way along the path as a princess would.

Despite her physical discomforts, it was hard not

to gape at her surroundings. Next to the stable stood the smithy, a dark building with an open front, where a trio of thick-armed men hammered at glowing chunks of metal. They did not look up as she passed, nor did the pair of wiry boys shoveling coal from a wagon beside the shop. There was no chance for anyone to recognize her; no one even looked at her.

Her stomach rumbled as they passed the kitchen and for a moment, Daria wished she hadn't turned her nose up at her portion of the workman's lunch. They would be preparing the evening meal now, nothing fancy, but as hungry as she was even a simple meal would be a feast.

She lifted her eyes toward Eric in time to see him snatch a small loaf of bread cooling on a rack in an open window. It vanished into his shirt so quickly she wasn't certain she had even seen him do it.

She glanced sideways at the rack. Did she dare? Her stomach rumbled again as the breeze once more brought the scent of fresh bread. She shifted the weight of the bucket to her right hand, loosened her grip with her left and made ready to grab.

"Well, hello there! Aren't you a pretty one? Don't think I've seen you about the grounds. New, are you?

Daria's cheeks flushed. Four laborers lounged in the doorway of a long, low building. All were laughing and leering so she was unable to tell which one of them spoke. Her heart thumped as she lowered her gaze and quickened her pace.

"Come now," the voice called. "Don't be shy. We only want to be friends."

Daria glanced back and immediately regretted it. Two of the four left off their lounging and followed her. Fear raced through her veins. "Leave me be!" she croaked, her voice barely more than a whisper. "I have chores to do."

"Ain't nothing that important." The taller of the two reached for her arm. "Let me get a look at you."

Daria twisted, evading his grasp, and sent a panicked look toward Eric. He still did not look back, but she saw his shoulders tense. It was all she could do to keep from running up and clutching his arm.

But then they would both be captured. Daria forced herself to slow her pace, noting at the same time that Eric quickened his. She was a laundry maid; what would a laundry maid do if a pair of strange men harassed her? She thought of her own attendants; one was old, but the other was almost as young as she was and flirted shamelessly.

Daria's cheeks burned. That would not do, even if she could bring herself to bat her eyes and fawn over the man; there was too much of a chance that they would recognize her.

"Hey now." The tall man grabbed at her arm again. "We just wanna talk a minute."

Everything stopped. Daria found her tongue. "Remove your hand," she said firmly. "Else I will scream."

"Will you now?" He grabbed her other arm and pulled her forward by her elbows. His breath was sour on her face, and she saw he wore a slave's collar. "We might enjoy that."

"So will the soldiers patrolling the wall." The words emerged before she thought them, and Daria was startled by her own boldness. "Shall we find out?" Her eyes darted toward the ramparts, then back to her captor.

His hesitation was all she needed. She jerked her arms from his grasp and spun on a bare heel, resisting the urge to strike him across the face with the bucket as she did so. Indignant, she nearly collided with a barrel-chested man in a black uniform. She looked up, then quickly shifted her gaze to the ground.

A watchman from the city guard towered over her. "These lads bothering you, girl?"

Daria swallowed three times before she could speak. "No, sir," she answered softly. "But they are keeping me from my chores."

"Well, we can't have that now, can we?" He placed a meaty hand on her shoulder and she shuddered. "Back to the barracks with you, louts! You know better than to chase these poor girls while they're working. I catch you loafing again; you'll serve a turn on a galley. You see?"

"Yes, sir!" The two spoke in unison. The taller one even tipped his wool hat. "My apologies, young miss."

Daria forced herself to give a small nod of acknowledgement. The men bobbed their heads, turned, and scurried back toward their quarters. She waited, willing the soldier to release his grip on her shoulder. Instead, he spoke. "Look at me."

Trapped and breathless with fear, Daria raised her head as much as she dared, then lifted her eyes to his face. She did not recognize him, but that did not mean that he did not recognize her. She waited for the realization to strike his gray-stubbled face, but instead he said, "Be about your duties, girl, and don't dawdle amongst the laborers." His smile did not comfort her. "Next time, I might think you're wanting the attention."

"Yes, sir." Relief washed over her as she lowered her gaze and tightened her grip on the bucket. "May I go now, sir?"

"Of course." He patted her shoulder, then, just as she thought she was away, he slapped her on the rump as if she was a horse or a dog. Startled, Daria stumbled away from his touch and the sound of his laughter.

But still, she was away! She had actually gotten away with it. It was all she could do to keep the grin from her lips. Eric would be so proud of her.

But where was he?

Daria quickly scanned the yard, but saw no trace of her new comrades. A few moments ago, she might have panicked, but her success with the three men emboldened her. Eric couldn't have waited; he was in more danger of being captured than she was. He would have kept going toward the south gate, so she would do that as well. She concentrated on keeping a steady pace, when all she wanted to do was run. The closer she got to the citadel, the more likely it was that someone would recognize her, so she averted her gaze and pretended to be watching the workers clearing away the rubble.

Closer. Closer. The south gate came into view from the corner of her eye. It was here, she knew, that the fishermen brought in the best of their catch from the docks below. The closed gate was large enough for two wagons to enter abreast, but a smaller, person-sized door was cut into the thick wood.

The crowd thinned as she drew near, and conversation vanished with the crash of the waves. Once more, she scanned for Eric, but saw only soldiers and guards both on the wall and in front of the gate. Why so many, and in one place? She knew the answer as soon as she thought it, and her calm evaporated, replaced by panic. She froze, unable to move a step further. They were looking for her.

A hand closed on her arm. Only a lack of breath kept her from screaming. A voice spoke. "You're needed here, miss."

Eric! Daria almost sobbed with relief as he tugged her into a nearby building, where Simon waited, a gnawed chunk of bread in his fist. The shed stank of fish, every surface glistened with slime and scales, and she didn't care. It wasn't until after she stepped back that Daria realized she had hugged him. "Thank you!" she gasped.

Flushing slightly, Eric disentangled himself from her grasp. “Figured you could use some help.” He grinned. “Though you did all right with those workers back there. You sure you’ve never done this before?”

“Never,” Daria breathed as he handed her a chunk of the bread — her share of what he had stolen. Without thinking, she took a big bite. Nothing had ever tasted so good. “Now what?” she asked after swallowing. “Do you have another plan for getting past those soldiers?

“I just might.” Eric craned his neck toward the window. “What’s on the other side of that gate?”

“The docks. There are three ....”

“Wait.” Eric held up a hand, then knelt on the dirt floor. “Show me.”

As she had in the granary, Daria quickly sketched the dock area. Knowing what he was looking for made it easy. Eric studied the map, then nodded once. “We’ll meet here.” He jabbed a finger at a small building near the base of the third dock. “Understand?”

“Yes.” Daria watched him scrub out the map with his heel. “But shouldn’t we stay together?”

He shook his head. “Someone has to draw away the guards. You did good with just one, but I’m probably better suited for this.”

Her mouth went dry. “But what if you get caught?”

“I won’t.” Eric reversed his tunic once more and loosened the chain around his waist. “As soon as I draw them off, you take Simon and get out that gate. Don’t panic and run, but don’t dawdle either.” He paused. “And whatever you do, don’t let him get away from you.”

Daria looked at the boy, who was solemnly chewing the last of his bread. “Why?”

“I’ll tell you when we reach the docks, but for now, you’ll just have to trust me.” He searched her face. “Can you do that?”

She nodded without hesitation. Trusting Eric was the one thing she could do.

"All right." Eric pulled Simon to his feet, and reluctantly placed his hand in Daria's. "You follow her," he said slowly, looking into Simon's eyes. "Stay with her."

Eric shifted his gaze to her, and for the first time, she saw concern, maybe even a little fear. "Whatever you do, don't let him follow me. He's like a dog, like this, he might pull, but he won't put up a fight."

"I understand." Daria nodded and tightened her grip on the boy's hand. "Good luck," she whispered. "And don't get caught. You owe me a story."

"I always pay my debts." Eric smiled, saluted, then hoisted himself through the rear window and vanished into the yard.

Eric crouched between the fish shed and the stone wall and studied the soldiers. Four stood on the ramparts; two on either side of the gate. None carried weapons, but there was a rack of crossbows close by. That wouldn't be a problem. He would be well away before the men could reach their weapons.

The six on the ground were his main concern. One was older, another somewhat portly, which left four for him to outrun. Eric grinned without showing his teeth, and wiped his palms on his breeches. Finally, his fate was in his own hands.

He followed the wall behind the shed to where the building ended. Holding the chain balled up in his fist, he scrambled along the backside of a woodpile twice his height. He needed distance between himself and Daria and Simon.

Eric glanced back at the shed and swallowed dryly. He knew he could outrun the soldiers, but leaving Simon with Daria was a serious risk. “Just stay with her,” he whispered by way of a prayer, and leapt down from the stack of logs.

Once on the ground, he surveyed the yard. A trio of genuine laundry maids led a pony-cart laden with washing toward the gate, chattering as they went. Just what he needed. Eric slipped from his hiding place and fell in step behind them. The stack of washing kept him hidden from the soldiers’ view, but not from the girls. He held his breath and waited to be noticed.

It didn’t take long. The girl walking at the rear of cart saw him from the corner of her eye. She looked, then stared, her eyes wide. Eric let the chain drop from his hand and leered at her. She shrieked, her friends turned, wide-eyed, and commenced shouting as well.

This got the soldiers’ attention. Eric gave them just enough time to get a good look at him before he bolted, scattering the laundry maids like geese. As he passed, he swung the chain against the pony’s rump, causing it to panic and rear, upending the cart and blocking the path.

Perfect. Without looking to see if Daria moved, Eric turned heel to his handiwork with the soldiers in close pursuit. A glance back proved his prediction — four followed, while the other two stayed to aid the shrieking girls.

“Stop him!”

“He’s the one!”

Eric was not afraid. He grabbed the chain in his fist and aimed for the large knot of people clearing away the wreckage of the livery. His boots slapped against the cobbles and he pumped his arms as the damp sea air filled his lungs.

The quickest of his pursuers drew close. Eric dove beneath an oxcart, scurried along the damp cobbles and emerged amidst a sea of legs on the other side. "Stop him!" the soldier ordered, but to Eric's ears, the crowd only shouted encouragement. He glanced up. The livery had butted up to the outer wall, and only the back portion remained. Inspired, Eric dropped the chain inside his tunic and started to climb. Charred wood gave way beneath his hands and feet as he scrambled for purchase. A hand grabbed his foot. He kicked it away and hoisted himself onto the stone wall. He was up, but which way?

The soldier shouted to his comrades, who converged on him from either direction. The ones to the west were closer, so he scrambled to the south, toward the sea. The street below gave way to docks crowded with workers who were moving a mountain of heavy sacks toward a waiting ship.

The soldiers closed on him. Buying himself a few more feet, Eric sprang onto the wall's edge, then dove for the stack of grain sacks. Though his breath was gone, he managed to roll as soon as he landed, and when his feet hit the planks, he was running.

"Escaped galley slave!" the soldier bellowed. "A rich reward for whoever stops him!"

Behind him, the knot of pursuers multiplied. Ahead lay a small building, a stack of crates, and beyond that, ocean. He was trapped!

Eric scrambled up the crates, then turned. The crowd advanced as a single being, laughing and leering. A crossbow bolt thudded at his feet. He pivoted and looked at the ocean, and before he thought, he jumped.

He slammed into the water. The impact was harder than he expected, like a fall from a great height onto hard-packed earth. As he hit, he exhaled sharply. He kept falling. Eric flailed his arms and legs. Which way was up? Reflex forced him to inhale; salt water burned his nose and throat. He coughed and choked, sucked in more water. He struggled again, weaker now, and lost. Pain in his torso doubled him over, and he sank into blackness.

"He's coming around!"

"Come on, lad, breathe!"

Eric was thrown down hard over a rounded surface and heavy fists thumped between his shoulder blades. He coughed and gasped. Seawater pored from his nose and mouth as his gut twisted in agony.

"There you go, boy, bring it all up."

"How much was the reward?"

Eric fought to catch his breath. He opened his eyes and tried to focus on what was in front of him — wooden planks, bare feet, boots, and water.

"Clear a path louts!"

The space around him opened. Eric lifted his head as far as he could and saw Rialle standing over him.

"Well now," she said, smiling. "I was hoping we would meet again."

Eric struggled, but it was futile. He barely had the strength to lift his arms and legs, much less escape. His chest and throat burned as if had swallowed fire, and his protests emerged as a watery cough. His last coherent thought before disappearing into unconsciousness was the memory of leaving the unsuspecting Daria alone with Simon. Which of them was in the most trouble; he wasn't sure.

Chapter 20

"No, you have to stay here!" Daria tightened her grip on Simon's wrist and pulled him away from the window. Eric was wrong; he wasn't like a dog. A dog would have understood, eventually. This creature did nothing but moan and lunge toward the window.

She was tempted to let him go. He'll be an even better diversion than Eric, and it will be so much easier to escape without him.

Outside, a girl shrieked. Daria twisted in time to see a laundry cart spill, and a flash of gray that was Eric, disappearing into the crowd. All but two of the soldiers dashed after him. Those who remained hurried to the aid of the panicked girls.

Daria's indecision vanished. "Come on," she told Simon, hauling him away from the window. She picked up her bucket and led the way from the fish shed into the yard. Raised voices echoed off the stone walls, no doubt following the path of Eric's escape. She wanted to look back, to see if he had gotten away, but didn't dare.

The gate loomed over them. Twenty steps. Ten steps. Five. Daria flashed a quick smile at the unresponsive Simon. They had made it. She placed the bucket on the ground and seized the swivel-bar holding the door closed. One-handed, she strained at the rough lever, but it was too heavy.

Terror filled her throat. Daria glanced back to insure the soldiers were still occupied, then tried again. It still didn't budge. She needed both hands, but that would mean releasing Simon. Whatever you do, Eric had warned, don't let him go. But did she have a choice?

"Help you with that, miss?"

Daria swallowed a shriek and turned to see a tall man in peasant's garb carrying an empty basket on his shoulder. His lined face was deeply tanned and a smile creased his mouth.

"Yes, please," she answered, her mouth dry.

He swiveled the bar as if it were a twig, and swung the door outward. "There you go." He tipped his wide-brimmed hat to her. "Sometimes it sticks."

"Thank you." Daria bobbed her head and pulled Simon through the gate toward the stone steps leading down to the docks.

"Wait!" the man called.

No! Daria wanted to sob, wanted to run, wanted to do anything but what she did, which was stop and turn halfway. "Yes?"

"You forgot your bucket." He hurried down the steps and held it out to her. "You'll be wanting this, I expect."

Cold relief washed over her as she took the rope handle. "Thank you again." The man opened his mouth to address her once more. Daria cut him off. "I'm sorry, but we must be going. Our mother worries when we are late." Without waiting for his response, Daria turned and hustled Simon down the steps.

The steps ended at the center of the row of docks. All the activity seemed to be centered at the pier on her distant right. "It's about time something went our way," she told Simon, and set off toward the storage shed at the base of the third pier.

Inside there were stacks of sails and nets twice her height. Hauling Simon up after her, Daria clambered one-handed up the mound of musty canvas. Every surface was thick with dust, and strings of cobwebs hung from the rafters. There was a hollow area formed at the top. Daria batted away the cobwebs with her free hand. She supposed there were rats here too, but there wasn't much to be done about it.

Only when they were settled did she relax her grip on Simon's arm. Her fingers ached from the pressure. "You stay here," she whispered to him. "Eric will be here shortly."

When it didn't seem as if he would bolt, Daria released him completely. She braced for him to run, but instead he scooted into a corner, crouched, and drew his knees up to his chest.

"You're scared, aren't you?" she whispered. He didn't look at her, or give any indication he understood. "I'm scared too." It might not be a comfort to him, but speaking the words made her feel better. "It will be all right. It has to be."

Eric lay in an unfamiliar room; dimly aware that the odd sound he heard was his own teeth chattering. Breathing in made him cough until his throat burned, and his stomach heaved in reflex, though there was nothing left to come up. When the spasm passed, he huddled on the narrow pallet like a kicked dog and shivered so hard his bones ached. Grit covered the inside of his mouth and his skin felt raw beneath the rough cloth of his tunic and breeches. When he rubbed his face, he heard the clatter of a chain.

His eyes popped open, though there was little to be seen in the semi-darkness. Using strength he did not feel, Eric shoved himself into a sitting position and tried to take in his surroundings. His head spun and he was forced to steady himself with his hands to keep from toppling over. The chains rattled with his every movement, and he felt their weight on his wrists, at the back of his neck, and in his heart. He was a prisoner again.

Over the rough sound of his own breathing, he heard the roar of the ocean. He remembered the chase, then the jump and fall, and all that water. Just thinking of it made him tremble and his stomach heave. It was as if some great monster had devoured him in a single gulp.

Only someone had pulled him out. Eric looked around the small room, at the cold gray walls and the single high window. Pale light spilled in through the latticed opening, though he could not tell if it was dawn or dusk. Using his hands more than his eyes, he explored the confines of his prison. The chain on his collar led to the thick frame of an iron cot, and a much-shorter span linked the manacles on each wrist. Behind him was a single door, made of dark wood and crossed with bands of metal. There was no handle on the inside.

Moving as quickly as his aching muscles allowed, Eric shifted around so he faced the door. Even that small action made him feel better; at least he had done something. And the room was definitely growing lighter, he decided, which meant it was morning. An entire day had somehow passed since he woke in the granary with

Daria and Simon.

His stomach tightened. By the gods, where was Simon now? The thought of the mad magician loose in the streets filled him with a fresh sense of dread. Sure, Daria was with him, but she had no idea what he was capable of, much less how to control him. What would she think when he didn't show up at the storage shed, and what would she do? It would have been easy now, to think that Simon was no longer his concern, but what if he harmed that girl?

He had to get to them. Eric stood, or tried to; the chain was not long enough to allow him to stand. He looked longingly toward the window, but even if he could have reached it, it was far too small for him to crawl through.

But wait. What was that? Eric froze, and strained his eyes against the dim morning light. There, on the window-ledge, rested the familiar shape of his leather bound box. A small cry of elation escaped his parched lips. The lock was broken, and one side was a bit battered, but someone had obviously salvaged it from among his few possessions. And if the box was safe, then perhaps the contents were safe as well. The letter from Master Phineas would still be there; all he had to do was get it and show it and he would finally be a free man.

His hopes died in an instant. Someone had placed it there, out of reach, probably the same person who had pulled him from the ocean's maw. What would she want from him, he thought, what would gain him possession of that casket, that letter, and his freedom? He shivered again, though this time it was not from the damp or the cold. The answer came to him quickly; it wasn't what she wanted, it was who.

It was well past dusk when Daria gave up the hope that Eric was still coming for her. She huddled wide-eyed in the darkness, listening to the water slap the pier and wondering what would become of her. It seemed she had no options at all. She was alone — no, worse than alone, because if her promise to Eric meant anything at all, she still had Simon to look after.

She couldn't see him in the darkness, but knew he was there from the rhythmic sound of his breathing. Untroubled by his friend's absence, he had fallen asleep almost immediately, and now it fell to Daria to decide what to do about their situation. Hard as she tried, she could not convince herself that Eric had abandoned her. Whatever trouble she was in, his current plight was far worse. If he was still alive. Daria shuddered. She wouldn't allow herself to believe in that possibility either.

She could end it now. It would be so simple to leave the storage shed and turn herself over to the first watchman to cross her path. She would be taken back to the citadel and tended by her maids. A warm bath, clean clothing, a full stomach — all things she had once taken for granted. Was it really so horrible living under Vassant's hand? So simple. She saw herself climbing down from the stack of musty sails, but couldn't actually bring herself to do it.

With a sigh, she drew her knees up to her chest and scooted closer to Simon for warmth. He never stirred.

All right. If she wasn't going to turn herself in, what could she do? There just didn't seem to be any options. She needed to find her father, or at least find out where he had gone. But she would need help and there was no one to whom she could turn. The guards were Vassant's creatures; at least enough of them were that she didn't dare turn to them. And even if any of the servants would help, they had too much to fear from Vassant.

That left someone from outside the citadel, perhaps someone from one of the noble families still loyal to her father. She studied her memories of long-ago parties, and came up with several possibilities. If they would not oppose Vassant, at least they would shelter her until father returned.

She shifted and stretched, and felt some of the tension leave her shoulders. Just having a plan made her feel better, even if it wasn't a very good one. But it was enough to let her snatch a few hours of fitful sleep, enough to let the dreadful night pass into morning.

Chapter 21

It was nearly mid-morning when Eric finally heard movement on the other side of the door. He had passed the time making and breaking deals in his head, and trying not to think about his overpowering thirst or the empty pit in his stomach. All the while, his eyes remained fixed on the leather-bound box. He knew he would only have one chance to strike a deal with her, and he had to be prepared.

The door swung inward. Two soldiers filled the opening, thick, beefy men wielding pikes. "Where is she?" Eric croaked, the words rasping across his tender throat. "I must speak to her."

The two soldiers moved to either side of the door and Rialle stepped between them, her pale blue robe rustling against their leather armor. "And so you shall," she said, favoring him with a smile that was completely devoid of warmth. "You have a lot to answer for, my friend."

Eric fought to keep his breathing under control and his gaze on her. He dry-swallowed his fear and faced her. "I've done nothing to deserve this treatment."

"Really?" She shook her finger at him as if he were a naughty boy. "I cannot speak for other places, but here in Legerdemain, runaway galley slaves are hanged."

"I am not a galley slave." Eric interjected. His eyes darted toward the casket of their own accord. "You know that."

"What I know is that thirty-seven slaves and one honest merchant died in the fire you started to cover your escape." She shook her head. "Did you think we would not want to find you and make you pay for your crimes?"

Eric swallowed again. His mouth was so dry it was hard to speak. "I did not start that fire."

"Then tell me." Rialle arched a brow. "Who did?"

Eric stared at her. "I don't know." It was a lie, and they both know it. "I didn't see anything but a chance to run. So I did."

"I see." Rialle pursed her lips. "And what of your friend, Simon? Did he escape as well?"

Eric's heart raced. This was it. "If I give you that information," he said slowly. "What will you give me?"

Rialle looked at him for a long moment, and a genuine smile touched her lips. "You're trying to bargain with me? Now, after all that has happened?" She laughed. "I don't have to give you anything."

She crossed her arms and walked toward the window, deliberately staying out of his reach. "If I cared to know, I would simply have your tongue loosened with a whip, or perhaps call Lord Vassant to question you. Then you would be sent to the galleys, though I can't imagine there will be much left of you in either event."

Everything she said was true, but Eric remained firm. "I am far more useful to you alive," he said carefully. "You wouldn't have pulled me out of the water just to send me to the gallows."

"Don't count on it." She gave a sharp laugh. "I've been told I'm quite vindictive." She paused. "But the truth of it is I genuinely do not care what happens to you."

"Then let me go."

"I could." She produced an iron key from her bodice, displayed it for him, and then closed it in her fist. "Just so long as I get what I want."

"And what is that?" Eric's legs ached from crouching, and he steadied himself with his hands.

"As you are not foolish, you must know why I am interested in Simon." Rialle opened her hand and displayed the key once more. "The real question is — what do you want?"

She handed the key to one of the guards, who approached Eric and unlocked the chain holding him to the pallet. "Come." Rialle gestured with a languid hand. "We don't have to discuss terms right now. Be assured that if it's in my power, it's yours." She picked up the casket and tucked it under her arm. "If you help me, of course."

Eric stood slowly, steadying himself against the wall with both hands. His head spun and his stomach rolled, but outwardly he remained calm, unwilling to show weakness in her presence. She gestured for him to follow, and passed between the two soldiers into the room beyond. Eric followed, though he was unsure his legs would hold him.

This chamber stood in stark contrast to the one he had just exited. Bright sunlight flooded through a pair of open doors, which lead to a balcony overlooking the ocean. Eric glanced out, thinking to judge it as an escape route, but the sight of all that water made his stomach roll. One of the soldiers positioned himself by the chamber door, while the other blocked the balcony exit. Eric swallowed a smirk; if only they knew he would rather face Rialle than the smothering water again.

With a deep breath, he turned his back to it and scanned the small parlor. Though little more than a dozen paces across, the chamber was filled with heavy pieces of furniture. Chests and cabinets lined every wall, a pair of wide armed divans flanked a small hearth, and a round table with a white marble top filled the rest of the room. Bright tapestries hung from three walls, and a rich emerald carpet felt soft and strange beneath his feet.

A servant entered, bearing a silver tray laden with food that she placed on the table. The rich smell of roasted meat filled the room. He glanced once at the tray, mouth watering, then deliberately looked away.

"I thought you might be hungry." Rialle absently placed the box on the table beside the tray and dismissed the servant with a wave. "Be seated," she told him. "You are not a prisoner here, but my guest."

Eric took a step, then stopped and raised his manacled hands. "Do you treat all your guests like this?"

"An oversight." She nodded to the guard at the door, who stepped forward and removed the feathers. "But I am afraid the one around your neck will have to wait."

Eric rubbed his wrists. "Until you get what you want?"

"Precisely." She gestured toward the table. "Sit. Eat. Then we will discuss your situation."

With a deep breath, Eric settled himself on the straight-backed chair, letting his shaky knees collapse. He linked his fingers tightly beneath the table to keep from snatching at the food. Though he was starving, he didn't trust her, not even enough to touch the meal she offered.

Rialle took the chair opposite him. "It's all right, see?" She tore a chunk of flesh from the fowl's breast and slipped it between her lips.

Eric salivated as he watched her chew, then swallow.

"As you so wisely surmised, I have nothing to gain by harming you."

Hunger overcame fear. Without taking his eyes from her, Eric unlinked his fingers, reached over and pulled away a plump leg. Grease ran down his chin as he took the first bite, and it was all he could do to keep from groaning with pleasure. While he stripped the meat from the bone, Rialle sampled the bread, cheese, and fruit, showing in turn that each was not poisoned. Finally, she poured a goblet of straw-colored wine, took a long sip, then pushed it across the table toward him.

"Easy," she warned him with a laugh as he picked it up and took a deep drink. "If it's been as long as I think, you might make yourself ill."

He stared at her over the rim. "I've been hungry before," he said flatly, and took another sip. "I know how to take care of myself."

"I don't doubt that you do." Rialle filled a second goblet with wine and placed it untouched on the table before her. "You've been a slave all your life, haven't you?"

His cheeks flushed, and Eric knew he had answered her question without saying a word. "Does it make a difference?" he asked, reaching for a chunk of bread.

"Not really." She crossed her arms and leaned back in her chair. Her icy gaze made him uncomfortable. "What about Simon?"

"I don't know." Eric chewed the soft bread and swallowed. "I suppose so. He can't take care of himself."

"That's what you did," Rialle said, almost to herself. "You were his keeper."

Eric nodded and tore away the second leg and thigh. Whether it was food, or the wine, or the warmth of the room, he felt his fear of her drift away with the ocean breeze. When she questioned him about Simon, he answered eagerly, even feeling a sense of relief at being able to speak freely about his dangerous charge. She listened with interest as he spoke of years of labor with only the promise of freedom to sustain him. "I took care of him," he said finally. "I took care of both of them."

"I understand." Rialle nodded in sympathy. "And I can take that burden from you." She placed a delicate hand on the box. If you will help me."

Eric stared at the singed leather and the metal bands. Sixteen years of hope, all stored in that battered little box. The memories washed over him, enveloping him just as the water had, threatening to over turn his sense of balance. Words tumbled out; he told her everything, his desire for freedom, his fear of Simon, his respect — no love — for Master Phineas.

The words spun out of control, and Eric gripped the table with both hands to steady himself. Why was he telling her this? When he spoke of the recent past, of meeting with Daria, he saw Rialle's eyes widen with what could have been fear or glee. Why was he saying so much? He was usually so careful, so controlled. As the answer came to him, he lifted his face to Rialle. "What have you done to me?"

"You are a clever one, aren't you? Most people like to talk so much they don't even notice." Rialle smiled slightly and nodded toward the wine. "Just a little something to make you a bit more forthcoming."

"But you tasted it." Eric spoke slowly, trying to make sure the words he spoke were his own. "I saw you."

"I tasted from one side of the goblet. You drank from the other." Rialle chuckled. "Don't worry; the effects only last for a short time. You will be back to your old, taciturn self in a few moments."

Eric sat back in his chair and glared at her, eyes wide. "You didn't have to do that."

"Perhaps not." She shrugged. "Last time we spoke, you weren't entirely honest. How am I to help you, if I don't know the true situation?"

Glowering, Eric seized control of his tongue, unwilling to say more in his muddled state. How much had he told her? He tried to remember, but could not tell where his memories ended and his words began. "I trusted you," he whispered.

"No, you did not." Rialle smiled. "But you shall."

Chapter 22

Daria tugged the chambermaid's cap from her head and shook the dust from it. What a sight I must be, she thought as she worked the tangles from her hair with her fingers. Her second night of escape had passed more easily than the first and she felt rested and ready to continue her quest.

Eric would be proud of her, she decided, and wondered once more what had become of him. Worry nudged at her, but she shoved it away. He had to have escaped; there was no other alternative.

Thinking of Eric brought to mind her other dilemma. She twisted and looked at Simon, sprawled and snoring among the folded sails. It would be easy to leave him there, just creep away as if they had never met.

Had she actually promised Eric she would take care of him? Daria tried to remember the exact words she had used. She sighed. It didn't matter; she was as responsible for Simon as if she had sworn a blood oath.

She squared her shoulders, tucked her hair back

into her cap and nudged Simon with her bare foot. “Come on,” she urged, careful to keep her voice low. “We have to get moving.”

He didn’t stir. She shifted to her hands and knees and crawled to him. “Come on, Simon,” she said. “It’s time to go.” She placed a hand on his cheek. “Wake up.”

Before she drew her next breath, he was awake and on her, pinning her back against the sails as a wolf would a lamb. “Where is this?” His words ran together. “Where is this?”

Daria tried to speak, but fear silenced her. What was he? She closed her eyes and swallowed hard as he leaned closer.

“Where is this?” he demanded. His breath was hot against her face. “Do you fear me?”

She nodded and clamped her teeth together to keep from crying out. “That’s good,” he laughed. “You should. He did. But he was always too quick for me to catch. You were slow. I caught you.”

His words came so quickly she hardly understood him. His fingers dug into her wrists and his body pressed her against the sails. She felt his breath on her neck, and for a terrible moment, she thought he might bite. “What are you?” she whispered.

“Where is he?” He sat back slightly. “What did he tell you?”

“Eric?” Daria forced herself to look at him. Simon’s blue-black eyes glittered above her like a thousand stars. She didn’t remember them being so dark. “I don’t know,” she breathed. “He was supposed to meet me — us — here, but he never arrived.”

“Lost? He is lost?” Simon released her hands and sat back on his heels. “Interesting. Interesting. Interesting.”

Daria tried to squirm away, but her legs were

pinned beneath him. He cocked his head rapidly from side to side. "If he is lost then I am free."

Daria seized the notion. "Yes you are. Go, quick, before you are spotted. I won't tell anyone."

"I shall I shall." He leaned over her again and placed a hand on either side of her head. "Tell me one thing. Where is he? I must know. I must."

"I told you I didn't know." Daria whimpered. "Eric was ...."

"Not him. Not him. Not the Keeper." Simon spat the name. "The one with the fire. The One who Glows."

Daria shook her head. "I don't know what you're talking about."

"Him!" Simon prodded her with his fingers. "The one with fire. The One who Glows."

Her mind raced. It was a puzzle, and if she didn't solve it, he would kill her. "Tell me more," she urged. "I want to help you, but I need more."

"Him!" Simon pounded the sail beside her head with his fist. "He glows. Like this." He straightened and opened his hands. Flames danced from his fingertips. "Like this. Like this."

Daria gaped at him. He wasn't a demon. "You're a magician!" she breathed. No wonder Eric kept him close.

"I am. I am." Simon cackled. "When they let me be I am." He threw back his head and marveled at his surroundings. "I am."

"You want Lord Vassant." She said it more to herself than to him. She looked up at him. "That's who you're looking for. Lord Vassant."

"If he is the One who Glows then yes." Simon clapped his hands together and the fire went out. "Yes yes yes."

"Oh, he glows." Daria struggled to order her thoughts. "Why do you want him?"

"Why do you question me? You fear me."

"I do." She forced her voice to be calm. "But I also know where he is. Why do you want him?"

"Bargaining with me? You bargain with me?" His face twisted in a grin. "I don't think you will like my bargain." He leaned close, but did not pin her down. "I will learn from him. I will take what he knows. I will kill him. Do you like my bargain?"

"I like your bargain." Daria masked her smile. "Will you like mine?"

"Perhaps. Perhaps. Perhaps." He laughed. "Tell it to me and we will see."

"I can get you to him." She spoke carefully. "Would you like that?"

"Aaaaah." Simon beamed with pleasure. "You will do that, yes, you will."

"I will do that," she repeated. "But you must do two things for me." When he did not stop her, she continued. "You must promise not to hurt me and to protect me."

"You give me the Glowing One." Simon rocked with each word. "And. And. And."

"And you must kill Lord Vassant." She smiled at him. "Will you do that?"

"Yes!" Simon chortled with glee and bounded down from the sails. "Yes! Yes! Yes!"

Daria took a deep breath and shoved herself into a sitting position. What an unlikely ally! She had no reason to believe he stood a chance against Vassant; no reason to believe they wouldn't be stopped as soon as they reentered the compound.

"We go! We go!" Simon paced a path in the dust on the floor. "Before he comes."

"Don't worry." Daria climbed down the pile of sails. "Lord Vassant won't come here."

"Not him," Simon said emphatically. "Not the One

who Glows. Him."

Eric. Daria shook her head and wondered if she was beginning to understand him. "We need Eric," she told him.

"No. No. No." Simon shook his head rapidly.

She stopped and looked at him. "Are you afraid of Eric?"

"Me? Fear? Me?" Simon's eyes popped open. "The Keeper fears." He grinned, leaned toward her, and spoke in an exaggerated whisper. "He never lets me free."

Daria's heart thumped into her throat. She trusted Eric a lot more than she trusted Simon. She looked at the agitated magician. "We made a bargain." She reminded him. "You protect me; I take you to Lord Vassant."

"We made a bargain." He repeated, rocking on his heels. "You take me to the One who Glows. I do not hurt you. I kill him. We made a bargain."

"Agreed." Daria picked up the bucket and placed a hand on the door. Her plan was as crazy as he was. "Stay close," she told him and opened the door.

Simon followed her out onto the dock. Daria shielded her eyes against the bright sunlight, and guessed it to be nearly midday. Beside her, Simon exclaimed. "Glorious. It is glorious."

She looked at him. His head tipped back as he lifted his face to the sun, and he held his arms out wide. "It is glorious."

Daria twisted her head to see if anyone noticed and placed a cautious hand on his arm. "Stop, please," she warned. "We mustn't draw attention to ourselves."

"But it is glorious." He turned and faced the ocean.

"Come!" she urged, and tugged his sleeve. "We haven't much time." When he didn't respond, she added. "We have to catch the One who Glows, remember."

"Ah! Ah!" Simon reoriented himself and allowed her to pull him along the dock like a toy on a string. Some of the laborers had stopped to look at them, but Daria imagined Eric's voice in her ear; pretend you belong. But how, dragging a mad boy with the mind of a child and the fire of a magician.

Simon stopped again. Daria turned, prepared to drag him if she had to, but was halted by the expression on his face.

"He calls," the young magician whispered reverently, lifting his eyes to the main keep. "Can you feel him? He calls."

Chapter 23

I think it is time for you to meet my magician.” Rialle placed her fingertips on the table and stood gracefully. She nodded to the soldiers. “Bring him.”

Eric stood of his own accord and followed Rialle into the stone corridor, flanked on either side by her ever-present guards. The two men towered over him and their armament jangled in time with his nerves. His gaze darted left and right, mentally mapping the halls, gauging possible escape routes. Rialle had promised him the letter if he helped her, but she was not the one who had consumed the truth potion.

“Where is Lord Vassant?” she demanded as the servants skittered out of her way. Those brave enough to respond pointed toward the lower levels. They descended one set of stairs, then another wider one that emerged in an open gallery.

Bright ocean light streamed through a pair of tall, latticed doors on the side opposite the stairs. Lord Vassant stood framed in the brightness, his back to them, his hands outstretched on the stone rails.

Rialle signaled for them to stop, then approached the magician as if he might shatter. "Have you found ...?" she started to ask, then her gaze shifted to the scene below. A sound that might have been a laugh emerged from her throat. She snapped her fingers at Eric. "Come," she ordered, and pointed.

Eric hesitated. The guards dragged him onward. As his eyes adjusted to the sunlight, he recognized the scene below as the courtyard through which he'd fled the day before. It was deserted now, save for a few brave souls who peered from windows or huddled against the perimeter, unable or unwilling to flee. A standing oxcart, a toppled stack of kegs, all spoke of tasks abandoned. The scent of charred wood hung in the salt air. At the center of it all stood Simon. Alert. Active. Alive.

Eric jerked back, out of sight. "That cannot be," he whispered.

"Yet it is." Rialle jabbed a finger at the scene below. "And that girl with him. Is she your thieving servant?"

Eric leaned forward and peered around the broader of the two guards. Daria stood just behind Simon, looking frightened but unharmed. A warning cry died in his throat. He turned to Rialle. "He'll kill her!"

"Pray he does not," she replied. "That girl is no servant. She is Princess Daria of Legerdemain."

"Princess?" Eric gaped at Rialle, then looked to Daria. He remembered the soft hand, the fine shoes, and the way she'd sniffed at the workman's stolen lunch.

Rialle barked orders at the guards. "Surround them!" She gestured a circle with her raised hand, then whirled on Eric. "Now do whatever it is you have to do to stop him. If she is harmed, you will beg me to send you to the galleys."

Eric hesitated. Neither magician had moved. From where he stood, he saw beads of sweat on Lord Vassant's skin, and the hair on Eric's arms prickled the way it did when Simon worked the stage.

Heart thumping, mouth dry with fear, Eric swallowed hard and turned his back to the courtyard. "First you give me the letter," he said, and held out his hand.

"Arrogant cur. You do not make demands. I do," she snarled and jabbed a finger at Simon. "Now!"

"No." Eric shook his head. "I don't trust you."

Her glare was sword-sharp. Without taking her eyes from Eric, she gestured to the guard on the right. "Can you bring him down without hurting the Princess?"

"Be a pleasure, milady." He dropped a bolt into the crossbow and raised it to his shoulder. "You want him dead or crippled."

"Crippled will be fine." She smiled at Eric. "Now you'll never know if I would have kept my side of the bargain."

I know, Eric thought, as the guard fired low. It seemed impossible he'd miss; yet the bolt flashed and vanished inches from Simon's left knee. The guard yelped and dropped the crossbow as it burst into flames.

"Fire on him again," Lord Vassant warned, "And it is you who will burn." He bared his lips in an approximation of a smile. "He is mine."

Chapter 24

Daria's nerves vibrated at a fever pitch as she followed Simon into the sun-washed courtyard. Too late to stop now. The courtyard was loud and bright, and she had difficulty sifting reality from her own racing thoughts Simon moved as if possessed, and Lord Vassant waited for them on a second story balcony.

"He glows," Simon whispered reverently. "Ah, don't you see it? He glows."

Daria didn't answer. In her mind, she saw her father's familiar face dissolve into Lord Vassant's cruel visage. The sight of him focused her rage to pinpoint precision. He doesn't glow, she determined, but he needs to burn.

"Remember our bargain," she told Simon, but he didn't seem to hear. She took an involuntary step back as Simon's laughter echoed off the stone walls. He spun drunkenly, arms wide, and the surrounding soldiers cried out as their crossbows burst into flames.

"Like that!" Simon shouted. "Like that!"

"Yes," Lord Vassant called back. "You learn quickly."

"I learn, oh yes!" Simon threw his head back and laughed again. "Show me more!"

"I'll show everything," Vassant promised. "But you must release the Princess."

"No!" Daria grabbed his shoulder. "You can't trust him."

Simon's head snapped around. The madness in his eyes caused her to flinch. "I learn from him. Then I kill him," he chanted. "I learn from him. Then I kill him." He spun back toward Vassant and shouted, "I do not hold her. No. I bargain with her. Yes."

Lord Vassant only stared. Daria filled the silence. "I am not his prisoner," she called. "We will surrender only to my father. My real father!"

"Stupid child." Lord Vassant sneered. "You cannot expect me to expose the King to this dangerous creature."

"Simon is not the dangerous one," she called back, then turned and looked around the square. "Ask yourselves, how long has it been since you last saw the King?" Her throat grew thick, but she refused to let her emotion reach her voice. "Ask Lord Vassant to produce him. Then I shall surrender."

Her eyes searched the balcony. She saw Rialle — the shrew was never out of her master's reach — but who was that beside her? Daria shielded her eyes from the sun. Was that Eric? What was he doing there? He did not appear to be a prisoner. Her heart froze. Apparently, she was not the only one who had made a bargain.

Chapter 25

Vassant moved toward the outer stair leading to the courtyard. "What are you doing?" Rialle hissed. Eric enjoyed the note of fear in her voice.

Lord Vassant ignored her, continuing his descent. "Stay with him," she told her guards. Eric hung back. She snapped her fingers. "You too!"

Eric shook his head. "If he sees me, he'll kill me. You'll never get him stopped."

Rialle grabbed his arm and forced him to follow. "Then you have more incentive to cooperate, don't you?"

As they moved down the stairs, Eric braced for an attack from Simon. It did not come. Simon stared at Lord Vassant in rapt fascination. Daria shifted slightly to the left, keeping Simon between her and Lord Vassant. Her eyes widened when she saw Eric, but she seemed more angry than afraid.

"What are you waiting for?" the Princess asked, her voice shrill. She pointed at Lord Vassant. "Kill him!"

Lord Vassant's head jerked back. Rialle cursed under her breath. "I shall I shall I shall," Simon chanted. "When I have learned all I shall and it shall be glorious!"

"Stop him," Rialle's fingers dug into Eric's arm. "Stop him now."

Eric froze, trapped between fear and curiosity. What would Simon do? He genuinely did not know. He strained his eyes and saw the pale blue circle of light surrounding both Daria and Simon.

Vassant saw it as well, and stopped just outside of Simon's reach. The expression on his face was one of genuine delight. "Call off your guards," he told Rialle, his voice almost conversational. "We don't need them."

Simon laughed. The sound almost made Eric stop him right there. "Don't kill him," Rialle warned. Eric wasn't sure if she was talking to Simon or Lord Vassant.

"Why would I do that?" Lord Vassant circled Simon, who watched with rising glee. The magician held out his hand above the ward, and the blue flames grew brighter. "What keeps me out, keeps you in. What do you fear, little one?"

The flames rose in a column, and then vanished, but not before Lord Vassant was forced to take a step back. Anger flashed across his face.

"Nothing I fear nothing," Simon cackled. The circle dropped. Lord Vassant reached for Daria, then yanked his hand back with a cry of pain. "Touch her not," chanted Simon.

"You're an apt student." Vassant regained his composure. "There is much I can teach you." He extended a hand. "Give me the girl, and your lessons will begin."

"Bargains? More bargains? She brought me here, bargained with me. Your coin is not good."

Eric knew he should stop Simon now, before anyone was hurt, but he also knew he couldn't until the letter was in his possession. His gaze darted toward the opened gate. Thanks to Simon, the guards no longer had their crossbows, but could he clear the distance before they skewered him?

Lord Vassant resumed circling. "If you are so powerful, why do you hide behind the girl?"

"I do not hide." Simon chattered. "She hides."

"I can offer you a better bargain."

"Don't trust him!" Daria warned. "Only my father can protect us."

"Don't trust him," Simon echoed. "Yes, yes, yes." He repeated as if to remind himself. "He Glows, and he lies."

Lord Vassant snarled and gestured. Flames shot from his hands. Simon deflected them and they splashed against the toppled pile of kegs. They burst and burned, spilling fire across the cobblestones.

"Stop him!" Rialle ordered. "How many deaths do you want on your hands?"

Eric took a few steps toward Simon, then turned and faced Rialle. "First you give me my letter," he said, as the flames grew higher.

Her eyes blazed with fury. "Not until I have my mage!"

Eric shook his head. "I don't trust you." He extended his hand. "Give me the letter."

"If Vassant kills Simon, you will have nothing to bargain with."

"Maybe Simon will win? Maybe they both will die?" Eric's heart thumped against his ribcage. "You decide. Is the future of an insignificant slave worth more than a pair of magicians?"

Rialle snarled, ripped the letter from her bodice and held it out to him. Eric snatched it from her grasp, spun, and shouted, “Simon! Sleep!”

Lord Vassant’s hands closed on thin air as the fire went out, and Simon collapsed. Lord Vassant groaned in frustration, and swayed as if his legs would no longer hold him. As Rialle barked orders to the soldiers, Lord Vassant knelt in front of Simon, who had fallen to his hands and knees. He took the boy’s face in his hands. Simon stared past him, his eyes vacant.

“Remarkable,” Lord Vassant whispered. “I sense nothing. It is as if he is gone. Completely gone.” His grip tightened and Simon howled in pain, a sound of uncomprehending hurt. Lord Vassant laughed and stepped back, leaving scorch marks on Simon’s face where his fingers had been.

Simon whimpered and scrambled toward Eric, who stepped back reflexively. A trio of guards converged on him; one struck the young mage on the back of the head with a cudgel, and he went limp.

“How could you? Why did you do that?” Daria screamed. Eric thought she was shouting at the guards, then realized her cries were directed at him. “I trusted you!”

Another pair of guards took hold of her. Daria fought wildly, but dwarfed between the two men, her struggles were futile. “Release me!” Daria ordered. “I command it!”

“How precious.” Rialle rolled her eyes and jerked her head at the guards. “Take her back to her chambers and see that she stays there, even it means nailing the door shut.”

She jerked her head at Simon. “That one goes to the laboratory. Fear not, and handle him gently, for he is quite valuable. Lord Vassant will go with you to insure he is safely contained.

It was over. Eric’s hand closed on the letter. He had held it so many times, but now it was really his.

He turned toward the gate, and faced a wall of pike-bearing soldiers. As he took his first step, he realized he would not be allowed a second one. Heart, mind, body — everything stopped.

He heard Rialle laugh and turned on her. "No!" he bellowed. "We had a deal!"

"And you believed me?" Rialle lifted her eyes.

Eric lunged at her. Before her guards could react, his hands closed on her throat and he rode her to the ground. His howls had no words — sixteen years of pent rage erupted in that single moment.

A pair of guards hauled him off her, cloth ripping beneath his clawed hands, and thrust him facedown on the cobblestones. A boot crushed the back of his neck; hands wrenched his arms to the small of his back and bound them there with a thick leather strap. A blow to the head left him dazed; a jab to the kidney stole his breath.

Gasping, he twisted his head as far as he could. Rialle had regained her feet. In her hand was the tattered parchment bearing Master Phineas' seal. "Daria was right," she snarled. "You are a fool." She crumpled the letter, tossed it onto the dying fire, and nodded at the guards. "Take him back to his quarters. Make him wish he was dead."

Not until I can take you with me, Eric vowed silently as they dragged him away.

Chapter 26

Daria fought her guards all the way to her chambers. She knew it was futile, stupid, even undignified, but she would no longer cooperate with them. She would no longer be led about like a lap dog on a little leash.

"You would not be treating me this way if my father were here!" she shouted as they pushed her into the hands of her nurse. "Where is he?"

Two of the soldiers ignored her. The third, an older man with close-cropped gray hair, shifted uncomfortably under her gaze. "It is for your own safety, Princess," he said, kindly.

"From whom?" she pleaded. "Who are you protecting me from?"

He didn't answer, though his eyes were thoughtful. One of the other soldiers motioned him away. "There will be a pair of guards outside your door at all times, Princess." He inclined his head in a bow. "For your protection, of course."

She watched them go, wishing she had something to throw at the door as it closed. Her rage was so hot, so fresh, that all she could do was stand and shake. She had been so close. If Eric hadn't ....

Eric. Daria bowed her head. Even he had turned against her. Tears formed behind her eyes, but she did not let them fall. Bethel reached for her. "Don't touch me," she snapped. The old woman jerked back as if slapped.

Daria softened. "I am sorry, Bethel," she said. "This has been a trying time, but none of it is your fault."

"Trying indeed, Princess." Her lined face wrinkled with relief. "Come, now, let me get you out of those nasty rags — wherever did you find them — and you can tell me all about your adventure."

Adventure? Daria stared as Bethel led her to the inner chamber where the chambermaid, Talya, hovered. What did they think? She had gone to the mountains for a few days?

She paused. What did they think? "What were you told about my absence?" she asked as the two servants lifted the dusty apron over her head.

"We were told not to concern ourselves, Princess," Talya replied, as if this was the most natural thing in the world. "That you would return in due time."

Daria looked at Bethel. "We are but servants," the nurse confirmed, but her expression did not match her words. "Shameful," she balled the apron and tossed it into the hearth.

Daria knew she had her first ally. She turned to the chambermaid. "Talya, go to the kitchen and fetch me a tray. Something warm, broth or stew." Though it was a ruse to get her out of the room, as Daria spoke the words she realized she was ravenous. The last she had eaten was the loaf Eric stole from the courtyard kitchen. Damn you, Eric, she thought as she watched Talya curtsey and hustle from the room.

As soon as the door thumped shut, Daria turned

and led her nurse to the window seat farthest from the door. “Oh, Bethel, I don’t know where to begin.”

The old woman opened her arms. “Tell me.”

Daria felt the tears welling in her eyes. “No,” she said, catching herself. “As much as I want to, I can’t. I can’t cry.” She covered her eyes with one hand. “I have to be strong.”

“You are strong, child.”

Daria bit her lip. Bethel was right, but if she kept talking, the tears would win. It would be so simple to lean forward and weep; she could even tell herself she was doing it for Bethel’s sake. But the time for that had passed. She took her nurse’s plump hand in her own and let the story spill out of her. How she fled when she discovered Lord Vassant was using some sort of glamour to impersonate her father, how she encountered two runaway slaves, and finally, how one of them betrayed her.

The anger drained away as she spoke. Her rage was replaced, not by complacency, but determination. By what right did Lord Vassant rule her? He was not King. Her father was King. In her father’s absence, she ruled.

Therefore, she would behave like a ruler.

Chapter 27

They dropped Eric on the cold stone floor of his cell. Blood seeped from his nose, from his mouth, from his wrist and his ankles, where they had bound him and beat him. He remembered every blow. Sleep would be a release, unconsciousness more so, but his mind raced with rage, awake and aflame. He knew he should move, crawl to the pallet, but the effort lay somewhere beyond him. Even breathing brought a pain worse than he had ever imagined.

He concentrated on every breath — inhaling, exhaling through his mouth. He couldn't reach up and feel his nose, but he was sure it was broken. He felt the blood oozing down the side of his face and trickling down the back of his throat. The taste of it made him gag; reflex made him retch, and what remained of the poisoned feast rose from his stomach in bitter bile and he choked.

Though it was dark, his vision was white with pain and he nearly blacked out. A familiar voice spoke. "Roll over. Do it or you'll die."

Fighting unconsciousness, Eric dug in with his heels and turned onto his left side. His ribs grated together and brought a fresh cry of pain to his swollen lips.

"Trust a man who spent the last dozen years of his life as a miserable drunk to know a thing or two about vomit." The voice spoke again. "You always were a trusting fool, Eric."

Eric forced his eyes open. Despite the total darkness, despite the pain, despite the fact the man was dead; Master Phineas towered over him like a disapproving parent. "You should have listened to me, Eric," he said with a cluck. "You should have used him when you had the chance."

"You're not real," Eric slurred, the words emerging as a moan. "You're dead."

"Aye," the shade agreed. "And you will be too if you don't escape the reach of that grasping shrew." He gave a rusty laugh. "You didn't actually believe she was going to let you stroll out of here, did you?"

His mind spun. Rialle. That bitch. How had he ever trusted her? How had he ever believed her? He had wanted his freedom so badly, for so long, that his desire made him blind — worse, it made him stupid. His whole life, he had survived on his own cleverness and now, when he needed it the most, it had failed him. Thinking every breath could be his last, he cursed her, damning her to Otherworld until time froze.

"You're not gonna die, boy. Not here. Not yet." Master Phineas squatted next to him. "She thinks she has you beaten." He placed a ghost hand on Eric's cheek. "She thinks Simon is the dangerous one."

If Eric could have summoned the breath to laugh, he would have. Dangerous? This whimpering wretch? Except, inside he knew it to be true, the rage that kept him awake was keeping him alive.

As he lay there shivering on the cold floor, Eric found the only way he could will himself to live was to imagine her death at his hands. He had never killed anyone, never even considered it, but now it was the only thought that sustained him. If he had the chance — and he would, because she needed him to work Simon — he would do what he should have done in the courtyard and order Simon to strike her dead.

Eric's consciousness ebbed and flowed through the long night. His thoughts grew less structured, and he wasn't sure if he was awake, dreaming, or delirious. Master Phineas' shade was long gone. The scene in the courtyard spun out before him. Simon battling Lord Vassant. Rialle's cold laughter. Daria screaming, "How could you! How could you! How could you!"

"I didn't know," he murmured. "I'm sorry, I didn't know."

"Of course you didn't." A woman's voice spoke.

Eric strained against the darkness. Something touched him. He jerked, sending a fresh wave of agony through his bones.

"Be easy, son, and let me be about it, for I haven't long and must be quick."

The touch returned — a pair of hands. Who are you, he wanted to ask, but he couldn't form the words.

"A friend," she answered, as if she'd heard him. Her fingertips ran the length of his body and she made a "tsk" sound with her tongue. "Excessive. Unnecessary. But like her." She reached beneath his tattered shirt. Her hands were cool against his fevered skin as she placed her palms against his ribs. The pain blazed anew, and she hushed him before he gasped.

Someone come to hurt him again? Eric tried to push himself away. A hand closed on his cheek. "You be still and I'll be quick," the voice scolded.

As her hands worked over him, the pain in his ribs

dulled from agony to ache. His breathing cleared and he sighed in relief. "Better better better," she chuckled. "You'll live, and be able to move when you need to." A hand cupped the back of his neck. "Now, up with you and onto the pallet. This cold stone will kill you quicker than a cudgel."

"I can't."

"You can," she scolded.

Eric braced for the stabbing pain and rolled onto his stomach. When it didn't come, he pulled himself to his knees and swayed drunkenly. "Where?"

"Left. Not far."

Eric crawled, groping ahead with his right hand. His fingers closed on the wooden frame. He heaved himself forward and collapsed onto the straw mattress. The room spun around him and he clasped the edge of the pallet to steady himself.

He had to be dreaming or delirious, he decided.

"Not quite," she told him. "But it's best you remember it so." Her hand covered his eyes. "Now, sleep, and be easy, for the worst is yet to come."

Chapter 28

Daria allowed them to think they had won. Though her nerves were as taut as the head of a drum, she played her part. She was pleasant with everyone, ate what was placed before her, and pretended to be entertained by the small amusements Bethel arranged to fill the hours.

In a way, it was no different from what she and Eric had done in the courtyard. She pretended she belonged. Thinking of Eric first made her sad, and then it made her angry. He had betrayed her, and there was no excuse to be made for that.

She funneled her anger into observation. She noted how the servants and soldiers came and went, what they said when they thought she wasn't listening, and the way they looked at her in silence when she asked about her father.

Her self-control was rewarded at the end of the second day. When the scullery maid came to retrieve the tray from her evening meal, Daria glimpsed the gray-haired soldier who had spoken kindly to her. Though he appeared attentive to his duties, she saw his gaze drift to the interior of the room. Twice she managed to catch his eye and mouthed, Help Me. His eyes widened, but he did not nod nor shake his head either. She decided that was a good sign.

That night she dreamed of Mara. The old woman smiled and spoke to her, but she was so small, so far away, that Daria could not make out what she was saying. Still, she felt comforted by her presence, and was dismayed when Bethel woke her from her slumber.

"Quickly, Princess. Come. You have a visitor."

Daria's eyes snapped open. It was dark save for the faint light from the open door to the next room. "What?"

"Hurry, else we'll be discovered."

Daria leapt from the bed, stepped into a dressing gown and followed Bethel into the sitting room. A broad-shouldered man stood silhouetted in the glow of the banked fire. "You asked for my help, Princess?"

Daria thanked Bethel and hurried to meet the man. "Thank you for coming." She inclined her head in a little bow. "I am indeed in need of assistance."

He returned her bow. "How may I serve you?"

She indicated the chair to the right of the hearth. "Please, sit." She perched on the edge of the opposite chair. Her palms were damp and her heart thrummed against the base of her throat as she spoke. "Do you know what's become of my father?"

"Alas no, Princess." He looked at his hands, his expression hidden in shadows. "But it is bad business, I fear."

Her blood chilled. "How so?"

He lifted his face. The steel in his eyes matched the gray in his hair. "I have served your father since I was a young man, and hoped to do so until my days pass. It has been an honor to serve, and a greater honor to claim that our good King knew me by name." He paused and looked down again. "The last few times I've seen him, there wasn't a flicker of recognition on his face."

Daria thought, then spoke. "I'd wager Lord Vassant does not know your name."

"No, Princess." His head jerked up. "And that's as I want it. I've no use for that spook or his high-handed trinket." His face grew thoughtful. "You think he's done something to the King to make his mind go soft?"

"Worse than that." Daria studied him. Her need to trust him took the form of an ache. "Has anyone else noticed this change in my father?"

"There's rumors." He shook his head. "But those who ask too many questions disappear."

Daria's heart filled with rage. "The rumors are true." Her voice was barely audible. "Lord Vassant is using some sort of glamour to impersonate my father. I have seen it with my own eyes. That is why he does not recognize you."

The soldier jerked back. "But what of the King?"

"I do not know. But I intend to find out. Will you help me?" He nodded. She continued. "Right now I need information." She set her mind to business. "There is one who has the power to defeat Lord Vassant. He was captured at the same time as I was. Do you know what happened to him?"

"Which one, Princess? There were two."

"Two?"

"Yes, Princess. There was the slave mage who battled Lord Vassant in the square. He's been taken down to the Witch's Pit."

"But what of the other one? I was led to believe he was in league with Rialle."

"Unlikely." The soldier shifted uncomfortably. "I am told he attacked her in the courtyard and she had him beaten for it."

Eric didn't betray her! "Where is he now?" she asked, startled by her own relief.

"If he lives, he's locked away in a cell near her quarters."

Daria drew a sharp breath. She had imagined her imprisonment was unbearable; now she knew it could have been a thousand times worse. "First we must make sure both of them are still alive and, if so, see they stay that way. Can you do that?"

"The first, certainly. As for the second." He shook his head. "I will see what I can do."

Her mind raced. "Are there others who feel as you do?"

"Yes, Princess. A few. I've already spoken to them." He stood. "I must get back to my post, before I am missed."

He was almost to the door when Daria called. "What is your name, soldier?"

He dipped his head. "I am Del, Princess."

"Del." She smiled and returned his bow. "I shall remember that."

It was evening when they came for her.

Daria mentally counted to five, then lifted her head from the book she was pretending to read. One of Rialle's soldiers filled the doorway to her sitting room. He did not smile when he spoke to her. This was a hard man — not a soldier who had served since her childhood.

"Madam Rialle wishes to speak to you."

She held his gaze for the space of a dozen breaths, then looked back down at her book. "If one of the servants wishes to speak to me, she knows where to find me." She gave a deliberate pause. "Especially since she has gone to such extraordinary trouble to see that I remain here."

"My orders are to bring you to Lord Vassant's salon. Now." He punctuated the last word with a step toward her.

Daria contemplated her options. She could refuse, but he might have her carried to the salon. These men had done it once; there was no reason to believe they wouldn't do it again.

She carefully placed a silver filigreed marker between the pages, snapped the book shut, and stood. "As it happens, I wish to speak to Lord Vassant. Perhaps I will be fortunate enough to find him there."

The walk from her chambers to the magician's salon seemed endless. Daria set her head high and her shoulders back, every bit a princess and not the prisoner she was. She would not appear frightened, though her pulse pounded with trepidation. I have allies now, she reminded herself. I am no longer alone.

The four soldiers surrounded her, two in front, and two behind. She didn't ask why there were so many, or why she was being led through halls she had lived in all her life. She had heard "for your protection" so many times it was easy to pretend she believed it. Nerves made her want to laugh and she covered her mouth with her hand. Did Rialle really think it took four men to stop her from running away again?

They halted outside the salon door and the guard who had spoken stepped in to announce her as if she were arriving at court. Daria took two steps, then stopped. Rialle sat like a contented cat in a high-backed wooden chair at the head of a carved table. She wore a pale blue gown shot with threads of silver and gold. Her long blonde hair was woven into an elaborate crown. Daria sneered inwardly. Rialle might dress in fine clothes, but she would never be anything more than a servant.

"Sit." Rialle dismissed the soldiers and gestured to the seat at her left. "Would you join me for refreshments? I can have something sent up from the kitchens."

Daria crossed her arms. "I think not."

"Suit yourself." Rialle gave a delicate shrug and poured a stream of straw-colored wine into her goblet from the carafe at her elbow. "Forgive me if I indulge. I have had a most trying morning."

"Forgive me if I don't feel any sympathy for you." Daria moved toward the arched doors leading to the balcony overlooking the ocean. "Where is Lord Vassant?" she asked. "I wish to speak to him."

Rialle sipped from the goblet, her eyes never leaving Daria. "He is trying to help that poor unfortunate creature who nearly killed him in the courtyard. As am I."

I doubt it, Daria thought. Her gaze traveled around the room. Diffused light entered through the doorways, spilling across the wine-colored rugs. Thick tapestries covered two of the three remaining walls, swallowing the sunlight and muffling the ever-present rush of the ocean. Two chairs and a divan boxed the hearth, and a sideboard and a cloak rack flanked the door.

Her thoughts turned to Eric. Was he still alive? It was time to find out. Daria turned to the arrogant servant. "What is it you want?"

Rialle placed the goblet on the table. "Lord Vassant asked me to look in on you, to ensure you were well after your misadventure."

Daria's dulcet response did not match her stony demeanor. "You may tell Lord Vassant I am well, and I appreciate his concern." She paused and tilted her head. "I might ask the same of him, after his battle in the courtyard."

"It was a small act meant only to ensure your safety as well as the safety of all those poor souls trapped in the compound. It could have been a terrible tragedy." Rialle inclined her head. "Are you sure you wouldn't like some wine? It's quite good."

Undoubtedly poisoned, a small voice in Daria's mind added. "Thank you, no," she said. "I prefer to keep my wits about me." Her pause became a smile. "I was not aware servants were permitted to drink on duty."

Rialle's pale eyes flashed with a lightning strike of rage that was gone as quick as it had come. "You still do not realize what has happened here." Rialle smiled coldly. "With the right connection, a servant can become even more powerful than a princess."

Daria glowered. "What do you want?"

Rialle let the smile reach her lips. "Lord Vassant is most curious about the slave who threatened you. I believe his name is Simon. Any information you can provide will be most helpful."

"Why would I help Lord Vassant?"

"Because in doing so," Rialle paused between each word. "You will help all of Legerdemain, and perhaps even save the life of that poor mad creature."

"Is he in danger of dying from Lord Vassant's assistance?"

Rialle sighed impatiently. "If killing him was all we wanted, I would have ordered it done while he was helpless. Lord Vassant wishes to study him, help him regain some semblance of sanity."

"How benevolent of him." Daria narrowed her eyes. "Unfortunately, I don't believe you."

"Pity." Rialle ran a finger along the edge of the table. "If we cannot control him, we will have to kill him." She paused, then lifted her eyes to the Princess. "And his friend."

Eric was alive! Daria struggled to control the tremble in her voice. "Eric and Simon are under my protection. Hold them, if you must, but they are not to be harmed."

"Your protection is meaningless. The only way you can save them is to assist Lord Vassant." Rialle stood. "What did you see when you were with the slave mage?"

"I saw two frightened boys fleeing for their lives." Daria placed her hands on the table. "Yet they were willing to risk those lives on my behalf."

Rialle stood. "How did Eric control the magician?"

"Kindness," Daria snapped back. It took all her nerve to stand up to this gilded harridan. "Did it occur to you to just ask him what you needed to know?"

"As I have asked you?" Rialle strode toward the door and jerked it open. "Kill the slave housed in the third floor cell."

"You wouldn't dare." Daria spoke through her teeth. "You may dress the part of a lady, but you're nothing more than a serving wench."

Rialle's delicate face twisted in a sneer. "Stupid girl." She slammed the door shut, seized a claret-colored cloak from the rack and flung it to the floor. "Tell me again what I would not dare to do."

Daria started to reply, but the sound died in her throat. What she had taken for a cloak rack was a statue of her father. She had never seen it before. The likeness was striking. It was as if ....

The eyes moved. Daria's knees buckled. Rialle grabbed her by the arm and yanked her forward. "Do you think a couple of worthless slaves can stop me?" Rialle raged. "Do you think I will allow a sniveling princess to stand in my way?"

Chapter 29

Eric sat on the low pallet, his back to the wall, watching the square of sunlight travel across the mottled stone. His legs were drawn upward; his arms lay on the tops of his knees. His expression never wavered. Those charged with watching him reported he hadn't moved in two days.

That was on the outside. Inside, he seethed. Sixteen years of being a slave, being owned and at the mercy of others, boiled down into the space of this tiny cell. Rialle, Master Phineas, the nameless man who set him to stealing before he could barely speak, they all had owned him. He had never run, never shirked. He had toiled tirelessly for each of his masters. Through it all, he had clung to the foolish belief his obedience would be rewarded.

He glared at the floor and the shattered pieces of his leather casket. Rialle's guards had smashed it, tromped his meager possessions with their heavy boots, mixing leather, wood, glass, and metal with his blood. She thought she was breaking him. She was only making him stronger.

He shifted slightly. His fingers and toes were stiff and swollen. His jaw creaked when he moved it, but his inner rage kept the pain at bay.

Eric tilted his head and gave a little shake. There was something else. Something he should remember, but did not. What? He squeezed his eyes shut, but no image came.

The door creaked inward. Eric glanced up without moving his head. Two shadow-faced guards escorted one trembling servant girl. He heard the thump as she placed the tray on the floor, heard her exhale as she lifted the untouched tray from that morning. He heard the whispering as they wondered why he hadn't eaten in two days. As the door closed, he heard one of the guards offer to hold him down while the girl force-fed him.

He ignored them as he ignored the new tray. Rialle had poisoned him once; there was no reason to think she wouldn't do it again.

Rialle. The thought of her turned his hands to fists and his heart to stone. Sixteen years as a slave, and this was the first time he had ever hated anyone. The emotion was so dark, so fierce, it felt as if he were drowning once more. And this time, there was no one to pull him out.

Two lights flickered in the darkness of his rage. Two flames kept him fighting for life. First was Rialle. She needed him. Alive. And he needed her dead.

Chapter 30

Darkness swallowed the cell. Hours passed. Eric stayed quiet. Rialle would come to him. She had no choice.

Pale light seeped through the gap at the bottom of the door. Boots scraped the tile outside. The hinges screeched inward; torchlight leapt at Eric. He shielded his eyes with his forearm as two broad-shouldered figures filled the open door.

Eric did not resist as the two soldiers hauled him from the pallet and shoved his face against the wall. One wrenched his arms back while the other clapped a pair of thick manacles around his wrists. He felt the heavy weight of a chain attached to his collar. They spun him away from the wall and shoved him toward the door. Eric staggered but did not fall. He knew they expected him to ask where they were taking him, but he kept silent.

They marched him through the cluttered sitting room into the blackened hall. None of the torches were lit; the circle of lantern-light danced around them like a spell. The only sound was the slap of his bare boots keeping time with their steps.

Eric stopped when they stopped, walked when they walked, the manacles rattled in time with his steps. He paid no attention to the path they took. This time he wasn't coming back. He would be dead by sunrise, but all he felt was his white-hot need for vengeance.

"Better days," a voice whispered. The lamplight vanished. Eric jerked his head up and strained his eyes against the sudden darkness. The guard on his left gave a cry of surprise. Eric heard grunts, then a blow, and a body hit the ground. The chain fell slack.

Instinct kicked in. Eric lowered his head and darted away from the struggle. He made three steps before being brought up short. "Be still!" a low voice growled. Someone hauled him back and shoved him against the wall.

Eric struggled against the weight of his captor. "Who are you?" he stammered.

A gloved fist covered his mouth. "Quiet!"

Before he could protest, he heard the sound of a second booted man moving toward them. "Hall is clear."

"Then we go. Quietly." The first man pulled Eric away from the wall. He stumbled over the prone form of one of the guards, but his new captor's grip on his arm kept him upright. Eric heard the sound of something heavy being dragged across the stone floor.

He had no illusions that he was being saved; twice they ducked into rooms to avoid being seen. The corridors became a maze. They passed through a narrow door, the space around them tightened, and the air smelled of damp and dust. "Up," the voice grunted, and they ascended a steep column of stairs that ended abruptly at a wooden door.

Eric's guard knocked and the door swung inward. "Thank goodness you've come!" A servant woman greeted them with a shielded lantern and a face lined with worry. "It's bad business gone worse, I tell you." She waved them inward.

The man put a hand on Eric's shoulder and propelled him into a small sitting room with a banked fire and the outlines of furniture just visible in the lamplight.

"Is she ready?" his captor asked.

"Daria?" Eric exclaimed, looking from one to the other. "This is her room. Where is she? Is she safe?

"Hush, lad!" The guard looked alarmed. "Them outside will hear." He looked at the old woman. "Is the Princess ready, Bethel?"

"Bad business," the woman repeated. Her voice was thick, as if she had been crying. "They took her away just before dusk, wouldn't say to where. I tried to get a message to you."

"Blast!" The guard grimaced and shook his head. For the first time, Eric noticed he was wearing the silver and black of a city guard. "Then it was all for naught." He jerked his head at Eric. "I could have left this wretch where I found him."

The old woman looked Eric up and down. "This the poor boy she was going on about?"

"Aye," said the man. "Can't imagine what we'll do with him now."

Eric heard enough. He jerked away from his captor, faced the pair and demanded. "What is going on here? And where is Daria?"

"That's Princess Daria, to you," the old woman scolded. "You best remember that."

"Princess Daria, Daria the Lady's Maid, what does it matter?" Eric's mind whirled. Perhaps it was a rescue after all. Daria had obviously overcome her anger toward him. He balled his fists in the small of his back and rattled the chains. "If you want to save her, you have to get me to Simon."

The pair exchanged glances. The guard shook his head. "Not so fast, lad. The plan was we get the Princess out of the citadel to safety, then deal with those who wish her harm. It was she who asked me to bring you here."

"Then she is a clever girl." Eric turned to the woman. "Do you have any idea where they took her?"

Bethel shook her head. "There's guards still posted outside the door, but they won't speak to me."

"Vassant's men?" Eric asked. She nodded. Eric felt a chill. He looked at the guard. "Where is the slave who was captured at the same time I was?"

"I don't see ..." he began.

Bethel cut him off. "Answer him."

The guard scowled. "Down below," he grunted. "In the Witch's Pit."

Eric felt a flash of relief. At least Simon was still alive. "Can you get me to him?"

"I might," the guard replied. "If I was in the habit of taking orders from a slave."

Eric glared at him. "You want to stop Lord Vassant? So do I. You get me to Simon; I'll have the means to do it."

The guard's face hardened as he chewed over Eric's demand. The old woman spoke. "Can you get there, Del?"

He shook his head. "The door is witched; even if we do get past it, Vassant's pet bitch has men stacked deep between here and there. I got men behind me, but too few to take her."

"Then find the Princess." Bethel looked at both of them. "Get her to safety. Then we worry about getting to the other boy."

Eric nodded. "Agreed," he said, and shifted to show his bound wrists to the guard. "Get these off me."

Del crossed his arms and shook his head. "How do I know you won't run off?"

Because I want to watch Rialle burn, he thought, but aloud he said, "Daria trusted me. You have to trust me too."

After consulting with Bethel, Del removed the chain from his collar. Eric turned once more and displayed his wrists. He heard a clicking sound, but the weight of the manacles remained. "The right one is unlocked," Del said. "One good pull and your hands are free." Before Eric could protest, he added, "Easier to explain if we're spotted. I'm expected to be escorting a prisoner, not ramblin' about in the company of a slave."

Eric's stomach tightened. Not a slave, he reminded himself. Bethel brought fresh water and a cloth. "You look a fright," she scolded as she washed the remnants of blood from his face. "Daria did trust you, you know," she added, mostly under her breath. "You won't let her down, will you?"

He studied her fleshy face, and saw her expression shift from worry to hope. "We'll find her," he promised.

Moments later, he and Del were back on the narrow stairs, headed down. They descended two flights, and exited left through another narrow door. "She must still be in the citadel," Del said under his breath. "I've friends in the outer guard; they would have alerted me if she had been moved."

"Do you think she's in danger?"

Eric heard him sigh. "A week ago, I wouldn'ta thought it possible. Now I don't know." He jerked Eric through a pair of doors and onto an outer walkway. "Wait here," he said, pressing him into a corner "Stay out of sight."

Eric pressed his back against the damp stone. The night was cold and black, and the ocean-wind lashed at him like a scold. Faint light floated up from the yard below; spitting torches gave silhouette form to Del and another guard, their heads bobbing together in conversation. The sound of the water swallowed their words.

Run, a voice inside whispered. Daria's hastily drawn map came to his mind. Though it was dark, he was sure he could find his way. Once free, he could disguise himself, hire on with the first caravan heading east, and be free of Rialle, Vassant, even Simon, for the first time in his entire life. Simple.

Except it wasn't. Eric stared at the inky water. Why did Daria matter that much to him? He barely knew her, her life distant from his. In any other circumstance, she wouldn't have spared him a second glance. Was it Daria who kept him rooted to the spot or was it revenge?

Del returned and motioned to Eric to follow him back into the citadel. "They took her to Lord Vassant's chambers," he said. "We find him there — you may wish you were back in your cell."

"Then let's get Simon first," Eric urged. "Even the odds."

Del grunted a negative. "We'll never make it. Besides, I saw that freak in the courtyard. Bad enough we have one of them madmen on the loose — we don't need a second."

With a grimace, Eric followed the guard on a circuitous path through the darkened halls. His nerves sang; he hated not knowing where he was going, and he hated trusting this stranger. If he thought he had a chance of finding Simon on his own, he would have bolted.

Lord Vassant's chambers lay at the south end of a long shadowy hall. A pair of torches snapped on either side of the open arch, their flames more blue than yellow. There were no guards, and the corridor was as silent as a crypt. Del started to enter. "Wait," Eric whispered. His skin prickled with the sense of magic. "It may be warded."

"You can tell?"

"Aye." Eric crept forward and studied the opening. He strained his eyes for the pale blue light signifying a ward. Nothing. The feel of it was maddening; like an all-over itch. The smell was there under the salt tang of the ocean; a fire-and-lightning scent that made the hair on his arms prickle.

He heard the creak of leather as Del shifted behind him. Then he heard something else. A rustle. Eric held his breath and strained to listen. The silence hammered in his ears and the darkness in the chamber defied his vision. When he could hold his breath no longer, he heard it again. This time it was followed by a sob.

"Daria!" Eric shouted before he thought. He jerked his hands free and was through the door. "Where are you? Daria!"

"Eric?" Her voice was close. "Eric, is that you?"

He reached toward the sound. Their fingers brushed, she clutched at him, and was in his arms sobbing. "The torch, bring the torch!" he told Del. A circle of light surrounded them. Eric looked down at Daria's tear-stained face. "What is it," he asked. "What did they do to you?"

"Not me." Her voice was hoarse; he felt her sag in his arms as if too weak to stand. She looked up at him, then back over her shoulder.

Eric followed her gaze to a marble statue. It was a crowned figure of middle-years, with a kind face and a regal air. This must be her father, he thought. Then a tear trickled down the statue's shiny cheek.

Del swore and dropped the torch. The room went black.

Daria pressed her face against his chest and sobbed again. "It's him," she cried. "Look what they did to my father."

"Light, get the light," Eric said as he tried to soothe the distraught Princess.

"Him, it's him," she repeated.

"I know. I'll help you. We'll get Simon. I'll do what I can."

"I knew he was gone." Her words were a tortured whisper. "I knew, but I never dreamed ...."

The light flared blue. Eric looked up. Lord Vassant stood over them, a ball of mage light in his out-stretched hand. "Well now." His face twisted to a grin. "Look what I've caught in my web."

Daria broke from Eric's grasp and launched herself at the grinning magician. "You!" she shrieked, her tear-streaked face twisted into a mask of fury. "You did this!"

"Yes, I did." Lord Vassant's laughter filled the hollows of the room as he batted her away as he would an angry pup. Daria stumbled backward; Eric caught her before she fell. "Let me go!" she howled, struggling to break free. "I will kill him."

Eric tightened his grip. "You can't touch him," he told her, his lips against her ear.

She whipped her head around, her eyes dark with rage. "He won't get away with it. I won't let him." She dug her elbow into Eric's ribs and clawed at him with raked fingers.

"Let her come." Lord Vassant extended a hand.

Eric's strength vanished and he hit the floor as if dropped from a great height. The weight of a giant hand pressed his chest against his spine. His breath left in a single rush as Daria lunged toward the magician.

Lord Vassant swept his left hand in an arc. Every torch, every lamp in the room blazed with light. He caught Daria by the throat with his right hand and lifted her chin. Eric tried to scream, but his voice was a croak. Daria clamped her hands over Lord Vassant's wrist and kicked at him with her feet. "I'll kill you," she shrieked. "I'll kill you."

"And I won't hurt you at all." Lord Vassant spoke as if they were having a conversation. "You know that." He drew her closer. "Why do you fight me?"

"No!" The word emerged as a curse. "I know what you're doing." Her eyes closed and her breathing relaxed.

As her hands dropped away, Eric's heart filled his throat. Dead?

No. As quickly as she had faded, Daria opened her eyes and smiled at Lord Vassant. "Papa" she said, her voice soft. "You've come back to me."

"Of course, my child." Lord Vassant shifted his grip from her throat to her cheek. "How could you think I wouldn't?"

"I was scared." She leaned into his touch. "I saw

the statue, I thought ...."

"Daria, no!" Eric managed a croak. Lord Vassant silenced him with a malevolent glare. His left hand shot out, and the pressure on Eric's chest intensified. His head jerked back, and his mouth worked silently as he gasped for air. He dug his heels against the floor and struggled to work free of the force holding him, but remained pinned. Blood rushed in his ears; he barely heard Rialle speak.

"What are you doing?"

Eric rolled his head to the left. Through blurred vision, he saw Rialle posed in the doorway. For a moment, rage blotted out his pain. Her gaze shifted from Lord Vassant to Eric, and then back again. "What are you doing?" she repeated. "Have you gone mad?" Her voice held the alarm he could not see in her face.

"Taking care of what you could not."

She looked at Eric again. "Kill him, and we may never make use of the mage below."

"Then I'll kill that one too." Lord Vassant waved a hand.

Eric felt the pressure on his chest lessen. He choked air into his starving lungs and hoisted himself to his elbows. On the floor, to his left, lay Del's lifeless body. Eric suppressed the urge to vomit; his bruised ribs ached and his temples pounded. "Daria?" he gasped, casting wildly around the room.

"Here." Daria stood at Lord Vassant's side, her arms wrapped around his waist in a loving embrace. Her cheek rested against his shoulder, and the look on her face was of utter contentment. "Have we met?"

Eric fought the enchantment. "What did you do to her?" he demanded.

Lord Vassant crooked a finger at him. "Come, I'll

show you."

Eric rose. It was as if the magician controlled his spine. He made the conscious decision not to obey, yet his feet slid across the carpeted floor. The magician reached out and cupped his chin. Lord Vassant's hands burned his skin. Eric tried to pull back, but his body remained rooted in place. Lord Vassant slipped through his mind. His eyes closed.

Fight you. I'll fight you.

"Why are you fighting?"

Eric opened his eyes. Daria stood before him, a smile filling her face. "Why are you fighting?" she repeated.

The relief he felt at seeing her safe overwhelmed his instinct to run. Tears welled in his eyes. "You're all right," he whispered.

"But of course. You thought I was Daria the maid, but I am really Princess Daria of Legerdemain." She gave a little laugh, as if this amused her. "Did you really think Lord Vassant would dare harm me?"

She placed a hand on his cheek. Her touch set his flesh on fire. Eric's senses blurred as he tried to make sense of his surroundings. He tried to move away, but she held him firm. How had they gotten here? "Where?" he said, unsure if he had spoken aloud or in his mind.

"We're still in the citadel," she whispered. Her voice tickled his ears. "There's one more thing you must do for me before I grant you your reward."

"Reward?" Eric heard her words, but the meanings slipped away before he could grasp them.

"Yes, silly." Daria dropped her hand from his face and linked her arm through his. "For helping me when I was in dire need. I don't know what I would have done if you hadn't been there."

Eric stumbled forward. Something was wrong. Something remained. "Your father?" he said aloud and tried to turn back.

"My father is a very busy man. He is the King, you know." She laughed again. "I am acting on his behalf, and I can give you what you desire above all else."

Eric halted and looked at her anew. Wrong, wrong, his instincts sang, but his desire was stronger. "My freedom?" he whispered, as if he dared not believe it.

"Now you've ruined the surprise." Daria set him in motion again. "It's a little thing for a princess. Just a scratch of a quill on a bit of paper. After all you've done."

Memories surfaced and vanished. "But what ... Rialle?"

"That bitch?" Daria laughed a bit too loudly. "We can have her hung, flogged, whatever you like. Vassant too. If Simon leaves anything for us to use."

"Simon!" Eric exclaimed. How could he have forgotten? "Where is he?"

"That's where we're going. To rescue Simon." She quickened their pace. "You need to show me how to make Simon perform, so I can stop Lord Vassant. That's the last favor I need from you before I grant you your freedom."

His instinct recoiled at this sudden change of fortune, but years of practice kept his reaction from his face. He was a slave and she was a princess, and she was leading him to Simon in the company of four pike-wielding guards. Their armament jingled. Questions nagged at him, but he held them at bay as he placed his free hand on his collar. It hardly seemed possible.

Their journey ended at the bottom of a long column of stairs before a heavy wooden door with an inlaid sunburst pattern. The face in the sun seemed to leer at him. Eric's flesh prickled. He was in the presence of magic.

Daria placed her palm on the sunburst, and the door swung inward. Two soldiers entered with them, while the other two positioned themselves at the doors.

Pale blue fog rose from the floor, making it feel colder than it was. The far wall and ceiling were invisible in the gloom. Beneath the chill lay the sharp, skeletal touch of magic. As his eyes adjusted, Eric realized the light emanated from a vast circle carved into the stone floor. The lines alternated gold and silver, fist-sized gems glittered around the perimeter, and raised letters in unfamiliar script filled the spaces in between.

His escort shoved him forward. Eric moved closer, but stopped just short of the outer ring. He counted seven circles inward. At the center lay a huddled figure.

"Simon," Eric said aloud.

Simon's head snapped up at the sound of Eric's voice. He struggled to his hands and knees and lunged toward him, but was brought up short by the ward on the inner ring. Thwarted, he keened like a whipped dog and sank back to the floor.

"Waken him." Daria pointed at Simon. "I want to see how it's done."

Eric nodded and started toward Simon, then stopped. It wasn't right. What had Master Phineas taught him about the magic of circles? The one on the floor of their wagon had contained Simon and channeled his magic. Would this one work the same way?

"Do it!" Daria ordered.

Eric forced his feet to move. As he passed through each ring, he felt a faint strike against his taut nerves. He wiped his damp palms on his tattered breeches and knelt outside the inner circle. Simon reached for him; Eric clasped his hand. "It's time," he whispered. He transferred his grip to Simon's wrist. "Wake up."

Simon snatched at Eric as he always did, only this time, he caught him, hauled him into the inner ring and pinned him as a wolf would a rabbit. "What is this?" Simon chortled. "You didn't even try."

Chapter 31

Eric lay back against the cold floor, unable to move, momentarily transfixed by the blue light of the rings reflected in the mad magician's eyes. Simon's touch burned through the mist in Eric's mind like the morning sun.

He realized it was all a trick. Daria hadn't escorted him to this room. Daria was a prisoner, just as he was.

Eric looked to the side without moving his head. Rialle stood at the edge of the ring, intent and wary. Bile rose from the depths of his being, choking him with rage. She had tricked him, tricked him again. The words "kill her" locked in his throat. Would Simon obey?

"She says wait." Simon's face was inches from his. Dried blood stained his mouth and jaw, and his right eye was swollen half shut. "Wait for the One who Glows."

"Why?" Eric answered.

Simon tilted his head as if listening, then nodded. "Play with them like cats." His face split into a grin. "We wait. We wait. And play."

Eric had never been this close to Simon when he was awake. His piercing gaze held the force of a storm. Could Simon be trusted? He felt a touch at the base of his mind. Wait, it persisted.

"You live, Keeper. Today." Simon rolled to his feet in a fluid motion and paced the confines of the circle. His bloodstained tunic hung in strips from his shoulders. Vivid welts showed against his pale skin. Eric clenched his jaw against the urge to demand Rialle's death.

Patience, the ring whispered.

Hang patience, Eric thought, but he forced the rage from his face and waited while Simon paced the confines of the ring. Rialle had to believe he was still in thrall, but the thought sickened him. "Where is this? This is different," Simon chattered.

"You don't remember?" Rialle walked the outer rim, watching Simon intently.

Simon's head jerked up. "You are his servant. The One who Glows. Fetch him."

"You are mistaken." She eyed him as if he were a bright toy. "I am Princess Daria, of Legerdemain. You are my servant. You will follow my orders."

Simon shook his head. "You are no one. No one. Fetch the One who Glows."

Rialle looked at Eric. "Tell him," she instructed. "Order him to obey me."

Eric fought to keep his expression slack and the hatred from his voice. "Why?"

"Don't question me!" Her eyes flashed with rage. "Do it."

Simon saved him the trouble of speaking. "I took this from him. The One who Glows." He held out his hand. Flames danced at his fingertips. Simon tilted his head again, as if listening to whatever spoke to him — to them — from within the ring. Whatever he heard amused him. He extinguished the flames, folded his arms across his chest and started to laugh. "Like cats," he chortled. "Like cats."

"What are you doing?" Rialle snapped. She turned to Eric. "What is he doing?"

"I don't know." Eric shook his head. "He's mad."

"Make him stop." Her voice grew shrill.

"Why?" It was out before he thought. "Why would I want to do that?"

Rialle whirled on him. Their eyes met, and Eric knew there would be no more waiting. Before she could draw breath to speak, Eric scrambled from the circle and shouted to Simon. "Kill her. Kill her now!"

Simon gave a low growl and lunged. Lightning scorched the air where his hands made contact with the ward on the inner circle. Simon's snarls became screams. Over the cries, Eric heard the sound of Rialle's laughter. Simon heard it too, but his attacks were caught up in the ward.

"Idiot," she sneered. "Did you think I wouldn't expect something so obvious?" Her contempt swelled. "You've known since we entered this room. Since he touched you. Correct?"

Eric glared at her. "How appropriate," she laughed. "I've taught you to hate." When he said nothing, she continued. "You could still come out of this alive, you know."

"What are you going to do?" he asked — his voice thick. "Offer me my freedom?"

"No. Your life." Rialle shot back. Any other slave would be dead by now."

"I'm not any other slave." He jerked his head at Simon. "Neither is he."

"You cannot hide behind your pet forever." Rialle leaned closer. "You may think you're ready to die, Eric, but I know better."

"I don't intend to die." He paused. "Alone." But

he knew that unless he could get Simon out of the ring, there was a stalemate.

Simon lifted his face and stared at the cavernous ceiling. “He comes.”

“Indeed.” Rialle nodded and smiled. “Lord Vassant will teach you, but we must have your cooperation.”

“Ah!” Simon exclaimed. “You bargain.”

“Yes!” Rialle seized his enthusiasm. “You cooperate, and I will make you more powerful than you can imagine.”

“Don’t listen to her!” Eric found his voice. “She cannot be trusted!”

“It is Eric you cannot trust,” Rialle inserted smoothly. “He is your Keeper. He kept you trapped, penned up like an animal. He uses you. He cannot teach you anything.”

But Simon wasn’t listening to either of them. “He comes.” His voice sounded strange, and the words that followed were barely intelligible. “He comes.”

Eric heard the outer door swing open, and the guards snapped to attention. Lord Vassant swept into the room, dragging Daria as a careless child would a doll.

Rialle frowned. “Why did you bring her here?”

“She grows tiresome.” Lord Vassant shoved Daria. She stumbled to her hands and knees. “I think I shall deal with her as I dealt with her father.”

Eric moved toward Daria. Rialle halted him with an upraised palm. “You stop right there,” she warned. “The Princess is not your concern.” Her expression shifted. “Or is she?”

“You won’t hurt her.” Eric’s heart hammered. “You wouldn’t dare.”

Rialle shook her head. “So many people telling me what I dare not do.” She jabbed a finger at the Princess. “She may be stupid, but I didn’t think you were.”

When he didn't respond, she advanced on him. "We can do without her, just as we have done without her father, the King. You saw it; if Simon had not cleared the glamour from your eyes, you would see it now." She watched as he considered this; then continued. "You may be willing to die, Eric. You may even be willing to take Simon with you. But tell me," she paused, her face a wicked mask. "Do you hate me enough to kill Daria?"

Eric didn't answer. He didn't have to. He looked at Daria, still kneeling where she had fallen.

"Enough!" Lord Vassant barked. "You distract me from my guest." He approached the circle and studied Simon. "What has she done to you?" he asked. "Brought you to heel? Women are like that." The blue swirls of light parted like mist as he crossed through the rings, stopping just outside Simon's reach.

Simon's focus never left Lord Vassant and the insanity was gone from his eyes. "What happened to that mad wretch I saw in the courtyard?" Lord Vassant asked. "This seems like a different creature entirely."

"Do you sense him?" Rialle asked.

"Oh yes." Lord Vassant moved closer. Simon did not react. "If anything, he's even stronger now."

Simon advanced. The ward around him flared. He gasped in pain and lurched back. Lord Vassant waved his right hand over the inner circle, and the flames died.

"Careful," Rialle warned.

"He won't hurt me," Lord Vassant replied. "He knows I am his master. Look." He reached out and placed a cautious hand against Simon's cheek. Simon leaned in to the touch and closed his eyes. Lord Vassant laughed. "He's only a little dog." He moved closer to Simon and placed both hands on his face. "It would be so simple. I could kill him right now, and he wouldn't even respond."

"But you won't," Rialle cautioned.

Lord Vassant released Simon's face, stepped back, turned, then extended his left hand and sent a fist-sized burst of fire at Simon's midsection. Simon screamed and staggered back, beating out the flames with his fists. The look on his face was one of uncomprehending hurt. Lord Vassant laughed and lifted his hand again.

"No!" Rialle cried. "I can control him!"

So can I, Eric thought. "Sleep!" he shouted, then ran at Simon, and caught the fading young magician before he hit the floor. Muscles straining, he hauled Simon clear of the confining rings where they collapsed in a spent tangle of arms and legs. Eric twisted himself free, seized Simon's wrist and cried, "Wake up! Protect the Princess!"

Simon responded with a roar, and the soldier standing over Daria screamed in pain as his flesh erupted in flames. Daria's lethargy broke and she scrambled toward Eric.

"No!" Rialle shouted. "Kill him, kill them both." Her lips twisted in a snarl.

Eric lunged toward Daria and pulled her to her feet. Together they retreated behind Simon, who stood braced in battle. Blood ran freely from a dozen wounds and a thin sheen of perspiration glowed against his white skin. His tunic was burned through, revealing blackened flesh.

"Kill them!" Eric positioned himself behind Simon and pushed the mage forward. "Kill them now!"

Fire consumed the air around them as the second guard aimed his crossbow. Simon cast him a glance and the guard's charred corpse dropped at his feet. Lord Vassant took another step back, then another, until he was completely out of the ring. Simon moved forward, the rings of light parting for him as they had for Vassant.

"No!" Lord Vassant insisted. "It cannot be."

"She says it can!" Simon shouted back. "She says you are not the teacher." His ragged laughter grew. "She says I can kill you now."

"She is dead!" Lord Vassant countered. "I killed her! I watched her die!"

"Wrong. You were wrong." Simon stepped back into the center ring. His eyes closed and he swayed. Eric wrapped an arm around Simon's waist to keep him from falling. "Keep going!" he shouted. "Finish them."

"She says I can," he whispered. The ring surged with power. "She says I can."

Lord Vassant's eyes widened. "Out!"

"But the Princess!" Rialle shouted.

Lord Vassant walked backward, retreating. "The witch will save her. Go!"

Rialle and the remaining soldier darted from the room with Lord Vassant right behind him. As the door thudded shut, Simon lifted his hand and sent a final blast of fire, melting the sunburst pattern.

"Sealed" Simon whispered, as his legs buckled and the magic vanished.

Chapter 32

Pale light rose from the rings like smoke from a dying fire. Eric eased Simon to the ground. The torches were long dead; if the mage light died as well, they would be left in total darkness.

The young magician lay motionless; his body a battered corpse. Eric placed a hand over his lips. Save for the occasional twitch and the faint rise and fall of his chest, there was nothing to indicate he survived the battle.

Daria's voice echoed in the cold air. "Is he alive?"

"Yes. Barely." Eric looked up at her. She didn't look much better than Simon. "What about you?"

"I'm fine — a little battered." She shoved herself into a sitting position and stood slowly. "I'll manage." She looked at Simon. "Is it safe? To come closer, I mean." Eric nodded, and she advanced. "What is he?" she asked.

Eric shook his head. "I don't know. Blood oozed from a dozen wounds on Simon's limbs and torso. He wasn't dead now, but he would be soon if Eric didn't do something.

"What do you mean, you don't know?"

"I've spent my whole life being afraid of him." Eric looked around the room for something to wrap Simon's wounds. "I've never given it much thought."

"You should have told me about him." Her voice was sharp, accusing. "We could have done things differently."

"Really?" Eric sat back on his heels and looked at her. "Perhaps I couldn't tell you, because I was too busy listening to you explain how you were really a princess instead of a thieving chambermaid." The words came sharper than he intended, but he was powerless to stop them. "Forgive me, Your Highness. Or is it Your Majesty?"

"That's not fair!" Daria shot back. "You don't know what's happening here. What's happened to my father."

"That's right, I don't. Because you didn't tell me."

"I am not the only one who wasn't completely honest." Her shock became outrage. "I am not the one who struck a bargain with Rialle. This is all your …."

"Fault?" Her accusation struck him like a slap. It wasn't the truth, not exactly, but it was close enough to sting. "This isn't even my fight. I was trying to protect you." He pointed at Simon who seemed to be slipping away as they spoke. "From him."

"And he saved us both." Daria's voice softened. "Eric, what are we going to do now?"

"I don't know." His gaze shifted frantically around the room. "Is there another exit?"

Daria shook her head. "We're trapped."

"Then it's up to him." Eric pulled his tunic over his head and tossed it to Daria. "Tear this into strips. We'll need bandages."

They both jumped as a heavy thud sounded at

the door. The sound repeated, followed by a crack of wood. "They're coming," Daria whispered. "We don't have time." She dropped the tunic and picked up a short sword dropped by one of the dead soldiers.

"Can you use that?" Eric asked.

Daria grasped the hilt with both hands. "I can try."

Despite everything, Eric smiled. "Then I can try too." He stood and claimed a sword from beside a still-smoking body. The hilt was hot to the touch. "I've never done this before," he said as he hurried to Daria's side. "But I will not die on my knees."

Daria gave him a grateful look, but before she could reply, Simon spoke. "Retreat."

They spun to face him. His lips moved, though he showed no sign of regaining consciousness. "Retreat," he repeated. "I will provide the way."

The floor beneath them grew warm, and the pale blue light rose, though just from the inner circle. Eric looked for the source of the magic as an arch formed above Simon. "Both of you hurry!" Simon said, using a voice not quite his own, yet still familiar. "I can't hold this open for long."

Not understanding, yet afraid not to obey, he caught Daria by the hand and pulled her to the center of the ring. They stood over Simon, still holding their weapons, as hammering at the door grew louder. "What now?" Eric asked, looking around him. "What now?"

The answer came in a column of solid light rising in the center of the ring. "Fear not," a familiar voice whispered in his ear, and they were all falling as the floor melted beneath them. The light vanished with an audible snap. Before he could react, they landed right where they began.

Stunned and bewildered, Eric lifted his eyes. The circle was the same, but the chamber was smaller, barely large enough to contain it. The air was warm and wet. He heard the clatter of metal. Daria's sword fell as she crumpled to the ground beside Simon.

"No!" Eric shouted, fearing another trap. He caught a flash of movement from the corner of his eye. He spun around, glimpsed an old woman with long white hair and amber eyes. She wore a tattered robe the color of red wine and clutched a worn staff in her gnarled hands. She swayed as if drunk or exhausted, but seemed immensely pleased with herself.

"Who are you?" Eric asked, still clutching the sword.

"A friend." She cackled. "You may come in now, boy."

A wizened little man hustled through an arched opening in the stone wall and rushed to the old woman's side. "You've over-extended yourself, my dear. I told you, I told you."

"Ah, but it was worth it." She tilted the staff toward Eric. "See? A fine day's work, wouldn't you say?"

The little man gaped at them, retreated a step, and rubbed his hand along the back of his neck. "Strangers!" he exclaimed. "Strangers! Here!" His bald head bobbled with agitation. "Nothing good will come of it, not at all."

"Hush now," she ordered, but her voice was kind. "Be a good lad and fetch me the Princess."

"Stay away from her." Eric clasped the hilt in his fist. His muscles screamed with fatigue yet he pointed the sword at the pair. "You stay away!"

"Easy, boy." The old woman extended a hand. "Your friends need help. I can help them." She moved closer. "I can help you too."

"Why should I trust you?" Eric staggered as he cut at the air with the sword. His voice broke. "Stay back."

The old man moved with a speed that belied his years. Eric managed one feeble swing before the sword was knocked from his hands and the old man was behind him, wrenching his arms back. Eric snarled and kicked, but his struggles were futile.

"Be still!" The old woman ordered, and advanced on him. Eric leaned away from her outstretched hand. She clasped the side of his neck in her gnarled fingers and squeezed. Eric felt the shock of memory; hands, her hands, healing him, her voice, whispering guidance. He sagged against the old man.

Eric met the woman's amber eyes, and she smiled. "It's all right," she told him. "You don't have to fight anymore."

Chapter 33

Rialle watched the soldier heft the axe over his shoulders and drive the head into the thick wood of the scrying room door. A second man struck in alternating rhythm; they had been at it for hours. The oak was old and unyielding, like the witch who had fashioned it. Like her, it would fall in the end.

Vassant also watched. Rialle had suggested he retire to his chambers while the men worked. She assured him she would call him as soon as the door fell, but he would not be swayed. Instead, he paced the landing twelve steps above them, his boots clicking on the stone. The hem of his robe was black with blood.

Maragause had built the room, enchanted the door that now barred their way. The melted sunburst leered from the middle of its halo of splinters. You're dead; she told the old woman's memory. I don't care what he says, I saw you die.

Vassant insisted it was Maragause he had battled, not Simon. The crone had used her web and the fly caught in it to drive him from the room. Rialle remained skeptical. She feared his vanity would not allow him to admit his defeat by a feeble-minded slave. If they had lost the Princess due to his arrogant posturing ....

A hole appeared in the door, than another, and another. The wood splintered with a mighty crack and fell inward. The two soldiers stepped back. Rialle covered her mouth and nose with her hand as the corridor filled with the stench of stale smoke and charred flesh. "Do you see them?" she asked. "Are they still alive?"

Mindless of the smell, Vassant descended the stairs and strode into the scrying room without fear. "Follow him," she ordered the soldiers, who traded their axes for crossbows and kicked past the rubble of the fallen door.

Rialle picked her way around what remained of the soldier foolish enough to point a crossbow at Simon. She scanned for signs of Daria and the two slaves, but saw nothing. Save for Vassant and the two soldiers, the room was empty.

"She has them." Vassant jabbed a finger at the center of the ring, and glared at her. His eyes glistened in the semi-darkness. "She has been here."

Rialle bit back a contradiction. There was no gain in arguing with him when his blood was up. Instead, she ordered the soldiers to stand down and watched Vassant pace around the circle, mouth and hands in motion with his feet. "Do you want torches?" she asked.

"No need." Vassant waved his hand over the outer ring and brought the hazy blue mage light back to life. "She thinks to trick me," he said. "I defeated her once. I can do so again."

"Are you sure it wasn't the boy?"

"Nonsense." Vassant circled again, as if seeking an entry. "What magic he has, he learned from me. He lacks the intelligence for something so intricate. No." He pointed again. "This was Maragause."

Rialle heard one of the soldiers clear his throat. It would not do to have Vassant appear mad in front of the men, but she was not ready to send them away. She crossed her arms and moved closer. "Can you tell where they went?"

"Not yet." He parted the rings with both hands, and stepped through the empty space. His pale skin grew luminescent in the mage light, while his robe looked black as coal. "But I shall."

Chapter 34

Eric slept as the wagon swayed. The warm sun touched his face with the softness of a mother's hand. He relished this time, traveling from town to town while Master Phineas slumbered in the back of the wagon, or sat beside him on the bench. He heard the old man's voice, telling him everything he knew. Eric watched the space between the horses' ears. His mind wandered and he dosed. He let the team choose the pace, but never slept deep enough that stopping wouldn't waken him.

It wasn't a bad life, better than that of most boys his age. Back then, he had no idea it was unheard of for a slave to know how to read, handle money, or have an opinion. When Master Phineas placed the letter of manumission in his hand, Eric knew what it said, and knew what it meant. The only thing he didn't know was why the letter didn't just free him now, instead of when the old man died.

"Just shows how much I trust you, boy." Master Phineas told him. "There you stand, with a letter making you a free man upon my demise, yet I have no fear of turning my back on you." He laughed. "Consider it an honor, boy, 'cause that's what it is. An honor."

An honor? The older he got, the harder it was to believe.

The scent of food stirred his hunger. Unusual, but not uncommon; the road wandered past farms, huts, and hovels, and much of the cooking was done outside. His mind lazily surveyed the wagon's stores, trying to remember what he had stocked away for their own evening meal. Strangely, he could not remember.

This alarmed him. The wagon stopped, and his stomach lurched. It took intense effort to force his eyes to open, and more still to stir his unwilling limbs. Every muscle whimpered in protest as he hoisted himself into a sitting position and shook the fog from his head.

This was not the wagon. Eric's heart jumped as the present dashed memories from his mind. Where? The last three days rushed at him; Lord Vassant, Rialle, Daria — where was Simon? There was the beating, and the ring, and then — what?

His head swiveled as he studied his new surroundings; a small room with a low ceiling and walls of stone. The pallet on which he sat was barely off the ground, leaving him eye-level with a crude wooden table groaning under stacks of moldering books and unrecognizable objects. More oddities hung from the walls and ceiling; a jumble of colors, textures, and smells he didn't recognize. There were chairs and tables, more furniture than floor space, and all seemed abandoned or scavenged.

Eric's stomach rolled and rumbled; the smell of stew had followed him back from his dream and made its way into an iron pot tended by an old woman with long white hair.

"You!" he exclaimed, and scrambled back as far as he could, which was not far at all.

"Yes, me." The woman laughed. "I was beginning to wonder about you, boy. Thought I might need to prod you with my stick."

Eric stared at her. It was she who saved them — brought him through the ring. Further back, she healed him after the savage beating. She had saved him twice, yet he could not stem his fear. "Who are you?"

"Maragause, of course. You may call me Mara, most do. Or did." She laughed again. "They think I'm dead."

"Are you?" Eric asked. A darker thought followed as he looked around the room again. "Are we?"

This amused her immensely, and she had to stop stirring just so she could laugh about it. "Do you feel dead?" she asked, when she regained control.

Eric took a quick mental inventory and decided he was alive, if for no other reason than he was far too sore to be anything else. "I don't suppose so," he answered. "But I never sleep like that. What did you give me?"

"Bit of ground sea slug. Some bracken. Oh, and virgin's blood." The old woman glared at him as if he were a fool. "I gave you a safe warm place to sleep, that's what I gave you. You might consider a bit of gratitude."

Eric tried to shake the mist from his mind. His limbs ached from idleness, and the inside of his mouth was as dry as a desert well. "Thank you," he said, finally.

"Much better." She lifted the spoon from the pot, sniffed at the contents, and shook her head. She hobbled to her feet, and reached for an opaque jar on the shelf above the hearth.

"No you don't!" The old man bustled into the room, arms waving. "You'll ruin it!" He tossed Eric a cloth bundle and snatched the jar from just beyond her fingertips. "You tend the magic. I tend the cooking."

Eric sensed glee in the old man's denouncements,

and suspected that this was not the first time for this particular argument. He cleared his throat.

They both looked at him. “Where am I?” he asked.

“That, my young friend, is difficult to explain.” Mara sighed and relinquished her position by the cook pot. “Accept my assurance that you and your friend are safe, the explanation would take hours, and you would still be none the wiser.”

“Friend?” His heart dropped. “Daria! Where is she?” He rose and started forward; his gait unsteady. He caught himself on the edge of the table. “What did you do with her?”

“Easy with your suspicions, boy.” The old man caught him by the elbow and propelled him back to the pallet. “We didn’t pluck you from Vassant’s web out of malice.”

“Well,” Mara chuckled, amending his statement. “Not malice toward you, anyway.”

“Where is Daria?” Eric braced himself with his arms and gathered his strength. “If you’ve hurt her.”

“That’s Princess Daria, to you, boy.” Mara grew sober. “And she is asleep in the scrying room. I’m using the ring to help her mend.”

Relief washed over him. “She’ll be all right?”

“‘Course she will.” The old man glared at him as if he were half-daft. “And you’ve questioned Milady Witch enough for one day, methinks.”

Mara waved a hand. “Let the boy ask. It’s not a wonder he’s confused.” She looked at Eric slyly. “What’s a wonder is why he hasn’t asked after the other one. The little mage.”

Eric felt another jolt. Simon. How could he have forgotten? “Where is he? He’s very dangerous.”

“See for yourself.” She gestured with her staff toward the left of the hearth.

Eric stood, slowly this time, and braced himself on the table. He craned his neck over a stack of musty books to see where she indicated. His hands tightened on the rough wood.

Simon sat cross-legged in the corner beside the hearth, busily engaged in dismantling some sort of mechanical toy. His dark hair hung over his forehead, and his pale brow was knit in concentration.

"Don't look very dangerous to me," the man snorted.

"He is," Eric insisted. He stared at Simon. The boy had been hurt, hurt so badly they thought he might die. Now he was healed and dressed in clothes Eric had never seen before. Eric looked to Mara. "How long was I asleep?"

"Difficult to tell." She shrugged and laughed. "I don't keep track of things like that." Noting his expression of alarm, she added. "Don't worry. It could not have been more than a day or two."

A day. Or two. Eric shook his head. "But he was wounded. Badly."

"Oh, aye." She placed a hand on Simon's shoulder. Eric braced to put him to sleep, but Simon only blinked a few times and looked around. His gaze passed over Eric without recognition, but his face lit up when he saw Mara. He whispered a few nonsense words and reached out for her.

"Good to see you too," she said, and took his hand. "He seems fit enough. Does he speak?"

Eric shook his head. "Not when he's like this." He hesitated. "Though I haven't seen him like this very much, at least not until recently."

"What do you mean, like this?"

"Alert. Awake. But not magic."

Mara snorted. "He's magic, make no mistake of that. I feel half my age, just touching him."

Eric looked back at Simon. "Then why isn't he trying to kill me?"

"I don't know." She released Simon's hand and patted him on the head. "Why does he normally try to kill you?"

Eric had no answer. Even so, he felt vaguely uncomfortable being this close to Simon when he wasn't dormant. "I don't know," he said. "He has been there most of my life, yet I don't know much more than you do. He was always just there."

"You don't know where your Master acquired Simon?"

Eric shook his head. "He owned Simon before he purchased me. I don't even know how old he is. We were both owned by Master Phineas, a traveling showman." He spoke methodically. "Simon made the magic from inside the wagon. I took care of — well — I took care of everything else." He paused, the words stuck in his throat. "Lord Vassant killed Master Phineas."

"I'm very sorry for that." Mara nodded. "You must have been a devoted servant."

"No!" Eric lashed out. "I despise being a slave. I was to have been freed upon Master Phineas' death, but Rialle ...." Frustration stopped his speech. The thought of her burned a hole in his stomach. "I tried to kill her. Rialle." He shook his head. "I meant to kill us all."

"I know, boy." Her voice took on a gentler tone as she hobbled around the table. "It was I who cautioned you."

Eric sank down on the pallet and cradled his head in his hands. Never had he felt this weary. "I don't know if I should be glad I failed or sorry."

"Don't be sorry. You're still alive, Simon is still alive, and the Princess is still alive." She placed a hand on the back of his head. He felt better. "I'm being a terrible hostess," she said, changing the subject. "Get dressed and I'll feed you."

Eric picked up and unfolded the bundle of cloth. It was a tunic simular to the one Simon wore. He pulled it over his head and sat back on the pallet. He nodded and let her lead him to the hearth. The old man pressed a wooden bowl and a chunk of brown bread into his hands. "I am Gabriel, by the way." He shot a withering glance at Mara. "Ungrateful wench can't be bothered to introduce me properly."

Mara snorted and lowered herself onto one of the chairs. "I wasn't aware protocol required me to introduce a servant."

Eric used the bread to shovel the stew into his mouth, his gaze darting between the bickering pair. He was so hungry he was halfway through the bowl before he realized how awful it tasted. He tried to force himself to stay alert, reminded himself he was still not safe, but with a full belly and such harmless-looking hosts, it was difficult to remain on guard.

"Good?" Gabriel asked after Eric emptied his bowl. "Would you like more?"

"Perhaps later." Eric stood and looked for a place to wash the bowl. "May I see Daria?"

"Of course." Mara stood. Gabriel snatched the empty bowl from his hand, muttering something about extra housework and ungrateful guests. Eric started to protest, but Mara waved him off. "Let him be," she said. "He's happiest when he has something to complain about. Now come."

Eric followed Mara down a narrow corridor to the scrying room. The circle was the same as the one in the citadel, but the chamber was barely large enough to contain it. The pattern on the floor extended up the walls, covering even the ceiling. The light streaming from the ring was blue, but warm and comforting.

Daria lay in a nest of blankets in the center of the

ring, her dusky skin pale in the mage light. Her hands were folded across her stomach, her dark hair fanned out over a pillow. Eric's first thought was of a pyre, and his stomach chilled. "How is she?"

"Alive." Mara answered. "Praise be, though it was no certain thing." For the first time, she sounded as old as she looked. "She has no physical wounds, but Vassant has been at her mind in ways I can't yet touch."

The cold in Eric's stomach intensified. "What do you mean?"

"My powers are limited, and those I have, I've tapped for now." Mara jerked her chin at Daria. "I can find no reason for her not to awaken, yet she does not. Something is keeping her from us. Something I can not reach."

"Lord Vassant did something to her mind. To our minds." Revulsion washed over him as the memories resurfaced. "She called him Papa, as though she believed he was her father."

"Undoubtedly she did, the poor child." Mara clucked softly. "Such a small spell, yet so cruel. But that would not account for what has happened here." She twisted her head. "What did you see?"

"I saw Daria. I thought we were escaping." Eric closed his eyes and shuddered. "But it was Rialle. She tried to get me to make Simon cooperate."

"Aye, she is a wicked creature, and it is no small part of my responsibility." Mara placed a hand on his shoulder. "In many ways, she is more of a monster than Vassant. At least he has an excuse."

Eric opened his eyes and looked at Daria. "There is no excuse for this."

"Perhaps not." She gestured toward the glowing rings with the tip of her mottled staff. "What we do with this weighs hard and heavy on the mind. The rush of it is like a river. Some of us can stand against the current.

Some, like Vassant, are swept up by it. Some are stolen away entirely."

"Like Simon."

"Aye. He's a rare creature, that one." Her voice held a strange note of awe, which faded when she spoke again. "But for now, let us tend to the Princess. Then we shall concentrate on Vassant and Rialle.

Eric nodded. "Is it safe to approach?"

Mara waved a hand over the outer ring and the light flared. "It is now."

Eric crossed the bands of warm light and knelt beside Daria. Up close, he saw the rise and fall of her chest, but could not shake the illusion that she was lost. He raised his hand to touch her face, then stopped and balled his fists at his side. It was not his place. He was a slave, and she, a princess.

Instead, he took her hand. It was cool and soft against his rough skin. "I'll help any way I can." The words were out before he thought them.

Mara leaned on her staff and studied him. "Will you?"

"Of course." Eric's suspicions flooded back. He reminded himself he did not know this woman or her cantankerous servant. "Why?"

"There are things I need to know about what is happening out there." She drew a small stool to her side and settled heavily. "Things only you can tell me — but it won't be easy."

"What do you need to know?"

Mara closed her eyes and let her head drop back. Eric started to ask if she was all right when the light around him flashed and surged. He opened his mouth to cry out, but no sound emerged. It was as if he were drowning all over again, except this time he was able to breathe.

Mara spoke to him as she had back in Lord

Vassant's circle, her words emerging in his mind. "Fear not. Remember what you will."

Memories flooded back. Everything that had happened in the last six days poured from his mind into the swirl surrounding them. Eric released Daria's hand and braced himself against the onslaught. He saw Master Phineas die again, saw Rialle emerge from the crowd, heard the screams of the slaves as they died in the livery fire.

"Stop it," he growled. "Make it stop!"

It did not stop. He met Daria, they fled, and there was the suffocating ocean and Simon's outburst in the courtyard. Rialle again, and his anger sang at her betrayal. Mara stole images of the citadel, of the guards, of everything he saw, even the final horrible memory of the statue with the eyes of a living man.

"Stop!" he screamed.

The light died back. Mara's head rolled and her eyes were hollow. "I never imagined," she whispered. "What has he done?"

"What did you do?" Eric staggered to his feet. "Why did you do that to me?" Mara held up a hand, halting him while she composed herself. Eric would not be halted. "You had no right."

"I had to know." Her voice was matter of fact as she stood and tottered unsteadily. "You offered to help."

Eric fought the impulse to take her arm. Let her fall. "I would have told you anything you needed to know. You didn't need to take it."

"I did. There was no other way." Her gnarled fingers twisted around the staff as she turned to leave. "I saw all I needed to see."

Fuming, Eric followed Mara back to the main chamber, where Simon and Gabriel were engaged in a spirited — if one-sided — conversation. Simon bobbed his head eagerly and rattled strings of nonsense words to which the old man replied with a few words of his own.

"You understand him?" Mara asked.

"All that?" Gabriel jerked his chin at Simon. "Not a chance."

"It's gibberish," Eric stated, still angry. "It means nothing."

Mara silenced Eric with a wave of her hand. "But you recognized the words."

"Aye." Gabriel bobbed his head. "It's Kataran."

"What?" Eric exclaimed. "What is Kataran?"

"Not what," Gabriel snapped. "Where. Katara is an island, on the other side of the world. I was there ages ago when I sailed with my first master."

"So you can talk to him?" Mara asked eagerly.

Gabriel shook his head. "Only enough to order a meal or buy some trade goods." He paused and grinned. "Maybe buy something that would make the lad blush. But talk to him?" He shook his head.

Mara's brow knitted a frown. "We need a translator."

Eric looked at Simon, who continued to stare at the old man with a sense of wonder on his face. "It's just nonsense," he said, mostly to himself. "It doesn't mean anything."

Chapter 35

The wait for the translator was excruciating. Eric sat, stood, paced, and poked at the stacks of books and scrolls smothering every flat surface in the room. But every time he stopped, every time his mind drifted he found himself staring at Simon. "Just a fool," he whispered to himself. "He's nothing but a fool."

"Ah, here it is." Mara emerged from behind a stack of books, clutching a thick volume. Eric suppressed the urge to help her and watched as she carried the heavy tome the rest of the way to the worktable where she deposited it in a puff of dust.

"Look here." She opened the cracked leather binding to the first page. "Do you recognize this?"

Eric's curiosity got the better of him and he joined her at the table. Mara's gnarled finger rested on a blotchy illustration of blue, green, and gold. "No," he replied, unsure of what she meant to show him. "What is it?"

Mara frowned, then lifted a few more pages. "How about this?" She placed a gnarled finger on the left side of the page.

Eric leaned closer. This one was mostly pale brown, with lines of green and darker brown. The left edge was the same deep blue as on the first illustration. Just above her yellowed fingertip lay a drawing of a city with thick gold bands leading away from it.

"A map?" he exclaimed. "It's a map!"

"Clever boy." Mara turned back to the first illustration, and pointed to a section in the middle of the page. "Now this?"

The image coalesced and Eric recognized other details on the landmass she indicated — rivers, and drawings of the mountains they had traversed on their way to Legerdemain. But the others, those beyond the blue of the ocean, those he had never seen before.

Mara gestured toward Simon. "Come." He stood and joined them at the table. She took his hand and placed his finger on a much smaller mass in the upper left corner. "Katara," she told him. "That's your home."

Simon did not react, but Eric felt a stab of conscience. Simon had a home? He studied the place she indicated, and tried to guess the distance from there to where they stood now. He turned to Mara. "How could he have gotten here?"

"Who knows?" Mara shrugged and sent Simon back to the hearth. "Slave dealers aren't particular." She looked at him. "Do you know where you're from?"

Eric shook his head and stared at the map. He should know something so important. "It was a long time ago. Maybe, if I studied it, I could figure it out." He looked over at her. "If you don't mind."

"Of course not, son, of course not." Mara patted him on the shoulder.

"We've time, before Gabriel returns. The old fool probably wandered into a tavern, or got distracted by something shiny." She snorted. "Could be days."

Eric settled himself on a stool in front of the open

book. Some places he recognized, but most he did not. His anxiety abated somewhat as he deciphered the drawings and strange notations that gave him a sense of place in the world. He ran his fingers over the pages, tracing roads and rivers, and remembering himself in the middle of a vast desert.

He was soundly lost in the maps when Gabriel came clomping back through the doorway, followed by a tall man in a gray hooded cloak. Gabriel's bald head glistened with water, and his clothes were soaked through to the skin. "You'd best appreciate this, old woman!" he barked. "Had to march through the downpour on your miserable errand."

His companion pushed back his hood, revealing a dour, aristocratic face and a thick head of iron gray hair. When he saw Mara, he smiled. "Ah, Madam, what a sight you are for my weary eyes! When that whelp of yours was named Court Magician, I feared the worst."

"I am a tough old bat, as Gabriel is fond of telling me." Mara smiled and held out her hand. "Welcome, Artur, it is good to see you as well."

Artur swept his cloak from his shoulders and tossed it to the scowling Gabriel. He took her hand and kissed it as if she were a princess. "As always, I am at your command. That the boy?" he said, nodding at Simon.

"That is Simon," Mara explained. "And Eric, my other guest."

Artur dismissed Eric with a glance, walked to the hearth and peered down at Simon. "From Katara, you say?" He added something in gibberish.

Simon's eyes lost their blank look. He sat forward and Kataran words tumbled from his lips in an excited stammer. He rose and seized the translator by the arm, speaking so quickly Eric couldn't imagine anyone understanding him.

"Easy, boy, easy." Artur looked down at Simon and laughed. "You're a long way from home, magician."

"So that is Katara?" Mara asked eagerly.

"Oh, yes," whispered Artur, never taking his eyes from Simon. "I learned most of my languages aboard an explorer ship. Fifty years past, I was there, and I had no intention of leaving. They had to drag me back onto the ship. A beautiful place." He shook himself from his reverie. "An island far from everywhere, isolated — as it should be. Magic lives there."

"The people are all magicians?" asked Eric.

"Oh no, not all." He laughed. "It is still a random occurrence, like blue eyes or long fingers. But it is more common there than anywhere else I've been. And it is used more for good than the bastardized form we have here." He paused. "This one should have been trained by his elders, educated in one of their schools."

"No, no," Eric stammered. "He is feeble, Master Phineas said so. He said it was good we were around to take care of him because he could never survive on his own."

Mara shook her head. "Your Master Phineas lied to you about a lot of things."

Eric looked at Simon again. He'd begun rocking slightly, his eyes closed. "You don't think he's normal, do you?"

"Normal?" She laughed. "No. Special, yes. Artur, do you remember enough to question him?"

"Let's see. Ask away."

Before Mara and Eric could speak, Simon touched Artur's arm and said something. Artur shook his head, and asked Simon to repeat himself. Finally, he turned to Mara. "He wants to know where he is."

"Tell him he's safe," said Mara. "Among friends."

Simon shook his head. "He doesn't understand," said Artur.

Mara moved from Eric's side and sat down beside Simon. She took his hand and touched his cheek. "Tell him it's all right, that we understand. We want to hear his story."

Simon's memories were fragmented. He knew Master Phineas and feared him. He knew Eric; knew he was, like him, a captive. He thought that Eric hated Master Phineas too. But when asked about the performing, Simon recalled nothing. He thought the magic was a secret. He also wasn't aware Master Phineas was dead.

"It's puzzling," Mara shook her head. "He should remember more."

"So he is a fool?" Eric stated.

"I don't think so," said Artur. "He just seems confused."

Through Artur, a terrible tale of abduction emerged. Simon didn't know how old he was, nor how long he had been with Master Phineas. His most vivid memory was being taken from a place with a group of other children — five boys and six girls. They were snatched at night. Simon recalled being wakened by a jab. Before he could cry out, he was stuffed into a sack with two other children. He woke in the hold of a boat.

They went days without food, drinking rainwater that collected in the bottom. Several of the children died — the bodies weren't removed. Those still alive huddled in a corner. He didn't know for how long. Then they were taken and cleaned up and scattered. Simon spoke of Master Phineas with great fear. Even if Eric couldn't understand the meaning of the words, he felt the emotion behind them. They had lived in the same wagon, he and Simon, but the two of them had lived very different lives.

"The place he was taken from was probably a cathedral." Artur explained. "Those who took him and the other children knew exactly what they were doing. A young, untrained magician is priceless."

"Then why did they let the others die?" Mara asked.

"Obviously, something went wrong. Attacking a school like that was a big risk. I don't imagine the elders took it too kindly. Imagine a highly skilled magician, angry and on your trail."

"I can imagine that," Eric whispered. Mara gave him a sideways smile.

Artur continued. "Once they were far enough away, the thieves took those still alive and peddled them."

While they spoke, Simon waited with his hands in his lap like a well-behaved child hoping for permission to speak.

Eric's face grew hot. Had Master Phineas known? He couldn't have.

What must it have been like for Simon, a clever little boy, snatched from his bed and thrown into that animal existence? Eric recalled beating Simon, not because the boy had misbehaved, but because he had made Eric angry. The memory made him wince.

"We kept him on a chain." Eric didn't realize he spoke out loud until he heard his own voice.

"It's not your fault." Mara hobbled to his side. "You were as much a victim as he."

"No!" Eric jerked away. "That is not the Simon I know." He jabbed a finger at the boy. "That is not the monster I shared a wagon with for most of my life."

She placed a hand on his arm. "Then show me."

Eric looked at her. Her expression was set in stone. "All right," he said. "You want to see? I'll show you." He strode to the hearthside and seized the docile mage by the wrist. Simon whimpered but did not cry out; for a second his eyes filled with fear, then went blank. "This is the Simon I knew." He hauled the boy to his feet. “And this.”

The word to wake Simon died between his lips. Eric wasn’t as enraged as that, but they had to understand. “Follow me,” he said, and pulled Simon through the doorway to the scrying room.

The mage light in the scrying room rose as they entered. Eric heard Gabriel ask, “Stop him?” and Mara replied, “Let him be.”

Eric halted Simon at the edge of the ring. The light flowed toward them and danced around the dormant magician as if it sensed the power within him. Daria lay where they had left her, unchanged, her pale form barely visible through the haze. His heart thumped. “Can she be moved?”

“Briefly, yes.” She gestured to the old man. “Gabriel.”

“I will get her.” Eric motioned for Simon to stay, crossed the pulsating rings and crouched at Daria’s side. The memory of the mind-rape rattled around his head; Eric gritted his teeth and banished it. “I won’t hurt you,” he whispered, and gently lifted her. Daria’s slight form seemed nothing but rags and bones. Her head lolled back and her left arm dangled. Eric shifted his grip and cradled her against his chest, so her head fell against his shoulder. The faint touch of her breath on his neck showed she was alive. Without thinking, he placed a kiss on the top of her head, then turned and rejoined the others.

Gabriel waited at the edge of the ring. Eric reluctantly placed Daria in his arms. “Take her in by the hearth.” Mara instructed. “Make sure she stays warm.”

Eric watched the old man recede down the dark hall, then turned and faced Simon. “Come,” he ordered, and hauled Simon to the center of the ring. The light flared as they crossed. Eric spoke to Mara. "You know what he will become?" She nodded. "Then do whatever is needed to contain him."

Mara whispered a few words and waved her hand over the outer ring. The pale blue light surged beneath her yellowed fingertips, then settled back at knee-level. "Do what you will," she said softly.

Eric steeled himself and once again seized Simon by the wrist. "Wake up."

Simon lunged for him and the inner ring crackled. Eric rolled away as he had a thousand times before and sprang to his feet. "There is your magician!" he cried.

"Where is this? This is different." Simon placed a hand against the ward. Sparks danced across his palm and between his fingertips; it contained him, but caused him no pain. "Another cage."

"He speaks." Artur gasped. "As plain as you or I."

"When I choose." Simon's dark blue eyes locked on Mara. "You whispered in my ear."

"Aye." Mara moved closer, eyeing Simon as a bird would a worm. "You remember?"

"Yes, I do. Yes." His head rolled against his shoulders. "Kill him, you whispered to me, kill the One who Glows." A tremor of pain flashed across his face. "I tried, I did try."

"I know," Mara answered. "Who are you?"

Simon laughed. "You know who I am." He extended his arms to either side, his fingertips arcing against the wards. "You do not trust me."

"Not yet. But I might." Mara spoke as one would to a clever child. She paused in thought, then continued. "I trained Vassant." When Simon didn't respond, she added. "The One who Glows?"

Simon's head snapped up. "So you did. Ah, yes,

so you did." His breathing quickened. "You will train me. Yes you will."

"Perhaps." She considered it. "But you saw what he has become. I would have to know more about you." Her lined face crinkled in a wicked grin. "I would have to know who you are."

"I will tell! I will!" Simon turned three times in the confines of the ward, and hugged his arms across his chest. "A fine bargain, with she who taught the One who Glows!"

To Eric's ear, Mara's interrogation of the awakened Simon brought little information, but she seemed pleased with the things she learned. Though his words were strung together in sentences, they were the chitterings of a madman. His face twisted in rage as he spoke of Master Phineas. His words came so fast, and were filled with such venom he was impossible to understand. "We danced when he burned, and as he burns evermore we will dance."

"Do you remember your life before?" Mara asked.

"There was no before. Only now. Only this." He pressed a hand against the ward. When she asked again, he admitted knowledge of the stolen boy, but spoke of him as if he were another person. "We protect him," Simon repeated. He jabbed a finger at Eric. "My Keeper and I."

Eric looked at Mara. "I don't understand."

"I believe I do," she answered.

Before he could ask what this meant, she asked Simon, "What of your other captor? What of Eric?"

"My Keeper." Simon glared at him and his hands flexed. "He is necessary. A servant. Necessary."

"Necessary!" Eric spat the word. "You tried to kill me every time."

"I never hurt you. Never did. Never would." The words rattled off his tongue. "I protect you. Save you."

Eric looked to Mara. "I don't know what he's talking about. He's mad, crazy."

"You know. You saw." Simon extended a hand and flame leapt from his fingertips. "It was glorious." He smiled. "The fire we made was glorious, but you would have burned as they did. I protected you. I saved you."

"That's not true," Eric protested, though inside he knew it couldn't be otherwise. He should have died in the livery fire; they both should have. And yet they didn't. He backed away until his spine pressed the stone wall. He braced his hands against the wall and listened to Simon's unfettered ravings on his years of captivity. It was as if he'd dropped into a nightmare-laden slumber — inside he knew the opposite was true.

He heard muttered conversation, knew the others were speaking, but their words were swallowed by the outrage within him. He thought to show them a madman; instead he exposed the truth of his own pitiful existence.

"The Princess is waking up."

Gabriel's words cut through his despair. Eric snapped his head around; saw the old man carry Daria back into the room and lower her to the floor. Mara stooped over her, knelt and seized Daria's face in her hands.

Eric scrambled over and knelt opposite the old woman. When he reached for Daria's hand, Mara batted him away. "Stay back, boy," Gabriel warned. "Stay out of her way."

Eric wanted to argue, but knew he had no grounds. He sat back on his heels and watched as Mara's gnarled hands worked frantically over the girl's still form. Over the hammering of his heart, and Mara's muttered incantations, he heard Simon's voice rising in the background. "What happens? What happens?" he chanted. "The girl. I was to protect her. We bargained.

What happens?"

"Quiet!" Eric shouted.

"I will not! Will not!" Simon's words flew from his lips, punctuated by the crackle of magic as his hands struck the ward. "Bring her. Bring her. I will protect! We bargained. Bring her. Bring her now!"

Eric looked to Mara. Her eyes were closed, and her lined face pale with exertion. Her lips moved as she labored over Daria's prone body; her words lost amidst Simon's ceaseless babble.

"Bring her now!' Simon demanded, and the ward sizzled in response as he thrust both hands unto the blue light. His face twisted in pain as sparks clung to the lengths of his arms like a swarm of angry bees. Still he came, his words reduced to howls. The air around them filled with the smell of burnt hair and skin.

"Sleep!" Eric's voice boomed in the airless room. Simon sank to his knees and cradled his injured arms to his chest. At the same time, Mara sat back with a satisfied smile. "She will survive," the witch murmured, and collapsed at Daria's side.

Chapter 36

Daria dreamed.

In her dream, she was warm and loved, and fear was a vague memory. She was a pampered child again, sitting on the floor of her father's study, playing with a pair of faceless dolls. She felt the stiff weave of the carpet beneath her knees, smelled the smoke from the hearth and the spicy tobacco scent from her father's pipe. He was there sitting at his heavy desk, studying sheaves from a stack of parchments. Every so often, when he suspected she was watching, he leaned over and gave the orrery a push with his ink-stained fingers. The jeweled globes glittered in the lemony sunlight slanting through the high, narrow windows. She knew he was an important man, knew others addressed him as King, but to her, he was "Papa" and she adored him.

There was a knock at the door. Daria looked up. So did her father. His brow furrowed and the sound receded. "Who was it, Papa?" she asked.

"No one, my child." He smiled at her, but there was something unusual about his eyes. "Go back to your playthings."

Daria looked at the dolls. They had faces now, unfamiliar to her eyes but not to her heart. They were staring at her, pleading with her. She turned them face down, but the urgency she saw in their eyes wasn't as easily dismissed. "Wake up," they whispered. No, not a whisper, a faint shout, as if from a great distance. "Wake up."

The knocking returned, louder this time. Her father balled his fists and thumped the desk. "Be gone!" he shouted, and she shrank away from him, something she had never done before.

"Wake up. Wake up. Wake up."

Her father grabbed her arm and jerked her to her feet. "Come," he ordered. "You're in great danger."

"But ..." She reached for the dolls.

He pulled her away. "Don't listen to them."

How did he know? Before she could ask, he pulled her against his chest. Her face pressed against the soft pile of his robe. He smelled right, but felt wrong. She tried to pull away but he held her tightly.

Daria swooned, and the room vanished. Her struggles weakened. What was doing this to her?

"What's wrong?" Rialle paced the outside of the ring, as anxious as an expectant parent. At its center, Vassant sat cross-legged, his brow furrowed in concentration. He shook her off with a small movement of his head. The stress showed on him in a thousand ways; most telling was that he no longer cared about his appearance. The man seated in the center of the ring seemed more captive than captor; he seemed possessed by the urge to reach through and grasp what lay on the other side.

Vassant folded his arms across his chest, tilted his head to the side, and began to rock. Rialle bit back another question. Disturbing him would be dangerous, but she burned to know what was happening. The light around him ebbed and flowed as if the circle breathed with him, and the blue took on a deep, midnight hue.

Rialle looked at the door and wished herself elsewhere. The witch's scrying room had never been a pleasant place for her and now, with the scent of charred flesh and dark magic hanging web-like in the stale air, it was all she could do to remain. Her feelings didn't matter — she couldn't stay here long. They had a kingdom to run, and the questions were mounting. So long as Vassant battled Mara — no, Mara was dead — so long as he battled whatever lay on the other side of the ring, he could not settle the masses in the guise of King Lysander. The people listened to her, but only because the King appeared to back her words. If Vassant burned out

Doubts ate at her. She had friends — no, not friends, allies — who would help her get away.

Vassant's head snapped up, and a wild smile stretched from his drawn features. "She is not as wise as she thinks," he whispered, and his head rolled back in apparent ecstasy.

Rialle could not contain herself. "What is happening?" she demanded. The toes of her slippers stopped just short of the ring. "Vassant, speak to me."

"The slave boy, our mad little mage, I can feel him." His head lolled back and forth, and his voice took on a dreamlike-quality. When he looked back at her, his eyes were clear. "The witch forgets," he whispered. "She taught me well."

The air in the room settled heavily around them. Eric pulled Daria into his lap. Gabriel rushed to Mara's side, and lifted her as if she were weightless. "Ah, my girl, my bright one," he crooned. "You overtax yourself, I always tell you that."

"She's alive?" Eric asked.

"Aye, no thanks to you." The old man cradled the witch against his chest and rocked her as he would a child. "I told her not to meddle, 'twas best to let it be, but no, she insisted." He carried her from the room; his mutterings following behind like a tail. Artur shook his head in amazement, then followed the old servant down the hall.

Eric looked down at the Princess. Her color had returned, and she seemed to be breathing easier. "How did we get into this?" he asked her.

Across the room, Simon had pressed himself into a corner and sat rocking. Eric supposed he should go check on him, but didn't want to leave Daria. Was it safe to take her back into the ring? Beneath her closed lids, Daria's eyes fluttered wildly. What was she dreaming?

"Wake up," he whispered, and gave her a gentle shake. "I don't know what to do."

For lack of a better option, Eric carried Daria back to the center of the ring. It gave no resistance as he passed; instead, it seemed to welcome them as he laid her on the warm tiles. Master Phineas had taught him so many things, but the ways of magic were not one of them. He looked at Simon again. Was he the reason? The old man trusted Eric with his life, but not with his greatest secret?

Simon's hands and forearms were burned bright red from his attempt to escape the ward, and he cradled them against his chest. His eyes were closed and his face tight with pain. Could the circle help him?

Eric spoke. "Simon, come."

The boy lifted his head then slowly crept toward Eric. This time, the ring didn't change as he passed through. Eric shook his head. "I don't understand," he told Simon, who settled at his side and resumed rocking. "I don't understand any of this."

"Perfect," Vassant whispered. "Like a spider, I have drawn them to my web."

Rialle looked at him; certain he had finally lost his mind. "What are you talking about?" she asked.

By way of an answer, he raised his hands and the light surged around him. "Doors go both ways," he cried, and thrust his hands through the tiles.

Daria's body jerked. Eric looked down, thinking she might be waking but her eyes remained tightly closed. Her mouth twisted in a grimace and a moan escaped her lips. He pulled her closer, held her tighter, as if that would protect her better.

Beneath them, the tiles became warmer, then got hot, and the light surged once more, blue and black. He had to get out, get Daria out, but when he tried to move the strength drained from his legs and arms. He looked around wildly. The tiles blurred. Eric thought it was a trick of his eyes until a pair of hands emerged. The fingers flexed. A heavy gold ring with a blood red stone glinted on the index finger of the left hand. Eric recognized it as Vassant's just as the hands seized Daria's legs.

"Gabriel!" Eric shouted. He struck at the hands with his fists, but the grip was unbreakable. He heard laughter. "Leave her alone!" he shouted and struck at the hands with all his might. The grip only tightened, the laughter intensified.

"Insignificant slave," the voice taunted. "You think you can defeat me?"

"Maybe not." Eric's eyes fell on Simon. "But I know someone who can."

He reached across Daria and seized Simon by the wrist. The boy flinched, and guilt washed over Eric. Did he dare? Simon's eyes held nothing but pain. "You want revenge?" Eric whispered, then spoke aloud. "Wake up."

Simon uncoiled. He snatched at Eric, then halted when he saw Daria. "What is he doing, what is he doing?"

"Protect her," Eric ordered. "Do what you want to me, but don't let him get her."

Daria heard laughter. She tried to turn to see, but her father held her tighter, crushing her against his chest. "What is he doing, what is he doing?" the voice chanted. Someone yanked her from her father's arms and she fell backward.

Her father cried out in rage. No, not her father, but Lord Vassant! He had tricked her again! The second person — she remembered his name was Simon and he was mad — he pulled her forward and spun her around behind him. "I protect her!" He pointed at Lord Vassant. "Stay away from her. You touch her not!"

Daria flailed her arms and felt nothing. Her fall ended, and her eyes popped open. The person who held her was not her father, not Simon, but Eric.

Simon knelt and seized Lord Vassant's hands by both wrists. The disembodied hands snapped open. Eric pulled Daria away and out of the ring. Simon screamed. "I can't I can't I can't," he gasped, and his body crumpled.

Eric thought Simon had gone dormant, then realized he had reverted to the lost little boy he'd glimpsed in Mara's study. Lord Vassant's laughter grew faint. "A greater prize," he heard the magician say, and Simon slipped toward the void.

"No!" Eric and Daria shouted. Eric lunged and caught Simon around the waist just as his arms and shoulders started to vanish. He felt someone at his side. At first, he thought Gabriel had finally arrived. He twisted his head and saw Daria crouched at his left, her slender arms reaching for Simon.

"Get back!" he ordered. "It isn't safe."

"I know. I was there." Daria dropped to her knees and crept toward Simon. She took his face in her hands and turned his head so he faced her. "He's protecting me. I won't let Vassant hurt him."

"What are you going to do?" Eric asked. Simon

had stopped fighting; even seemed to be slowly drawing himself into the void. Eric leaned back and hauled at the semi-conscious mage, but the slick tile surface offered no purchase.

Simon slid farther forward, drawing the Princess with him. "Daria, please!" Eric shouted. "Get out of here now!"

"I know what I'm doing." She thrust her right arm through the iridescent tiles. Her voice trailed off as she slumped against Simon's back. "At least I think ...."

Daria found herself back in the study. It was as she remembered; the fire, the yellow light, the scent of spiced cologne. She looked at the desk. Her father was gone, but the orrery still spun, the jeweled orbs sparkled as they orbited the miniature sun. She stepped toward it and spied the young boy sitting cross-legged on the floor. He had shoulder-length black hair, pale skin, and eyes bluer than the ocean on a clear day.

She smiled and spoke his name. "Hello, Simon."

"Hello." He looked up. "Are you here for the lesson?"

"What lesson?" Daria moved closer.

"He told me to wait here. He said the lesson would begin when the others arrived. I was hoping it would be you." He poked at the doll lying face down on the floor, but did not pick it up. "I am eager to begin."

Daria crouched in front of him and rested her arms on her knees. "Do you remember me?"

He shook his head, then picked up the doll and held it in his lap without looking down at it. His eyes darted around the room then he leaned toward her and whispered. "I'm scared."

Daria smiled. "You know what?" she said. "Me too." She had stepped back into the dream, expecting to find the fire-throwing magician she had seen earlier, not this scared little boy. She reached over and smoothed the hair from his forehead. "What did Vassant do to you?"

"Not a thing, child, not a thing." Lord Vassant chuckled. "He's doing it all himself."

Daria stood and pivoted. Vassant stood in the shadows beside the hearth. "It's quite remarkable." He unfolded his arms and stepped toward them. "I don't quite know what to make of it."

Daria stood between magician and boy. "Stay away from him," she warned. "Stay away from us."

"Or what?" Vassant moved closer.

Daria held firm. "Stay behind me," she told Simon, then cast her gaze around the room, looking for a weapon. The hearth tools were closer to Lord Vassant than her, and there was nothing on the desk but papers.

And the orrery. Daria grabbed it. The base was sturdy enough to use as a cudgel. She lifted it high. "Stay away," she warned again.

Vassant laughed, and the orbs shattered, one by one, sending jeweled motes dancing through the rays of light. "I made this place," he said. "I control everything in it." He reached for her. "Even you."

Daria screamed and swung the iron base. Vassant laughed and batted it away. "Go ahead," he shouted and seized her arm. "The louder you scream, the quicker my third student will arrive. Then the lesson can begin."

Chapter 37

In two linked scrying rooms, worlds apart, two keepers sat watch over their respective mages. Rialle rocked nervously on her heels as she watched Vassant hold sway at the center of his web. His lips worked soundlessly and a mad smile mixed with his muted words. “Bring them down,” she whispered. “Bring them down.”

In the other room, Eric lay sprawled across Simon’s prone body — one hand holding the boy, the other holding the Princess. They were no longer being drawn downward, but they were still as lost to him as if they had been dragged into the void. It was up to him to save them, but he had no idea what to do. “Wake up, Simon,” he pleaded. “Wake up!”

Daria shrieked and tore herself away from Lord Vassant. "Stop him!" she screamed at Simon. She stumbled away from the enraged magician and dropped to her knees before the boy. "Stop him," she pleaded. "You're the only one who can."

"Why?" His blue eyes were wide with alarm.

"He's going to hurt us."

As if to prove her point, Lord Vassant loomed over them. "Don't listen to her, boy. My son. My child." He laughed. "She is weak. She is the one who doesn't understand."

Daria knew she should hide behind Simon, knew he wasn't really a little boy, but couldn't bring herself to leave him to face Lord Vassant. Instead, she seized him by the shoulders and gave him a hard shake. "Please, Simon, please," she urged. "Remember who you are."

"This is who I am," he answered. His eyes, clear blue like the ocean, lifted toward Lord Vassant. "That man is going to teach me."

"He's going to kill you!" Daria drew a deep breath, leaned back, and slapped Simon as hard as she could just before Lord Vassant yanked her to her feet. Simon's expression shifted from hurt to scared to empty in the space of an instant.

The room went black.

"Wake up!" A distant voice pleaded — Eric's voice. "Simon, wake up!"

Simon woke, and the light flared. "Touch her not!" he bellowed as his dream image shifted from scared little boy to enraged slave. "I protect her. You touch her not!"

"You don't tell me!" Lord Vassant pulled Daria back against his chest and wrapped his arm across her throat. "I tell you."

Simon lifted his left arm and extended his fingers, his hand palm down. "I tell you," he snarled, his eyes dark with rage. "She stands aside. Then we dance."

"You want to dance?" Vassant raised his right arm, mimicking Simon's stance. "Show me."

Daria braced for Simon's attack, but the young magician remained motionless.

Vassant laughed. "You're in my world now, slave. I created this place and I control it."

A flash of blue light spun from his hand and shattered against Simon's palm. Simon gasped and staggered back, then a grin split his face. "I see," he whispered, and his eyes grew glassy. "I see. I see."

"Simon, no!" Daria dug her fingers into Vassant's forearm and tried to wriggle free.

Vassant's grip shifted to her throat. "Stand down, boy," he growled. "Or I'll choke the life from her."

Daria's vision blurred and she fought for breath. Through a haze, she saw Simon take a step and forcibly link his fingers with Vassant. "I see," he repeated. "Now you show me!"

"No!" Vassant pulled away, releasing them both. Daria dropped to her knees.

Before she could suck in a breath, Simon clasped her arm and pulled her away. "Flee," he shouted, and thrust her behind him.

Daria snatched at him. "You come too," she insisted. "You can't defeat him alone."

"I can! I can!" He shoved her back. "I can!"

Daria held tight, and they tumbled backward. The study swam around her and dissolved in a whirlpool of blackness. Daria thought she had struck her head, but there was no pain. When she opened her eyes, Eric was looking down at her.

"You did it," he told her. "You saved him."

Rialle watched Vassant pull himself to his feet slowly. He seemed drained but satisfied. “You failed?” she asked.

“No.” He shook his head. “I know where they are. I know what the boy is.” When he looked up, he was smiling. “And now I know how to defeat him.”

Together they pulled Simon out of the void. He lay on the tiles, gasping, his eyes dancing wildly. “I see,” he whispered and raised his arm toward the ceiling. “I see.”

Eric placed a hand on his forehead. “Sleep,” he said softly, and the magician went limp. “Let’s get him out of the ring.” The two of them half-led, half-carried the exhausted mage out of the scrying room and into the main study.

“Do you think Vassant can come through after us?” Daria asked.

“I have no idea.” Eric shook his head as they eased Simon down on the pallet. “We need Mara, she would know.” Daria didn’t answer. Eric looked up and found her staring at him. “What?” he asked.

Her voice was strange. “How do you know Mara?”

“She saved us from Lord Vassant.” He gestured around the room. “This is her study.”

“Eric, you are mistaken.” The way she spoke his name gave him a chill. “Mara was the Court Magician before Lord Vassant. Lord Vassant killed her three years ago.”

Chapter 38

While Daria remained with Simon, Eric explored the cavern. It gave him something to do while his mind processed what she had told him about Mara, and it kept him from pestering her about what appeared to be a painful subject. Either the witch who had rescued them had lied to him, or she was dead. He didn't like either alternative.

And so, he investigated. There was the scrying room, the study, and the tunnel leading from it that did nothing but lead him back to where he had begun. His frustration grew. "I have a question." Eric looked at Daria, when he could stand it no longer. "If Lord Vassant killed Mara, as you say, why was he not punished?"

"I asked my father the same thing." Her voice was sad. "He told me that was how the position was decided. To become Court Magician, you must vanquish the current one."

"That doesn't make sense." Eric continued his study of the wall. "Maybe you get the most powerful one, but you also get someone who doesn't mind killing people."

"It is their way. It broke my heart when she died. I swore when I became ruler, that was the first thing I would change." Her voice trailed off. "Now it doesn't look as if I'm going to get the chance."

"Don't say that." Eric shook his head at the confusing walls, then returned to her side. "We will defeat them." But even as he said it, he knew he had no idea how.

"You said we." Daria gave him a gentle smile. "I thought this wasn't your fight, Eric."

"It is now." His voice grew thick. "I guess it was all along. Rialle stole something from me, something I wanted and waited for my whole life." Eric studied her face and spoke his heart. "I was supposed to be freed upon our Master's death. He promised. I had a letter written in his own hand." Frustration welled within him, and he looked away from her. It seemed he was falling from one cage into another, and then another again.

Daria touched his cheek. "What will you do? When you are a free man?"

"Learn a trade. I'm not afraid to work." He shrugged. "Though, as you said, now I probably won't get a chance."

Daria lowered her eyes and smiled. "Quite a pair, aren't we?"

Simon slept. At length, so did Daria. Eric watched over them, alternating between sitting on the floor beside the pallet, and pacing the confines of the study. To fill the time, he tried to work out the number of days that had passed since he guided the showman's wagon through the gates of Legerdemain.

It was easier to count the nights. The first he spent in the stable livery, thinking that was the worst that could happen. How wrong he had been.

The second was in the granary, where he met Daria. He looked at her, asleep on the corner of the pallet, Simon's head cradled in her lap. Of noble birth, yet nothing at all as he imagined a princess would be.

He had spent the third night in Rialle's personal dungeon cell, after she had him plucked from the ocean. Rage boiled within him. Had one or two days passed since he tried to kill Rialle? Since she had had him beaten? He thought two, maybe even more, judging from the way his injuries healed. No, that was Mara. He decided two days.

That made five. And now he sat here, where it was impossible to tell day from night, or the passage of time. A day and a half, Mara had told him when he awoke. It felt as if he had been awake for days. A week, by his reckoning. A week, yet it felt like a lifetime.

"You moved her. Why?"

Eric jumped and spun around. Mara stood in the doorway behind him. "You're alive," he exclaimed.

"That's debatable." She shrugged, then jerked her head toward Daria. "Why did you move her?"

"I didn't." Eric eyed Mara warily. She waited expectantly, her hawk-like eyes piercing through him. He swallowed and said. "She moved herself."

"The Princess awoke? Here?" Her brow knotted

and she waved him out of her path. Eric stepped back, then followed her to the pallet. Daria sat nestled in the corner, her legs tucked beneath her, her fingers tangled in Simon's hair. Both breathed easily, with the gentle rhythm of sleep.

Eric opened his mouth to speak. Mara shushed him, then placed her fingertips against Daria's forehead. The Princess sighed, her lashes moved against her cheeks, and her head lolled to the side.

"Good," Mara murmured. "It's not too late." She pointed at Simon. "Get him off her."

"He's hurt."

"He's fine." Mara turned and hobbled away. "Bring him back by the hearth. I'll see that he's fit. We'll be needing him."

"For what?" Eric asked. "Don't you want to know what happened?"

"I know what happened." She dismissed him with a shrug and headed toward the hearth. "Do as you're told."

Eric spoke before he lost his nerve. "Daria told me you were dead. That Lord Vassant killed you."

Mara stopped, paused, and turned. Again, she regarded Eric. "Am I not standing before you?" He nodded. She continued. "The Princess does not know everything." Her voice softened. "It is safer this way. Now bring the boy, or must I call Gabriel?"

"I'll get him." Eric turned and knelt beside the pallet. Not right, the voice inside him warned. Not right. But there was nothing he could do about it. At least not yet.

He placed a hand on Simon's shoulder. "Come," he urged, and gave the boy a gentle shake. "You need to move."

Simon's eyes fluttered open. He whimpered as a tremor of pain shuddered through his body. Eric guided him to a sitting position and let him gather strength before helping him stand. One week ago, I would have jerked him to his feet, Eric thought. One week ago, I would have struck him for moving too slow.

"It will be all right," Eric told him, though he himself felt no such assurance.

Mara waited at the hearth, and Eric reluctantly delivered Simon into her hands. As soon as she touched him, his expression shifted, and his eyes filled with light. Though it obviously pained him, he clutched at her with his injured hands and spoke urgently in words they could not understand.

The old woman's eyes were gentle when she looked upon him. She eased herself onto the stool, leaned her staff against the stone wall, and clasped his hands in hers. "With me," she told Simon. "Like we did it before. With me."

Simon settled on the floor at her feet. Mara closed her eyes and lowered her head; Simon did likewise. Eric leaned against the table and watched. At first, nothing happened, then he noticed the flesh on Simon's forearms slowly mending. The angry red welts dried and closed, imperceptibly at first, then with greater speed and the color faded from red to pale pink.

When it was over, Mara lifted her head, released Simon's hands and brushed the hair from his face. "There," she said softly. "Doesn't that feel better?"

"How powerful are you?" Eric asked.

"That wasn't me." Mara retrieved her staff. "That was him. I only showed him what to do. Now come. It's time for him to return the favor."

"What do you want from him?"

"I must know if Daria's father still lives. There are different ways of making a man into a statue. Most kill, but some do not. I must learn if King Lysander can be saved." She dragged herself to her feet. "I am going to open a portal to Otherworld and call to him. If he is within, he will answer."

"You can do that?"

"I can open it." She pointed a crooked finger at Simon. "But I will need that one's help to close it."

Chapter 39

While Gabriel hovered in the background, Mara hobbled around and around the ring, chanting and gesturing. She had been unsure of which face Simon should wear for the spell — the boy was more controllable, but would be more vulnerable to whatever lay on the other side of the portal. She decided to keep him dormant until they needed him, then wake him and risk the consequences.

As she spoke, the center ring filled with pus-colored fog. Mara's voice rose with the light. The column swirled and churned, and the stench of rotting flesh filled the air.

"King Lysander of Legerdemain, your servants call you forth! If your shade lies in this domain, speak to us! Aid us in our quest for vengeance on those who betrayed you. Our aim is pure, our desire just."

Faces swirled into existence, eyes and mouths agape in frozen screams. "Who dares!" a low voice moaned.

"I dare. I, Maragause of Legerdemain, command

you to seek within for the shade of our good King Lysander."

Its laughter sounded like the flapping of dusty wings. "Your hold on this plane is tenuous, witch. I smell death on you. You risk much asking for this boon. Haven't you cheated me enough?"

"I summoned you here to do my bidding." She slammed the butt of her staff on one of the symbols and the entity recoiled in pain. "I did not summon you to question my motives. If King Lysander lies within, bring him hence. Otherwise, begone!"

The entity writhed within the column of light. "It seems, witch, your pathetic pleas have been heeded. There is one who would speak with you. One freshly slain."

Eric's heart sank on Daria's behalf. A form coalesced before them and the smoke fell away as the figure of a man took shape. He's older than I imagined, Eric thought, until the figure turned around.

Master Phineas! Eric gasped and stumbled back against the wall. This wasn't the wreck of a man who died in the square, but the upright charismatic figure from Eric's childhood. His eyes burned with unworldly fire. It was all Eric could do to keep from sinking to his knees.

The shade turned slowly, its ghastly eyes creeping over the scrying room walls. When he saw Simon, a satisfied sound emerged from his husk-dry throat. "Ah yes," he said. "There is my boy."

"You were Phineas Delayne?" Mara spoke the name like an accusation.

"I am Phineas Delayne," the shade corrected. He extended a ghostly hand to Simon. "Come here, boy. I won't hurt you."

Simon took a step. "Stop him," Mara warned. "Don't let him into the ring with that creature."

Eric broke from his torpor, caught Simon by the collar and hauled him back. The boy whimpered, but did not fight. Eric's heart hammered against the base of his throat. The initial relief he felt from seeing his old master was quickly replaced by an all-consuming rage.

Master Phineas turned and faced Eric. "Well now," he said, looking up and down. "It seems you've managed to survive as well." He gave a dusty chuckle. "You always were a resourceful creature."

"What do you want?" Eric's voice was thick. "Where is Daria's father?"

"In due time, boy. In due time." He resumed his study of the rune-covered walls. "My compliments, Madam. You've crafted quite a focus ring." He paused. "Yes, yes, a fine ring like this, plus a powerful slave to fire it." He nodded at Simon. "All you lack is an advisor experienced in handling young Simon." He gave a courtly bow. "As it is, I happen to be available."

"So you did know about him!" Eric gave Simon's collar a shake. "What he is. What he was."

"What's to know?" the shade scoffed. "Twas the most fortunate moment of his miserable existence when he came into my possession. He's a danger to himself and others."

Eric's voice rose. "That wasn't always so, was it?"

The old man's head jerked back. "Listen to the tongue on you. Apparently your new mistress is as lax with discipline as I was." He shook his head and looked to Mara. "He's a good lad, but thinks much of himself sometimes." He bowed. "My fault. I offer my apologies."

"She is not my mistress."

The anger in Eric's voice brought the old man up short. His bushy eyebrows shot up like the hair on an angry dog's back. "You dare raise your voice to me, whelp? You forget who made you."

"I haven't forgotten." Eric jabbed a finger at Simon. "Did you make him as well?" He watched the shade's expression harden. "We know what happened to him. What he was. Did you do it?"

"Bah!" Master Phineas dismissed him with a wave. "I did not force myself into this plane to be insulted. I had thought to check the well-being of my beloved servants; and perhaps offer my services in your time of need." He shook his head. "Good riddance. I take my leave."

"Stay where you are!" Mara ordered. "I have not dismissed you."

"And who will stop me? You?" He looked Mara up and down. "Crone, you have stolen your time in this existence for too long. Oppose me, and I will drag you back to where you belong. You haven't the power to stop me."

"No." Eric seized Simon's wrist. "But he does."

"You wouldn't dare." The shade's words were strong, but there was a tinge of fear in its voice. "He'll kill you first."

"He won't hurt me." Eric tightened his grip. He felt as if he were flying, alive for the first time. He looked at Simon. "Wake up."

Simon grabbed him. Eric stood firm. The magician smiled and laughed. "You learn," he hooted. "Not quickly, but you learn. Now." He whirled and faced the ring. "Look! Look! Look what you've brought me!"

"Sleep!" The shade cried, his voice frantic. "Sleep!"

Eric whirled on Simon, ready to bring him back. The mage just laughed and laughed. "Not now!" Simon cackled. "Not anymore! Not ever again!"

The shade quaked and faded. "Keep him here, Simon," Mara instructed. "Watch me. You know how."

Simon's eyes flicked toward Mara. "I see I see I

see." He lowered his left hand and held it flat over a star-shaped rune in the outer ring. Purple light streamed from his palm to the floor, and a violet glow emanated from the metal.

Immediately, the shade stabilized. "What do you want of me?" Master Phineas whined at Mara.

"I want nothing from you." She pointed her staff at Eric and Simon. "I'm not the one you must answer to."

"Very well." Master Phineas turned slowly until he once more faced Eric. "What is it you want then, boy? You have accusations? Speak them. You have problems with the way I treated you? Speak up. And while you're at it, tell me where you'd be right now if I hadn't plucked you out of that thieves' nest. Show me another slave who can read as you can, write as you can, solve figures, and handle money."

Eric shouted at him. "Be silent."

"Show me another."

"Silent!" Simon roared and a shower of sparks erupted around the shade. "Silent! Silent! Silent!"

The shade howled and writhed in pain. "You will regret this, witch! When he finishes with me, he will turn on you."

"You will answer my questions!" Eric shouted. "Tell us how Simon came into your hands, or I will let him play with you until he tires."

The shade raised its hands. "I'll talk, I'll talk," it moaned. "Put Simon to sleep, and I'll talk."

"No more," Simon insisted. "No more."

Eric shrugged. "You heard him. Tell us about Simon's past. Did you know what happened to him?"

"Of course," the shade sneered. "I was there. I created him."

White rage roared in Eric's ears. Though the old man's ghost confirmed what he knew, learning that the master he had once revered was in fact a monster sickened him. "How could you?" he demanded.

"How could I?" Master Phineas laughed. "Magic and madness go hand in hand." He glanced at Mara. "You figured that one out long ago, didn't you, Witch? Everyone has a touch of magic, but sanity renders it useless. To create a truly great magician, one must first create a madman." He laughed and pointed a crooked finger at Simon. "We broke a lot of them before we got our wizard."

Eric couldn't believe what he heard. "You kidnapped and tortured children so you could travel the countryside performing tricks from the back of a wagon."

The shade's visage clouded. "I wasn't always the drunken wretch you remember. We had plans, great plans, but they came after us. We split up, fled, but they hunted us down, killing my comrades, killing the monsters we had created." He jerked his chin at Simon. "The Katarans are fierce, vengeful people. They find out he's here and breathing, they will come for him; kill him, and everyone standing around him." He paused. "By the time I was able to breathe easy, I had fallen too low to recover."

"Do you expect me to feel sorry for you?" Eric asked. "Pity you?"

"Of course not," the shade scoffed. "But I expect you to know what you're dealing with. Who you're dealing with." He pointed at Simon again. "That is a monster."

"You're the monster." He spoke to Mara without looking away. "Can this thing be destroyed?"

"Aye." Mara smiled. "I can't do it, but I can show Simon how."

"You wouldn't dare." Master Phineas' voice grew

shrill. "You're a hair's breadth from a shade yourself. You don't dare step that close to the edge."

"And you don't make demands on me. Not anymore." Eric stepped closer. "If you hope to avoid obliteration, tell us what we need to know. Does Daria's father, King Lysander, wait within Otherworld?"

"So that's what it is," he sneered. "She won't love you. When this is over, she won't even notice you."

"Answer me," Eric demanded. "Answer me, or I will turn Simon lose, and turn my back."

Through it all, Simon stared at the old man's shade as if hypnotized. His lips moved, but Eric had difficulty making out what he said over the rush of his own heartbeat.

"We danced when you burned. We danced when you burned. We danced when you burned."

The shade regarded Eric with a level of disgust that would have withered him a week ago. Now it only paled beside the hatred he himself was feeling. "What will it be?" he asked again.

The shade sighed. "King Lysander does not dwell in Otherworld. He remains among the living. Now leave me to my fate."

Eric nodded. "Let him go, Simon."

Simon raised both hands. The shade screamed in agony, writhed, then vanished in a swirl of sickly yellow fog. "Close it!" Mara commanded, and Simon slammed his hands down on the mage light. It vanished like a doused fire, leaving Simon gasping with exhilaration.

"More," he chanted. "More more more."

Mara beamed at Simon. "Later, perhaps. I think we've had enough magic for this session, thank you. You did very well." Her gaze shifted to Eric. "Both of you did very well."

"Did you know that would happen?"

Mara shook her head. "No, I fully expected King Lysander to appear before us. Praise be, it is not too late to save him." She turned to leave. "Now I think we all need a little rest."

"Wait." Eric drew a deep breath and waited for her to turn. "What the gatekeeper said. What Master ... that thing said." He paused, trying to find the right words. "When you battled Lord Vassant. He really did win, didn't he?"

She studied him before answering. "You don't know everything either."

"No," Eric agreed. "But I'm learning." The words left his mouth reluctantly. "What are you?"

Her gaze became painful. Still, he held it. "I am what you see before you," she said. "A stubborn old woman with a touch of magic."

"Then why does Daria believe you are dead? And don't tell me she doesn't know everything." When she didn't answer, he spoke to Simon without looking away. "The Princess is asleep in the other room. Go wake her."

Simon started forward. Mara halted him with an upraised hand. "Stay where you are, boy."

"That's what I thought," Eric replied. "You're the reason Daria wouldn't wake up. Why she sleeps now. You didn't want her to know."

"I'm trying to protect her."

"She deserves to know."

"Know what?" Mara's voice grew menacing. "That I've managed to survive this long on will alone, trapped like a scarab in a glass case, while a magician I created destroys my city on the whims of his power-hungry whore?" She spat. "Would that I had allowed myself to simply die. It would have been easier."

Eric digested her revelations, surprised only at the violence of her words. "Daria still deserves to know."

She glared at him. “Your late master was right about one thing. You cannot hope to be anything more to her than a friend.”

“That’s not what this is about.” Eric’s jaw tightened. “This is about which one of us goes in there and tells her the truth.” He paused. “Which one of us is it going to be?”

Chapter 40

"Madness breeds power." Lord Vassant shook himself from his trance and looked at Rialle. "Of course. It's so simple."

Nothing is simple, Rialle thought. "What do you mean?" She struggled to keep the frustration from her voice. For days now, she had kept watch over him, waiting impatiently as he peeled at the layers of the old witch's ring.

Vassant chattered, as pleased as a happy child. "The boy, that mad little slave, has no sanity to hold him in check." His lips curved in a smile. "He does not know what he cannot do, so he can do anything."

"And this pleases you?"

"It amuses me." He stood and adjusted his robes. "'Twas a shame I killed the old man so quickly."

"Can you do what she did? Open the ring and bring them here?"

Vassant laughed. "You do believe me."

Rialle sighed inwardly. "What do you mean?"

"You asked if I could do what she did. You too believe she is alive." He swept his arms around the ring and laughed again. "But to answer your question, no, I cannot. Once I have the boy back, then there will be no limit to what I will be able to do." He looked at the pulsating rings on the floor. His merriment vanished, and his face twisted in a sneer. "There is so much she did not teach me about this room. It's no wonder I had to kill her."

Rialle bit her tongue to keep from pointing out the contradiction in his words. "Have you learned all you can from the ring?"

"Until she activates it again."

Rialle watched him carefully. "If it's a doorway, we should close it. Permanently." She edged toward the door. "I can summon a work gang; we can have this cavern sealed within the hour."

"You will do no such thing." Lord Vassant held his arms out slightly from his body, and the mage-light caressed his palms. "How else will he come to me?"

"That's the idea." Rialle narrowed her eyes. "We don't want him back here." She pointed at the pulsating pattern on the floor. "We close this doorway, and no more Simon, no more Eric, no more sniveling Princess." And no more Mara, she thought.

"The ring remains open." His words were a giddy decree. "I have never felt this alive."

Aside from his seeming drunkenness, she had to agree with him. Was it the battle, or the presence of the more powerful magician that made it so? "And what if she comes back." Rialle moved to the edge of the ring, as close as she dared. "What if she comes back with our mad little mage at her side?"

"Then I will be here." Lord Vassant smiled. "Waiting for them."

Chapter 41

Simon had remained silent throughout Eric's exchange with Mara, but his bright eyes followed the conversation as a dog would a ball tossed between two people. Eric realized this was the first time they had ever been alone together with Simon awake and unconfined, and it was the safest he'd felt since coming to Legerdemain.

"You think she should know?" Mara had asked him, with a jerk of her knobby chin. "Tell her then. And be it on your head if it causes her more than a moment's grief."

Eric stared at the arched doorway where she had disappeared. Mara had done nothing but help him since they met, and still he did not trust her. Despite her claims of wanting to protect the Princess, he suspected her motive was revenge. It was a motivation he knew well.

Simon watched expectantly, still silent. Waiting to be sent away, dropped into dormancy, whatever happened when Eric spoke the word that rendered him harmless. Not this time. Not ever. An unspoken truce hung between them in the silent, sea-damp air.

Master Phineas' shade had one final lesson for both of them. They had been fighting the wrong enemy. "Come on," Eric told Simon. "Let's go see Daria."

Daria listened patiently while Eric once more explained their circumstances. He saw in her eyes that she doubted him and he couldn't really blame her. An undead witch, dreams that were not dreams, and at the center of it all, a stolen slave-mage made deliberately insane to fuel his power.

The best he saved for last. "The shade told us one final thing." He smiled and touched her hand. "Your father does not dwell in Otherworld. He is still alive."

Relief washed over her face and she flung her arms around his neck in an exuberant hug. That moment alone made everything worthwhile. "Oh, thank you, thank you," she cried. Happy tears tumbled down her cheeks. "I don't know what to say." She sat back and covered her face with her hands. "I didn't know. I imagined the worst."

"It's all right." Eric reached to touch the side of her face but stayed his hand. Not his place. "We'll do whatever it takes to restore your father," he promised. "Simon and I both will."

Eric looked up at Simon. Through it all, the boy hovered nearby, uncharacteristically silent. He stayed fixated on Daria. The shifting emotions on his face mirrored her own. "Yes, yes." His head bobbed in excitement. "We go back."

Daria looked from one to the other. "You will, won't you?" she said as if she was only just beginning to believe it. "Even though this isn't your fight?"

"It's our fight," Eric assured her. "They made it so."

She smiled and hugged her arms across her chest. "It's good to know I'm not alone anymore."

Eric started to answer, but was stopped by a crashing sound. He turned and saw Simon had stumbled against one of the tables. Books slid to the ground like a shifting dune.

Eric's brow furrowed. "Simon. Why don't you sit? Get some rest? You'll need your strength."

"Can't. Can't. Can not." Simon stood and began to pace. "Can not. Can't."

Eric realized Simon hadn't sat down or even stopped moving since they banished the shade. Reaching back, he realized he had never seen or kept Simon awake for so long. It was always brief bursts of activity and fear, followed by days and weeks of dormancy. "He needs to rest."

"What?" Daria asked.

"Simon. He's burning himself out." Eric caught the boy by the arm and forced him to be still. Simon's head whipped around. Eric's heart jumped at the flair of rage in his red-rimmed eyes. "You need to rest."

"Can't. Cannot. Can't." Simon muttered.

"Do you want me to help you?"

"Banished." Simon whispered. "Banished until needed."

"Until you wake."

Simon's head lolled to the side. He looked at Eric through narrowed eyes. "Do I trust you?"

"You do," Eric assured him. He saw a nod, and Simon's eyes closed. "Sleep," he instructed the boy, and caught him before he hit the ground.

"I should have thought of that myself." Mara spoke from the doorway. "A flame can't burn that bright forever."

"Mara!" Daria vaulted from the pallet and rushed to the old woman. "You're alive! When Eric told me ... I just didn't know what to believe."

"Alive is a tricky term for what I am, and I am sorry to have deceived you when you first arrived." Mara patted the girl's dark curls. "It is a joy to see you too, child. A pure and absolute joy."

Eric eased the now dormant Simon onto the pallet Daria had vacated. He brushed the hair from Simon's face, then turned and watched Daria exclaim and fuss over the old woman.

Not for you, his conscience warned. Not for you.

Chapter 42

While Simon slept, Gabriel passed the time teaching Eric to defend himself. "Can you use a sword?" The old man hefted an oily black blade from a rack in the corner. "This is a good 'en. Not too heavy, not too long, just right for stickin' in someone."

"Sorry, no." Eric shook his head. "Until a few days ago, I'd never even held one. I'm a slave. It would have meant my death."

"Hmph!" Gabriel replaced the weapon with a clang. "Staff? Dagger? Cudgel? Pointed stick?" Eric shook his head. The old man gave a grunt of disgust. "Is there anything you can do?"

"Well, there's this." Eric snatched a small green jar off the shelf behind Gabriel.

"What you gonna do?" Gabriel sneered, but his eyes never left the jar. "Juggle?"

"I suppose I could." Eric held up his hand. In the right, he held the jar. In the left, he held a battered leather coin purse. "Now that I can afford to buy a set of clubs."

Daria clapped and laughed, while the old man clutched at his belt. "You can get your neck stretched for stealing too, you know," he warned.

Eric sobered. "I never needed to carry a weapon. But there were times I needed to steal to eat."

"May those times never come again," Daria said.

May we all live to see them, Eric thought, but kept those words to himself.

Gabriel selected one weapon after the other, and tirelessly worked Eric. Mara and Daria sat side by side at one of the little tables, their heads bowed over sheaves of parchment. The old woman shook her head and scowled, but the Princess remained beautifully defiant. His attention lingered on her, and he was rewarded with a sharp rap on his thigh with the butt of Gabriel's staff.

"Mind me," he snapped. "Not the young miss."

"I know." Eric raised the staff wearily. "She's not for me."

"Nay." The old man darted his eyes at the pair, then motioned for Eric to lean close. "Bit of unrequited love is good for a young man. And you never know what's to come of it." He rapped the staff out of Eric's hand and sent it clattering to the stone floor. "Hah!" he said with a snort. "Maybe we'll get you a nice big rock."

"While you're doing that," Daria interrupted. "There is something I need to discuss with Eric." She approached, bearing a pair of parchment scrolls sealed with crimson wax.

"You best be certain you wish to do this, Princess," Mara said.

"More certain than I have been about anything for a very long time." Daria stood before him. She transferred the scrolls to her left hand, took Eric's hand and held it palm up. There were ink stains on her fingertips. "I would call this a gift, but in truth, I'm only returning something stolen from you a long time ago. Something that never should have been taken in the first place."

She placed the first scroll in his hand. Eric looked in her eyes as he unrolled the scroll, then transferred his gaze to the parchment. The first three words, Letter of Manumission, were all he needed to make out.

When he looked up, she was beaming at him. "With my father incapacitated, I am the reigning monarch. I have the authority to make it so." Her fingers touched his, anchoring him. "And so I have."

Eric gaped at her, then at the letter. He became aware Gabriel was standing behind him, but he was so detached he barely felt the hands on his collar. The old man grunted, the metal got hot, and the collar fell away.

Eric lifted his hand to his throat and felt nothing but bare skin. He closed his eyes and swallowed hard. Tears welled in his eyes. He did not want to cry in front of her, in front of any of them. He covered his eyes with his hand and squeezed them shut, willing the tears back.

"Say something," Daria laughed. "Otherwise I'll think you don't like my present."

Eric wanted to thank her, but his throat was choked shut. "It's all I ever wanted," he managed to say. "Thank you." He lowered his hand and lifted his chin. "Thank you."

Daria wrapped her arms around him in a quick hug, then stepped back. Her eyes grew sober. "Now that you are a free man, you have a decision to make, but I don't want you to make it right away." She fidgeted with the scroll in her hands. "I'm going back to fight Vassant. I'm going because I have to, and because I must save my father. Mara will help as much as she is able."

Eric started to speak. Daria hushed him with a raised finger. "Please hear what I have to say." She paused and swallowed. "Any debt you may feel toward me is paid. You've saved my life more than once. I would welcome your assistance, but you owe me nothing. You are a free man, and if you desire, you are free to go with my thanks and best wishes."

She turned and smiled down at Simon, then handed Eric the second scroll. "This is the second part of the present. It grants you ownership of Simon."

"No." Eric held it out to her. "He should be free too."

"And he shall." Daria glanced at Mara. "I was all for writing a letter of manumission for him this day, but Mara convinced me otherwise."

"Why?" Eric glared at the old woman. "He has suffered more than I."

"We may know what he is, but someone still needs to care for him," Mara explained. "When this is over, when you all are safe, then Daria can make arrangements for his care."

Eric looked at the scroll. Just the idea that he owned a slave sickened him, even if her reasoning was sound. He shook his head. "It shouldn't be me. It's just not right."

"None of this is right." Daria pressed the scroll into his hand. "But I will make it right again."

Mara lifted her head. Daria started to speak, but the old woman stopped her with an upraised hand. "He comes," she whispered, and hurried toward the scrying room. Eric and Daria exchanged glances, then rushed after her, with Gabriel trailing behind.

The stone chamber was filled with blue-black fog that crackled like lightning. "So this is how it was done." Lord Vassant's mocking laughter echoed through the room.

"Begone, traitor!" Mara boomed.

"You live." Lord Vassant mocked her. "Rialle said

it was impossible, but she does not know what you and I know."

Mara began an incantation, her lips working rapidly. His laughter rose with her rage, and the black fog swirled faster. Mara raised her staff and slammed it down on the glowing gem between her feet. "Begone!" she shouted.

At once, the fog drew inward, inhaled into the center of the ring. Lord Vassant's laughter faded with it, until it existed only in Eric's mind.

At the center of the smoking ring lay a body clothed in blood and tatters. Daria cried out and sank to the floor. Eric's blood ran as cold as the night wind as he recognized Daria's nurse. He turned.

"Where are you going?" Mara demanded.

"To wake Simon," Eric's jaw was so tight he could barely speak. "This ends now."

"Wait," Mara ordered.

Eric hesitated. "I've waited long enough." His fists clenched as he faced her. "I'm going to get Simon." He pointed at the ring. "Go back. Kill Vassant, Rialle, and anyone else who stands in my way." His blood seethed with vengeance. He wanted to charge through the portal and battle barehanded with whatever lay on the other side.

"And squander your new-found freedom so foolishly?" Mara asked.

Eric looked at Daria kneeling over the bloodied form of her nurse. Bethel's eyes were closed, but her visage was no less horrible. "Yes." The coldness in his voice shocked him. "I would."

"No." Daria looked up at him. Tears stained her cheeks. "Mara is right. We need a plan. It's just five of us against all of them." She looked back at the body. "We must see to poor Bethel."

Her tears stole the fight from him. He turned and

stalked into the other room. Daria was right. He kicked a stool into a pile of books, and the tomes scattered across the mismatched rugs.

The others followed warily, as if he were a coiled snake. Gabriel bore the nurse's body from the room as if she was naught but a doll, and Eric wondered if the man was truly what he appeared. He paced to and fro in the confines of the study, rubbing the back of his now-bare neck with his left hand.

It all hinged on Simon.

"I just wish we knew more about him." Mara studied the sleeping boy. "We can only learn what he tells us."

"Can we trust him?" Daria asked.

"We don't have a choice." Eric shifted from one foot to the other. "Forgive me, madam, but unless I am mistaken, you cannot defeat Lord Vassant."

Mara nodded an acknowledgement. "True. I couldn't then. I certainly can't now, at least not on my own. There are ways though." She paused. "We know Vassant draws power from Simon every time Simon enters the ring. While Simon has plenty to spare, it will defeat our purpose to let Vassant take it from him. We need to drain him, wear him out. This means I have to fight him without Simon in the circle."

She didn't need to finish the statement. Eric knew this fight she could not win.

"I won't accept that." Daria shook her head. "I won't let you risk your life for me."

"The risk is long past, child." Mara looked at Eric. "My life has been forfeit since the day Lord Vassant vanquished me."

Daria's eyes filled with tears. "I don't understand."

"I would have spared you this if I could." Mara placed a hand on her cheek. Her voice grew sad. "Eric has guessed the truth of it."

Eric felt a shiver. "You're a ghost?"

Mara shrugged. "More than that, but not much more. I only exist here because I prepared the way — I created this place as a haven. But once we go back to the citadel, I will not be able to pass beyond the ring." She nodded at Simon. "It will be up to him."

Eric knelt beside the slumbering mage. Now that his anger had settled, his conscience broke free. "It doesn't seem right, does it? We are risking our lives," he said. "We know what we are getting into. Simon doesn't. He never had a choice."

"Wake him, then," Daria said. "I'll ask him what he wants to do."

"He'll say yes. He would do anything for you." Eric looked down at the sleeping boy. "And he would do anything for me."

"Simon's power shields him, and they want him alive," Mara said. "I can teach him how to protect himself better than any suit of armor." Mara clasped Simon's wrist. "Wake up"

Simon shook his head. "Where am I? Where am I? Ah!" Recognition widened his eyes. "We still wait."

"Not much longer," Mara told him. "How do you feel? Are you rested?"

"Rested yes rested," Simon said, but he looked anything but.

Eric knelt beside him. "We're going back, Simon. Back to the citadel to rescue Daria's father. Do you understand?"

Simon's brow furrowed. "I protect her. I protect her."

"Yes," Eric agreed. "That is your job — you protect her. No matter what else happens."

"Eric, no!" Daria cried.

"He's right," Mara agreed. "That's the way it has to be."

"I protect her," Simon repeated. "I protect her."

"He will also be there," Eric told him. "Lord Vassant. The One who Glows."

Simon's eyes widened and his lips twisted in a gruesome smile. "I will kill him."

"Perhaps," Mara told him. "Will you let me show you how?"

Simon nodded. Mara motioned for him to come to her, and he knelt on the floor at her side. The old woman placed a hand on his cheek. He leaned into her touch like an obedient dog and they both closed their eyes.

"Best let them be," Gabriel grunted as he returned. "Might take a bit."

"We don't have a bit." Eric stood and dusted his breeches. He was ready. With a restless shrug, he turned and went back to the worktable where Mara, Gabriel, and Daria had worked out a diagram of the citadel. He traced the path from the scrying room to the study with his fingertips, then closed his eyes and did it from memory.

Daria came and stood beside him. "Are you ready?"

He nodded. "I'm ready." He looked at her. "Are you certain you want to come?"

She took his hand and squeezed it. "It's my duty."

Simon sat back on his heels and laughed. "Are you certain? Are you certain? Ridiculous and foolish it is. For certain?"

"Very certain." Mara stood and rubbed the small of her back with her hand. "And, I agree with Eric. I want this to be over with as well. Gabriel, is the way prepared?"

"Aye, madam." He gave a courtly bow.

Mara raised her chin and straightened her robes. "Let's be about it then."

Chapter 43

Rialle sat in the high-backed, ornate ironwood chair that had once been King Lysander's throne. The room was absolutely still, the doors and shutters closed against the throng of activity and the ever-present roar of the ocean on the other side of the citadel. She imagined she heard the dust motes spinning in the air over the rush of her own blood coursing through her body.

Being here, sitting in this chair gave her a hidden, forbidden thrill. No one came here anymore, no one ever saw her. She came here when she needed to think, and to remind herself how far she had come. She had accomplished so much, and yet this construct of wood and nails could still render her common again. Not her. Not common. Not after what she had accomplished.

She drummed her fingers on the broad arm of the chair and contemplated the task ahead. Vassant assured her that the insipid Princess and her street-born champions were trapped. Executing the traitorous nurse had been her idea, but sending her battered body as a gift was Vassant's. When last she had checked on the magician, he was playing with them like a cat dipping his paws into whatever lay on the other side of the portal.

All they were waiting for was for him to figure out how to open the portal wide enough to send a squadron of men through. Or, better yet, for Mara to open it. Either way, the men were waiting to burst through, snatch the Princess, and slaughter anyone else they found. She knew they would probably not take the slave-mage Simon alive, but she had let it be known that she would pay handsomely if his companion were delivered while still breathing.

Rialle smiled, and her fingers drummed harder. That one would be weeks in dying.

Chapter 44

Eric waited in the still, humid air of the scrying room while Mara stirred the magic that would send them back. In his hands, he held a smooth wooden cudgel, the only weapon Gabriel pronounced him fit to handle. The old man didn't know about the knife in his boot. Eric had no skill with either weapon, but that didn't matter. The only weapon he needed was his wits.

He needed to blend in. Be invisible. Now, instead of a slave's rags, he wore the homespun tunic and breeches of a shopkeeper's apprentice or workman's son. A pair of worn but still serviceable boots with a knife hidden in the leather, and an oversized cap completed his disguise. He looked as he felt — a free man, an honest laborer.

Daria stood beside him, unarmed, save for her fierce determination to save her father. She wore a long hooded cloak over her robes. She had been disappointed that she too could not disguise herself as a working boy, but if their plan worked, the time would come quickly that she would need to be recognizable as Princess

Daria of Legerdemain. She stood to his left, and when he glanced at her over his shoulder, she gave him a tight smile. You don't have to do this, she had told him. If anything, he needed to do it more than she did.

Mara's chanting filled the thick air, and the conjured blue light swirled around them. Simon stood at her side, rocking back and forth in time with her words, his mouth working soundlessly, his eyes rolled back in his head in apparent ecstasy. Mara took the boy's hand. Simon laughed. "He waits. The One who Glows he waits."

"So do I," Eric said as the floor vanished beneath them. There was a tug, a swirl, then a fall without a landing, and the room reformed. Lightning filled the air.

Eric placed himself between Daria and Lord Vassant, with Gabriel at his side. The old man held a heavy sword with a blue-black blade, and Eric believed he could wield it. But would it do any good against the magician?

"Welcome back," Lord Vassant spoke, but his words were directed at the floor. "I've been waiting for you."

"You're in my ring." Though she remained behind with Simon, Mara's voice filled the smoky air. "I suggest you stand down."

Lord Vassant feigned fear. "Oh yes, I'll do just that. After I kill you. Again."

"You're fading, boy. You were never the man or the magician you imagined yourself to be. You could have been, but you chose another path."

While Mara baited him, Eric led Daria and Gabriel toward the door. Lord Vassant gestured at them, and they were flung back against the wall. "No one leaves," he bellowed. "You will all watch me defeat her."

"Your quarrel is with me, not with them." The

smoke intensified, boiling black and blue. "You will deal with me."

Soldiers poured into the scrying room. "Are none of you loyal to the King?" Gabriel shouted, raising his mighty weapon. The blade glowed with red and gold as he swung at the nearest soldier. The man easily ducked the blow, but collapsed lifelessly just the same. Gabriel cackled a challenge to his comrades, and they swarmed as one on the sword-wielding old man.

"Go!" Mara spoke in Eric's ear. "Gabriel won't be able to hold them for long."

Daria stood transfixed by the battle. Eric grabbed her hand. "Come." She turned and followed him past the melee into the empty stairwell. "You know the way?" he asked.

"Like the palm of my hand." Daria mounted the steps, with Eric close at her shoulder. The cudgel was slick against his palms, and the stone cold beneath the thin soles of his boots. He wanted to caution her to slow down, but she was a creature inspired by vengeance.

They reached the first landing. Daria placed a hand on the door. "Wait," Eric whispered. He stepped up beside her and placed an ear to the thick wood. Hearing nothing, he stepped back and opened the door a crack. The corridor, like the stairs, was empty. "Remember," he told her. "Act as if we belong. Not like fugitives."

"We do belong," she replied, and opened the door the rest of the way.

The confrontation was better than Simon dreamed anything could be. In the space of a breath, She who

Taught invoked more mage-power than he had seen in his strange and hazy lifetime. He watched her, supported her, and fed the mind-numbing sleep spells she taught him to the blade of her servant. She who Taught would survive because he needed her to teach him these things.

No, her voice spoke sharply in his mind. That is not the bargain.

Not the bargain. Not the bargain. He felt the pull of the One who Glows. His voice whispered along the edges of Simon's mind, but she held firm, held him at bay. Simon yearned to lose himself in their spells, devour them both in a single swallow and become the sum total of all three.

Do it, she urged.

Simon shook his head. The One who Glows mocked him with laughter. Weak, you are weak!

Not weak. Not weak. Not weak.

Simon saw it all, and it was glorious. Focus was the word she gave him. Focus focus focus. But it was so hard, oh so hard, as she battled the One who Glows and their magic swirled around them in dizzying spirals. Could they see what he saw?

Focus, Simon, focus. She spoke in his mind. Yes, he would focus. If she fell, he would not learn, and there was so much to learn. An obedient boy, he did what he was told. Simon always obeyed.

He held out his hand and felt the magic flow from him, like that, and like that. It was hard to see past her, past the upraised staff, and the flashing glory that spun the air in the room. Never had he seen, never had he imagined.

Except.

Another voice spoke in his mind, this one tiny. I remember.

Simon staggered. He had seen, seen it, the he that

was that little voice.

Simon, focus! She who Taught screamed in his mind, blocking out the shiny memory. He snarled in reflex, then remembered the present. Help the Teacher, help the Princess, and help the little one. He gave the Teacher his full attention and waited.

You know what to do next.

I know I know I know. A pause. You will survive?

You know what to do.

Simon worried at this.

You know what to do. You promised. You bargained.

I did. I did. He gave her everything he had, everything he could, then broke contact and staggered back. Even from without, the battle was glorious; he longed to sink to his knees and revel in it. But if he ceased to be, who would protect the Princess?

Eric tucked the cap low over his brow and followed Daria into the hall. Heads up, eyes forward, they navigated the angled corridors, while servants and other functionaries passed without a second look. He should have asked the resourceful Gabriel for something more deadly to carry instead of the cudgel.

“Better days,” whispered Daria to the grunted greetings of a pair of guards who barely took notice of her. She looked back at Eric. The expression on her face said what she dared not voice — this was hopeless. “Keep trying,” he told her, and squeezed her hand. She squeezed back, and tried her greeting again, and again.

"Better days, better days."

"Eh?" One grunted. "Better days indeed."

Eric froze. Daria turned and revealed her face to the soldier. "Do you know who I am?" she asked.

His head jerked back in surprise, then he smiled and rubbed the stubble on his chin. "Aye, Princess, I do." His voice was low. "These are bad times, it's best not to be wandering unattended."

"I am not unattended," she replied, and stepped in closer. "The question is, are you ready to bring the bad times to an end?" His brows arched. Daria threw her hood back, and at that instant changed from a scared girl and became a Princess. Her shoulders went back, her chin went up, and her dark eyes filled with flint. "How many men are loyal to my father?" she asked. "Can we take and hold the citadel, if necessary?"

The man considered it, then nodded. "Most still believe they serve the King. Early on, those that saw the truth drew hazardous duty. The rest of us, when we saw that truth, kept silent and watched. Waiting for a ruler."

"Your wait is over," Daria told him.

The doorway swelled before them. Mara pushed through, and Simon followed unbidden, unwilling to be left behind. He splayed his fingers and felt the magic rush against his flesh and his skin tingled. The One who Glows saw him, and his face split in a wicked grin.

"You brought him here?" The One who Glows laughed. "One last gift for your favorite student?"

"You could say that." She who Taught looked at

Simon and smiled. "Good bargain," she told him, and with a gesture, knocked him out of the circle. Simon looked at her in astonishment, his eyes never leaving her as he struck the ground hard. He pivoted to rise, confused and angry, when she spoke the word that sent him away. "Sleep."

Eric's head jerked up, then he hunched his shoulders and tried once more to look inconspicuous. "What is it?" Daria whispered.

"Not sure." He replayed the images that flashed through his mind, images he was sure came from Mara. She was here now, on this side of the circle. He saw her, saw Simon cringing on the floor, dormant, but not dead. Saw Gabriel, his body crumpled, but his spirit?

He heard a single word. "Come." Then he heard nothing, and saw nothing.

Eric thought about telling Daria what he had seen, but didn't want to upset her. "It's time," he told her.

"So quickly?" Her eyes darted over his face, searching for the truth of what he had seen, and it took all his wiles to hide it from her. "Are you certain?"

He nodded. "You will be safe with them." Eric indicated the guard they had met, and his newly arrived comrades. He turned to go before his nerve failed.

Daria caught his arm. He turned, and she kissed him. "You are my hero," she whispered. "None of this would have happened without you. Thank you."

Eric swallowed the knot in his throat, and gave a tiny bow. "It is a pleasure to serve, milady." He smiled. "Now, go to your father. Simon and I will join you, and this will be over."

Chapter 45

Come,” Mara told him and so he came. Eric moved through the citadel like a shade, like smoke. No one saw him; no one even looked in his direction. Three floors above the battle, the magic flowed beneath him so strongly it drowned out the roar of the ocean. By the time he reached the stairs leading to the scrying room, Eric was moving at a dead run.

Smoking corpses lined the corridors. Gabriel’s blue-black blade lay on the floor at the foot of the stair, but there was no sign of the old man. The air pulsed with electricity. Mara and Lord Vassant stood at opposing sides of the magic ring, motionless, like the statue of King Lysander. Their eyes were closed. Eric’s ears heard nothing, but his mind was nearly sucked into a whirlwind.

This is what she wanted to protect Simon from, Eric thought, as the void widened and filled with howls. He felt as if he were standing at the edge of a precipice and the drop called to him. He had to get out of here, and he had to get Simon out of here.

Simon sat, rocking back and forth, tears streaming down his face, his mouth open in a soundless scream. Eric had to call him three times before he looked up. "Come," he shouted. But Simon didn't move. Eric skirted the ring, grabbed Simon by the hand, and hauled him to his feet.

"Come on, come on, it's all right," he said, to reassure both Simon and himself. They followed the wall back to the door, Simon close on his heels.

Eric stopped and turned. Could he do anything? Did he dare? Mara had forced a promise from him that he would not get involved once she engaged Lord Vassant. More importantly, that he would not let Simon get involved.

But could they save her?

A fading voice answered in his mind, and that answer was No.

Eric forced himself to turn away. Pulling Simon like a wagon, he mounted the stairs and returned to the citadel. It was difficult to be invisible now, with the cringing Simon in tow. There was no way they could get to Daria without being seen.

Eric heard Rialle before he saw her — her cold voice burned straight through his skull. He halted, and his skin dampened with sweat. "Waken," he told Simon, though they were not far enough from the maelstrom below.

Simon's head snapped up and his eyes brightened. "Where?" he started to ask, then he appeared to remember. "Now?" he asked. "Now?"

"Not yet," Eric whispered. "We have one more duty to attend."

His spirit freed, Gabriel went about the castle like a bottle imp, dousing lanterns and lighting fires, tipping buckets in the spirit of a poltergeist. Over and over, he whispered the words "Better days, better days, better days," until they reached the ears of a trio of older soldiers watching a work crew clean up the remains of the livery. Once their attention was caught, the spirit filled their ears with so much more.

Rialle scowled at the disturbances around her. Summoned from her reverie, she stalked the main floor of the citadel, looking for a culprit she knew she would not find. She knew who to blame, but could not point the finger without looking seeming insane. One crazy person was enough. She had dispatched all but two of her personal guards to help restore order. Where was Vassant? Most likely still sitting in the scrying room like a broody hen on a nest. She headed that way.

Rialle rounded the corner. The corridor was empty save for a servant. Always under foot, they were. "You, boy," she called. "What are you doing here?"

He didn't answer her.

"Fetch him for me," she told the man on her right.

The boy turned, then broke into a run. Rialle caught a glimpse of his face. Eric! Anger surged through her. "Get him!" she screamed. "Bring him to me!"

The soldiers rushed forward. Rialle suppressed the urge to run after them. It would not do to be seen racing about the halls like a harridan. They would catch him soon enough, and catch him they did. Eric fought, kicked and struggled, but the men were built like bears. There was nothing he could do but kick and curse.

Rialle smiled. If one was here, especially this one, then the other two could not be too far behind. It was shaping up to be a much better day than she anticipated.

Daria wished for Eric at her side, but it was not to be. She could only close her eyes and offer a silent prayer for his safety as her growing escort of guards led her through the citadel. She made sure everyone, soldiers and civilians alike saw her face; there was to be no mistaking who was in charge. “If you would follow me, then do so,” she instructed all those who hesitated. “If not, I want you out of the city by sundown.”

Eric stood before Rialle, eyes glaring, jaw clenched tight. She laughed. “We’re so much alike, you and I,” she told him. “Except, of course, that I am not so stupid as to throw myself into a hopeless battle that has nothing to do with me.” She pinched his chin between her fingers and felt him shudder with revulsion. “Yet here you are again.”

Her gaze strayed to his bare neck. “Well isn’t this interesting.” She traced a fingernail along his collarbone, and was disappointed when he did not recoil.

"You appear to have lost something. Not to worry. I'll find a suitable replacement."

Vassant joined them. The buzz of magic surrounding him was almost visible. "What happened?" she asked.

"You don't question me." He sounded almost drunk. "You don't question me."

The hell I don't, Rialle thought. She looked at Eric. "Where is your friend?"

"I have no friends," he said.

She struck him, an open-handed slap. His head jerked back, but he did not flinch. The stone-like expression on his face did not change. Vassant laughed. Rialle resisted the urge to strike him as well. "Do you have the strength left to pull the information out of him?"

Vassant leered with eagerness. "Another stupid question." He appeared about to say more, but stopped himself.

Rialle rolled her eyes. "Not here. Come, bring him." She led the way back into what had been the King's Salon, where she whirled on Eric. "Tell me where Simon is."

"Dead," Eric replied.

Vassant laughed and moved around behind her. "Do it now?" he asked.

"Wait," she replied. "Give him time." She glared at Eric. Her hatred of him colored everything, threatened to blacken her vision, swallow her whole. "I will ask you once more. Where is Simon?"

"I will tell you once more." Eric looked at her. There was no hatred in his eyes now. "Simon is dead. I put him to sleep, and then I killed him."

Her breath left. "Why?" she gasped. Everything slipped away. "Why would you do that?"

"Because it was the only way to keep him away from you." He gave a little laugh. "Imagine that."

Rialle's chest heaved. "You should have taken your own life as well. I would have cared for Simon, he would have been as happy as such a creature can be. You, on the other hand, will die so slowly you'll plead with me to sell you to a slave galley." She placed a hand on his throat. "The next collar you wear will be so heavy you won't be able to stand. I will have you brought before me every day, just so I can see you beg. Things can be worse, Eric. And I promise you, I will prove that to you every day for the rest of your worthless wretched life."

"Now?" asked Vassant.

Rialle was about to answer yes when Eric nodded. She turned, looked over her shoulder, and saw Vassant's features dissolve into those of Simon. She looked back at Eric and he was smiling.

"Go ahead," he told her. "Threaten me some more."

Chapter 46

During the walk from the scrying room stairs to Lord Vassant's chambers, Daria felt herself grow taller with each stride. These men supported her, and more than that, they followed her, because she had seized her birthright with both hands. Buoyed by their support, she felt certain their plan would succeed.

They met their only resistance in the corridor outside Lord Vassant's chambers. Here the men still loyal to the magician had regrouped to bar passage to anyone who might learn his secrets. Daria counted sixteen men, and wondered if they knew what secret they guarded.

Bennick, the man she and Eric had first encountered, stopped her with a raised hand. "Best stand back, Princess. We're going to have to fight our way through."

"No." She shook her head. "This battle is mine." Before he could stop her, Daria moved forward. Her men followed. Vassant's soldiers stiffened at their approach, but did not draw their weapons. "Stand down!" Daria ordered. "Surrender now and I will see that your lives are spared."

The men exchanged glances; a few smirked. Daria raised her voice. "I will not repeat myself." She folded her arms across her chest.

One man stepped from the group. He had long black hair held back by a thong, and a jagged scar on his right cheekbone. "My orders are to secure this citadel, these quarters, and your safety, Princess." He smiled and held out his hand. "Now, if you would be a good girl and come with me."

Daria glared at him. "What is your name?"

His dark eyes narrowed. "What does that have to do with anything?"

"Because I'll need it when I sign your death warrant." Daria stared him down, her anger fueled by every lie, every deception foisted upon her by Lord Vassant and his allies.

Her defiance amused him. "Go to your chambers, girl, and no harm will come to you." He stepped toward her. "Lord Vassant has personally assured your safety."

"Is that so?" Daria smiled at him. "Then there is nothing you can do to me, is there? Your threats are empty." She gestured with a flick of the wrist. "Either kill me now, or get out of my way."

Steel shifted on both sides. Daria stood firm. "You heard my orders."

"I will not surrender to a girl," the leader sneered.

"She is not a girl," Bennick shouted. "Princess Daria is the daughter of our King, who I serve with honor." He paused, his face a granite mask. "Who do you serve?"

Daria felt the tension between the men lessen. "This doesn't have to be a battle," she told them. "You open the way into that room, and I will show you the true nature of your master."

He hesitated and looked at his men. "We can hold you here as well as anywhere, I suppose." He jerked his head, and the soldiers divided to form a narrow aisle leading to the door to Lord Vassant's quarters.

Daria strode through with Bennick close on her heels. Swords remained at the ready; all it would have taken was a single misstep on either side for the battle to begin. The man closest to the door opened it, and Daria swept into Lord Vassant's parlor.

Daria's eyes went to her father, still frozen, his eyes staring out in horror. Around her, the men fell silent as they realized the fate of their King. Daria heard gasps and prayers as she placed her hands on the statue's chest, then wrapped her arms around its waist and lay her cheek against the stony surface.

"I'm here," she told her father. "Help is on the way."

Chapter 47

The soldiers on either side of Rialle reached for their weapons. Simon dropped them where they stood. Rialle backed away, but there was no place for her to retreat. The color left her face, and her jaw went slack. "Afraid?" Eric taunted. "You should be."

Her gaze dropped to the two downed soldiers. "Maybe not," she said. "They're still alive."

"They didn't betray me." Eric knelt beside the first man, rolled him onto his stomach, then bound his hands and feet with his sash. "Simon has already killed enough people."

Rialle smirked. "We're not alike at all then, are we?"

"No." Eric finished binding the second man. His hands shook with rage as he fought to control his temper. "I'm not afraid to get my hands dirty," he said as he stood, pulling the dagger from his boot as he did.

"You don't have the nerve," she sneered.

"That was true once." Eric grabbed her arm and yanked her forward. "Then I met you. Let's go."

"Go where?" Rialle halted. "Where are you taking me?"

"It's not where we're taking you. It's where you're taking us." At the door, Eric nodded at Simon, who once more assumed the form of Lord Vassant. "Take us to the King."

"The King?"

"I know. I saw him. We're going to restore him."

"You won't succeed." Eric saw a glint of panic in Rialles' eyes. "You said you didn't want any more killing, but if you tamper with that spell, his death will be on your hands."

"Quiet!" Eric dug his fingers into her arm and prodded her with the knife. "If you're so concerned about his wellbeing, why is your master using him as a cloak rack?"

"Vassant went too far. I told him so, many times." She paused, stopped, and looked at him despite the knife aimed at her side. "It doesn't have to be like this."

Eric stared at her. Was she going to offer him a deal? "Keep walking," he told her.

She did as instructed, but did not stop speaking. "You see the power we amassed. Simon is more powerful than Vassant; he must be, because he is here and Vassant is not." She paused and Eric knew she was trying to decide if her magician was alive or dead. "Imagine what we could do with a mage as powerful as Simon. He could impersonate the king as easily as he is impersonating Vassant, and do it better. The Princess wouldn't have to know." She looked at him, eyes gleaming. "I could even arrange for you to have her."

Eric shoved her hard against the wall. The knife moved from her stomach to her throat. Rage deepened his voice. "You disgust me," he told her. "There is nothing — nothing — you can offer me that will change the fact that you are a lying whore who sold her freedom." He leaned closer. "And if you ever speak like that about her again." He touched the blade to her flesh. Blood colored the blade. "Remember, we can do this without you."

Simon saw it all, and it was glorious. From three floors away, the battle screamed at him with glottal yowls, made his skin dance and rattle against his bones. The need outweighed the wishing, he had to help her, help her, help the Princess — the tiny thread he clung to in the ocean of madness. Help her. Help the Princess.

So big, it got so big. He liked wearing the mask of the One who Glows. They didn't know. No one knew. The Keeper knew, but he knew many things. So he played the game, he wore the mask, and walked the halls, all while the vortex of magic spun below him like the mouth of a sea serpent.

Focus, Simon, focus. I am, he replied in his mind, for it was She who Taught who gave the order. He reached for her, wanted to run to her. He felt her slipping and growing smaller and being swallowed. Anger flared within him. You promised. We bargained. Focus. Focus. Focus.

He tried. But she was falling slipping falling and the thought made him want to explode.

Eric knew the way to Lord Vassant's chambers. He didn't need Rialle. Part of him hoped she would give him a reason to kill her. Simon would do it, gladly and gleefully without a reason, but he didn't want any more blood on the boy's hands than was necessary.

Simon relished playing the role of Lord Vassant, and Eric realized that this day was probably the most fun that Simon had ever had in his whole life. He glanced over at the boy, and found he could see Simon's true face behind the glamour. Simon was smiling.

Rialle was not. Her jaw was clenched and she walked with her arms folded across her chest. Her eyes darted back and forth, searching the faces in the hall for anyone who might be an ally. Most just looked away from her and a few seemed to take actual pleasure in her predicament.

Then he felt it. For an instant, they all were connected through Mara's dying burst of magic. Vassant howled in victory. Daria stood before the statue of her father, her tear-stained face uplifted. A rushing swirl of mad voices that could only be Simon.

"I've done what I can," Mara said. "The rest is up to you." The link snapped.

Eric lost his concentration and stumbled, but righted himself before his captive could think of fleeing. He knew the cold emptiness he felt that followed the link could only mean Mara was truly dead. He looked over at Simon. The glamour of Vassant wavered. "Focus, Simon," he told the boy. "We still must help Daria."

"We shall we shall we shall," muttered the young mage.

"The witch is dead, is she not?" Rialle asked. "I see it in your eyes; she's really dead this time." She addressed Simon. "Who will be your teacher now? There is only one left. How will you learn from him if you kill him?"

"Be silent!" Eric told her, and looked at Simon. He was an empty void waiting to be filled with knowledge, and now, the only one who could fill that need was Lord Vassant.

Chapter 48

When Eric reached Lord Vassant's chambers, he shoved Rialle at the nearest soldier and went to Daria, still standing before the statue of her father. "You felt it?" he asked.

She nodded. "Eric, what are we going to do? What if Simon can't break this spell?"

Eric looked at Simon. The boy had dropped the pretext of being Lord Vassant and Eric had let him be. Simon paced the room, rubbing his hands back and forth. His gaze was distant, and his lips worked silently.

"Simon! Focus!"

"Trying," Simon muttered. "Trying. Trying."

"Can you save my father?" Daria asked. "Can you undo the spell?"

Simon shook his head rapidly. "She says not now. Not with He who Glows about. There are things I must do first. Things that must be done."

Eric and Daria exchanged glances. "What things?" Eric asked, but all Simon said was, "He comes. He comes. He comes. He comes."

The war within Simon raged on. Simon was active and alive. He had never felt so much, heard so much, tasted so much in his life. The madness threatened to swallow him.

Burn them all. Burn them all.

No. He would not. He bargained. He promised. He bargained.

He hugged himself tight and tried to find her, but she was gone from this world. All he found was the white-hot power of the One who Glows coming at him. I know you're out there, I can see, smell, feel you. Just come to me and it will all be over. It will be glorious and we will dance.

So easy it will be. So easy.

Eric watched Simon struggle, and struggled within himself as to what to do next. His faith in the boy's ability to face Lord Vassant wavered. He heard the mutterings of the soldiers, knew they feared Simon and wanted to take him down.

Daria edged closer to Eric. "Look at him," she whispered, her voice revealed her panic. "He can't do it, can he?"

"He can," Eric told her. "He has to."

"The soldiers?"

"Will all be killed in an instant." He looked at her. "Lord Vassant is coming. I can feel it, I know you can too. Simon is the only one who can face him."

Lord Vassant appeared in the doorway. The whites of his eyes glowed blue. "Don't engage him!" Eric shouted as the soldiers approached. "You can't touch him. He'll kill you."

"You are correct." The magician's head swiveled on his neck. "Where is he? Where is that boy? I've killed the witch and taken her power, plus what he gave her." He raised his hand. "I am unstoppable."

"Out, everyone, out!" Eric ordered. The soldiers retreated, but Daria remained on her knees in front of the statue. He seized her shoulders. "Come, we have to get out of here."

She shook her head. "I won't leave him."

"We'll come back." Eric pulled at her, but she jerked away from him. "It's not safe here."

Simon stared at Lord Vassant, his face a blank. Eric would have given five years of his life to know what was going on in the boy's mind.

"There you are." Lord Vassant crossed the threshold and stopped opposite Simon. "You've grown so small and quiet, I hardly noticed you."

"You killed her," Simon stated.

"I did." The magician rubbed his fingertips together. Eric saw sparks. "I can kill you too. But I don't have to."

Simon watched him, mouth open, eyes filled with wonder. Daria squeezed Eric's hand so tight he flinched. "He's going to betray us," she whispered. "Eric, he's going to betray us."

Eric shook his head, but it was faith that kept him going, not what he was watching. Lord Vassant extended his hand. "Come," he told Simon. "I can show you so much."

Simon cocked his head. "Can you show me how she died?"

"Of course, Little One, of course." The magician waggled his fingers. Blue light spun like spider's webs. "Can't you feel it?"

Simon's head bobbed, and his body swayed. "Glorious," he whispered. "It is glorious."

"I don't want to hurt you. I want to teach you."

Lord Vassant advanced. So did Simon.

"Stop him," Daria whispered. "We can still get out of this, but you have to stop Simon."

"No." Eric spoke loud enough for everyone to hear. Simon did not turn, but Lord Vassant looked at him as if he just noticed Eric was there. "Simon won't betray us. We made a bargain." His mouth was so dry he had trouble speaking. "I trust him."

"There is no betrayal. We all work for the common good." Lord Vassant looked beyond Eric to Daria. "Ah, Princess, it pleases me to see you are safe." He gave a little bow. "You know I only want to serve you."

"As you did my father?" Daria spat back. Eric felt her trembling, but her voice remained firm. "Tell me some more lies."

"That was regrettable." He smiled. "But what is done can be undone." His smile broadened. "Have your boy there call off his pet monster, and I will restore your father."

Eric felt her falter. "Don't listen to his lies, Daria."

"That is a complicated spell." Lord Vassant took a step toward them. "Do you honestly think that mad creature can break it? I am your only hope. One false step, one wrong breath and King Lysander will die within his marble prison." He placed a hand on the statue. "Are the lives of a couple of slaves worth the life of a King?"

Eric turned and looked at Daria. Tears filled her eyes as she whispered. "We have to, Eric. It's the only way."

"Daria, no! Don't believe him!" Eric cried.

She shook her head. "I can't take the chance. I can't." She looked at him, eyes pleading. "Eric, I know the word. It won't be on your head. I've done it before, I can do it now." She lifted her face. "Simon, sl ..."

Eric grabbed her, spun her around and clamped a hand over her mouth. She kicked and struggled, but years of hard labor gave him the strength to restrain her. "I'm sorry, I'm sorry, I'm sorry," he whispered into her ear. Then his voice rose and he shouted, "Simon, now!"

Chapter 49

Simon stood on the edge of a cliff, arms outstretched. He had seen so much, so much, in the past few days, more than he ever imagined.

Now, the One who Glows stood before him, offering to show him more. All he had to do was jump. The One who Glows touched him, called to him, caressed him, and beckoned. Come. Be with me. Jump.

"Focus, Simon, focus."

The words of his Keeper reached him from a distance. There were more words, but it was difficult to understand. "Betray," the tricky word "Bargain." And a word he never thought to use. "Trust."

Simon hesitated. Lord Vassant laughed. "This is too easy." He lifted his hand and beckoned to the boy. Eric's faith waned as the entranced Simon stepped forward, his eyes never leaving Lord Vassant's face. Daria growled and kicked in his arms, and Eric knew — he knew he should stop Simon. But he could not.

The two magicians drew close. Lord Vassant

opened his hand for Simon to clasp. "That's it, little one," he crooned. "Come to me. Let me show you what we can do."

Their hands touched, and their fingers intertwined. Eric felt the tingle of magic singing against his skin. He could only imagine what it must be like for them.

They touched. Simon nearly dropped to his knees. Every inch of his flesh, every fiber of his body sparked with illumination. It was glorious, glorious, larger than the sky and deeper than the water that stretched forever, and he wanted to bask and revel in the glow.

"Simon. Focus."

Two words drew him back. Two words spoken in the voice of She who Taught. Alive, he thought gleefully. Alive.

"Not alive. And not much time. Focus, Simon. Focus, and remember."

Lord Vassant's eyes grew wide, and for a moment, he was as frozen as the statue of Daria's father. "No, no, no." His voice grew desperate. He tried to pull away, but Simon did not release him. The young mage brought up his other hand and clasped the older man by the throat.

"Take it," Simon chortled. "She tells me to take it all."

Both mages cried out, but only Simon's head was thrown back in delight. The sound emerging from Lord Vassant's mouth was not human, not animal. It was the sound of something escaped from Otherworld.

The charge around the linked magicians grew. Blue sparks of mage fire showered from where their skin touched, the arcs growing as Simon's glee intensified. A bloom of light and power boiled around them like a thunderhead, and there was no ring to contain it.

Eric grabbed Daria by the arm. "Out now!" he shouted. Somewhere at the back of the room, he heard Rialle scream. Dragging Daria, he managed two steps, then the force of the mages' combined power slammed them to the floor.

Eric rolled to his side and looked behind them. Bright blue light swallowed the two figures limned in purple. "Focus, Simon. Focus," he whispered, and shielded his eyes from the light.

Simon focused. It was glorious. His world, their world, became a swirl of magic, and it was glorious. Singing, screaming voices swept through his shattered mind. He drew the One who Glows to him, clasped him to his chest. And they danced.

"Take it, Simon! Take it all!" She who Taught exhorted. "Take it in payment for all you've lost!"

Simon took everything. He feared he would burst. The struggling eased and ceased. His arms grew empty. The One who Glows was gone. His once-seductive voice was now only an echo among many.

As was hers. "One last gift," she told him, "and then I must go."

As it began, it ended. Simon dropped to his knees and cradled his head. The body wants to heal, she told him. So does the mind.

The voices in his head swelled in protest; all three of them, the child they shielded, the shell who hid them, and the mage who protected them all. They wept, and they were one. The witch called Maragause joined her steadfast companion in Otherworld. Their dance was over.

The mage light faded. Eric scrambled to his feet. Two forms lay in the center of the floor. The nearest, a wizened husk of a man, recognizable as Lord Vassant by the robes he had worn. The second, Simon, hunched on his knees, his arms wrapped around his head.

Eric touched his shoulder. Simon looked up. He studied Daria, then Eric. "Simon, you did it," Eric whispered.

Simon looked at him, but did not appear to understand. "Sleep," Eric told him. But Simon did not respond. Eric knelt at his side. Simon drew back. "It's all right," Eric said, and held out his hand. Simon did likewise. Eric clasped his wrist. "Wake up."

Simon gave him a curious look. Eric smiled, transferred his grip to Simon's hand, and helped him to his feet. "Well done," he told the boy. "Well done, my friend."

Eric looked back at Daria, and was surprised to see tears glistening in her eyes. "What's the matter?" he asked. "Don't you see what has happened? He is mended."

"That may be." She spoke through tears. "But if he is no longer as he was, who will restore my father?"

Chapter 50

The light was bright, brighter than he had known, brighter than he remembered. Simon listened to the buzz of conversation around him. The words came to him if he paid attention. There were no teachers now, no one to guide him. He had only his lessons.

The lessons the old one, Maragause, had taught him. That Simon had not liked it; but he was greedy for the knowledge and this Simon was glad. He liked learning, and liked the old woman almost as much as he liked his friend Eric. What was the lesson? Something familiar in the room called to him. Something from the lesson. The statue. Yes. The statue of the man. Simon stood and began to remember.

Rialle opened her eyes. Her head throbbed and she tasted blood from her swollen lip. She rolled on to her hip and propped herself up. Then she remembered and her blood became ice.

She saw them. Their attention was focused on the slave-mage, standing before the statue of the King. She stared at the statue, the unconscious body of the soldier set to guard her, the puling Princess and that bastard Eric. But where was Vassant? She spied the smoldering robes on the floor, and she knew that all was lost.

She wasted no pity on the dead magician. Her thoughts shifted to self-preservation. Rialle slipped a slender dirk from the folds of her robe when the soldier stirred. She jammed the blade into his throat. His eyes popped open, blood gurgled from the wound, and his mouth worked futilely. Without a second look, she withdrew the blade, wiped it on his uniform, and crouched behind the desk to study her adversaries.

Simon circled the statue slowly, his eyes traveling over the marble surface. After his second pass, he looked at Eric, who nodded.

"What is he doing?" Daria asked.

Eric replied. "Remembering."

Simon halted and held his hands out, his palms inches from the statue's face and began to chant. The statue's eyes registered alarm and fear. Simon's lips moved soundlessly and he resumed circling, moving his hands rapidly up and down the statue.

"Nothing's happening." Daria spoke in a small

voice.

"Give him time," Eric replied. Then he felt his skin tingle, and knew the magic had begun to work. "He will do it."

"No, he won't." Rialle appeared on the opposite side of the room, a dagger in her right hand. She stepped over the body of the man they had set to guard her. "I won't permit it."

Eric cursed, and looked to Simon. Rialle laughed. "He can't help you. He's locked into the spell. If he breaks it now, the King will die. So will he." She wagged the blade to and fro. "So will you all."

Eric placed himself between Rialle and Daria. He could call for the guards, but she was too close to Simon, and could plunge the dagger into his neck before they would subdue her.

Their eyes locked. "You will die too," he told her.

She raised the dagger. "So long as I do not die alone."

Simon studied the statue of the man in the spell and wished for the quiet voice of Maragause to tell him what to do. She was gone. The spell was cleverly made, a snapping trap that would eat him as soon as he touched it. Yet he had to touch it. In the new calm of his mind, he heard the aching need of the man inside. The word "king" meant nothing to him, but this man was Daria's father. For that reason alone, he knew he had to touch the statue, break the spell.

Simon followed the path of the spell in his mind, from the casting to the disastrous unmaking at his own hands. Powerful as he was, and he knew he was powerful, it was not a thing he could contain. He would free the man, and kill the man in a single action.

Eric stepped toward Rialle, then stopped. "Afraid?" she laughed.

No, he almost answered, for it was another thing entirely that stopped him. Through sheer force of will, he kept his face expressionless while a familiar presence touched his mind. What do I do?

Break the spell, Simon. You can do it.

But when I do it, it must have a place to go. I cannot control it.

What do you mean?

Simon showed him, a burst of blackness that sucked the life from those it touched. The ring? Simon asked.

No time. Eric looked at Rialle, who advanced once more, her knife upraised. An idea flashed through his mind. Watch me, he told Simon and lunged for Rialle. He grabbed her right wrist with both hands and shoved the dagger upward.

"Don't you touch me!" she shrieked, and clawed at his face with her free hand. Eric twisted his head away and wrenched her arm down, sending the dagger clattering to the floor. He used his body weight and wheeled her toward Simon. A place to go, he told Simon.

With the speed of an adder, Simon reached around, grabbed her by the throat and pulled her close. Stand down, he told Eric, who reluctantly released his grip on Rialle. Simon placed his right hand flat on the chest of the statue and tightened his grip on the struggling woman. With a satisfied smile, Simon closed his eyes and concentrated.

Magic swarmed around them, and the room filled with buzz of a riotous mob. "No!" Rialle screamed, and raised her hands to flail at him. The spell passed from the King, through Simon, and into Rialle. It rose from her feet up her legs. The folds of her gown paled to white and grew solid. She struggled as if mired in sand, but the mortification spell moved up her body, covering her hips, her stomach, her heaving breast. She opened her mouth for one final scream and her head snapped back. And so she stood, arms outstretched, head thrown back, her face twisted in horror.

The air around the King shimmered, and the marble-edge began to blur. Color formed, first his skin, then his clothes. Finally, the statue heaved a great breath and dropped to its knees. He was alive.

"Papa!" Daria cried, and threw herself into his arms.

"Easy, child, easy." His voice was a hoarse whisper and he gasped for breath. He wrapped Daria in his arms and rocked her tightly. "It's all right now. Everything will be all right now."

Would it? Eric looked at Simon. He had dropped to his knees; a thin sheen of perspiration covered his pale skin. He was watching Daria and her father, swaying in motion with them.

After a few moments, Daria helped her father to his feet and sent for a physician. Eric watched her fuss over him, and placed a hand on Simon's shoulder. "You did it," he told the boy.

"You both did it." Daria held out a hand to him. "Come," she said. "I want you to meet my father."

Eric stood, drawing the unsteady Simon with him. Together they approached the King, who had seated himself on the edge of the heavy wooden desk.

"Papa, these are my friends, Eric and Simon."

Eric started to kneel. The King stopped him with an upraised hand. "Not necessary. I know what happened. I saw everything." Color returned to the King's cheeks, and he grew steadier by the moment. "I saw everything that transpired, and I know what these young men went through on your behalf." He extended a hand to Eric. "You have my thanks, and whatever the gratitude of a king may provide for you."

Eric took the proffered hand. "I was happy to be of service. Daria has given me the only thing I ever wanted, my freedom. I ask that same boon for Simon."

"Consider it granted." King Lysander wasted no time. He ordered the papers drawn up, and while the physician fussed over him, he gave Daria the honor of signing Simon's manumission papers. She did this with a flourish then embraced him as she had embraced Eric, then embraced Eric again for good measure.

"Thank you," she whispered in his ear. "Thank you for everything."

Chapter 51

The season turned to summer, bringing heat, and the only respite came with the ocean wind. The doors and windows of every building on the south side of the city were thrown open to catch the breeze, and servants and citizens alike arranged their tasks to take advantage of the fresh air. Wisps of clouds chased across the azure sky and sunlight sparkled against the waves.

Eric still had no use for all that water. He sat on the ledge of a third floor balcony in a rare block of shade and watched as Daria and her friends made ready for an outing aboard a small sailing vessel. He smiled every time she looked up but, when she waved for him to join them, he shook his head.

In amongst the ladies and laborers was another familiar figure. Simon. Daria and her friends indulged him like a favorite brother, including him in their diversions as if to try and make up for all he had missed. He was strangely solemn now, and reluctant to use or even discuss his magical abilities. In his own words, the magic "confused his mind," and from the tone of his voice, Eric believed it frightened him, more than a little. The physicians brought in to examine him added little information — no one had ever seen anything like Simon — but to Eric's untrained eye it seemed Simon had picked up his life where it abruptly ended, as a young boy who was far from home. No one knew how much Simon remembered, but it appeared he held no grudges, not against those who had stolen his childhood, and especially not against Eric.

That was the hard part. Eric watched Simon throw back his head and bask in the bright sunlight. Nothing gave the boy more pleasure than being outdoors, and his once-pale skin had darkened with a healthy glow. Seeing him so happy should have made Eric happy as well, but it had the opposite effect. It was impossible for him to watch Simon enjoying his freedom without remembering the years he'd spent chained up in the front of that wagon. Simon didn't blame him; no one blamed him, but none of that mattered. Eric blamed himself.

"You're not joining them?"

Eric gave a start. Daria's father had joined him on the balcony. King Lysander, he reminded himself. "No sir," he said. "I don't like being this close to the ocean."

The King chuckled. Eric's dislike of the ocean was well known, and a source of mild amusement. "Simon seems to enjoy it."

"Simon likes anything that takes him outside." There it was again, the guilt again. The silence grew between them, as it often did when Simon was discussed. No one could teach him, because there was no one like him — at least not in Legerdemain. Maybe, on the whole continent.

Each waited for the other to speak, and it was the King who broke the silence. "I've made the arrangements. When the winds change in the fall, I'll send a courier ship to Katara and tell them of their lost son."

Eric felt a chill. “Will Simon accompany them?”

The King shook his head. “Absolutely not. Simon is under my protection now. I’ve made him legally my ward. Anyone who wants to claim kinship must convince me that have his best interests in mind.” He sighed. “And I am not as trusting as I once was.”

“That’s very kind of you, Sir.”

“I owe him that much. More, actually, but this is what I can do now.” Another pause. “What about you?”

Eric’s brow furrowed. “What do you mean?”

“Do you have family out there?”

“I don’t know.” Eric shrugged. It wasn’t something he ever thought about. “I wouldn’t even know where to look.”

The King leaned on the railing and looked out over the ocean. “I hope you realize that you will always have a place in my household, so long as you desire.”

Eric felt his throat tighten and it was a few moments before he could answer. “Thank you, sir.”

“Don’t thank me quite yet. Because I’m not at all sure that remaining in Legerdemain is in your best interest.”

Eric grew cold despite the heat. When he could bring himself to look, he found the King watching him thoughtfully. “My daughter gave you a powerful gift. What do you plan to do with it?””

Eric looked back out at the water, but this time the apprehension he felt came from within. What would he do? It was a question he had been avoiding. In truth, his life as a free man wasn’t dramatically different than his life as a slave. The trappings were much improved — he had finer clothes and plenty to eat. And, he mentally added as he looked down at Daria again, the company was more agreeable. But he still spent every day feeling the grip of responsibility. Responsibility for Simon. Responsibility and guilt.

Daria watched as her father joined Eric on the balcony. She was too far away to hear his words, but she knew what he had planned to say. They had discussed it the night before while sitting in her father's library; his calm, measured words speaking painful truths she hadn't wanted to voice. With the scratch of a quill, she had granted Eric his freedom, but so long as he stayed here, he'd never truly be free.

It all sounded so reasonable when her father said it, but now, faced with the prospect of his departure, her heart nearly broke. Though they had only known each other a brief time, Eric had become her truest friend. Chambermaid, thief, or princess, it made no difference to him, and she adored him for it.

She tore her gaze from the two men and looked at Simon, standing at the bow of the boat. His head was tipped back, and he seemed to be enjoying the sun and spray in equal measure. It was hard to look at him without sharing his joy, and she smiled despite herself. If Eric could find that same happiness in Legerdemain, she would beg him to stay.

"The decision is yours, Eric." King Lysander spoke the words in Eric's heart. "You can remain here, watching over Simon, watching my daughter, for as long as you want." He paused. "Or for as long as either of them will allow it. But that's no life, certainly not one to be recommended. If I didn't know how you felt about sailing, I'd send you with the courier ship to Katara. You're the ideal choice; you know Simon better than anyone, and while you might not realize it, you read people very well.

"I'll go," Eric said, before his nerves betrayed him. Already, the water was closing in around him.

"Of course you'll go. And you'll be miserable every moment. That's why I won't permit it."

"But Simon is my responsibility."

"No." The King's voice was gentle but firm. "I just told you. Simon is my responsibility now."

Eric thought to argue, but knew he had no ground. He watched the little boat carrying his friends sail away from the pier and into the harbor. Daria waved at them from the deck. He knew he could never be anything but a friend to her, and that wasn't enough.

The King turned to leave, but paused. "Think about what I've said, Eric. You have your freedom. You can do anything."

Eric nodded. By week's end, he had signed on with a caravan heading back over the Eskell Divide. He had never had to say goodbye to anyone who mattered, and it was both easier and harder than he imagined. Simon listened and nodded as though he understood. Eric had thought he might ask to join him, but the boy seemed happy here, comfortable in the security of the royal household.

Daria spent their last remaining days together insisting she would not tell him goodbye, but on the morning of his departure she was waiting for him in the stable. Saying little, she helped him equip the fine horse her father had given him, then waited as he led the beast out into the misty morning light. Her final gift to him was a small, leather-bound book of painted maps. A purple ribbon marked the page that showed Legerdemain.

"So you can find your way back," she told him, and then she kissed him goodbye.

Sword & Science

Presents

Prodigal

Book Two
of the
The Shattered Mage Saga

Eric has gained his freedom, but is not yet free from the ghosts of his past. A mysterious stranger offers him the chance to return to Legerdemain. Will his journey put the past to rest, or will he risk everything for the woman he loves?

---

www.swordandscience.com

P. S. RAMSEY lives in Southeastern Michigan in a little house by the railroad tracks. Her earliest fiction was pounded out on a portable typewriter and featured the many adventures of her vast herd of Breyer model horses. Then, like every other fantasy writer in the known universe, she discovered Tolkien and computers, and her imaginary world has never been the same. In addition to various jobs in auto-related industries, Ms. Ramsey is involved in canine rescue, and while she insists she is not a crazy dog lady, her home is frequently overrun by Border Collies.